What the critics are saying…

"This is a well plotted, smooth flowing, action packed story from the first page…I highly recommend this one to anyone who enjoys a well-written vampire/werewolf read. This one's a keeper!" ~ *Luisa, Cupid's Library Reviews*

"This book was delicious and sensually erotic. The relationship and consequent friction between these three characters was spine tingling." ~ *Dianne Nogueras, eCata Romance*

"Skye, Rico and Gian are all terrific characters with complex personalities. It is fascinating to watch the relationship development between the three of them. The sex scenes are hotter than a whole box of firecrackers and left me searching for a glass of ice water… *Ms. Strong* is a talented author with a very creative imagination. I recommend this book to anyone who enjoys tales of vampires and magic." ~ *Susan White, Just Erotic Romance Reviews*

"Once again, *Jory Strong* crafts a strong paranormal romance with a leading heroine who can kick some serious butt. Skye is not a woman to mess with… Though this story has a thrilling plot and an equally thrilling romance with two alpha males, it is Skye who is the heart and soul of this story. Kudos to *Ms. Strong* for creating such an unforgettable story! *Skye's Trail* is not to be missed by fans of the paranormal genre." ~ *Sarah, A Romance Review*

"From the first page until the last, you won't be able to put this book down." ~ *Donna, Fallen Angel Reviews*

JORY STRONG

Skye's Trail

THE ANGELINI

ELLORA'S CAVE
ROMANTICA PUBLISHING

An Ellora's Cave Romantica Publication

www.ellorascave.com

Skye's Trail

ISBN # 1419952749
ALL RIGHTS RESERVED.
Skye's Trail Copyright© 2005 Jory Strong
Edited by: Sue-Ellen Gower
Cover art by: Syneca

Electronic book Publication: April, 2005
Trade paperback Publication: October, 2005

Excerpt from *Binding Krista* Copyright © Jory Strong, 2005

Warning:

The following material contains graphic sexual content meant for mature readers. *Skye's Trail* has been rated *E-rotic* by a minimum of three independent reviewers.

Ellora's Cave Publishing offers three levels of Romantica™ reading entertainment: S (S-ensuous), E (E-rotic), and X (X-treme).

S-*ensuous* love scenes are explicit and leave nothing to the imagination.

E-*rotic* love scenes are explicit, leave nothing to the imagination, and are high in volume per the overall word count. In addition, some E-rated titles might contain fantasy material that some readers find objectionable, such as bondage, submission, same sex encounters, forced seductions, etc. E-rated titles are the most graphic titles we carry; it is common, for instance, for an author to use words such as "fucking", "cock", "pussy", etc., within their work of literature.

X-*treme* titles differ from E-rated titles only in plot premise and storyline execution. Unlike E-rated titles, stories designated with the letter X tend to contain controversial subject matter not for the faint of heart.

Also by Jory Strong:

Skye's Trail
The Angelini

Trademarks Acknowledgement

The author acknowledges the trademarked status and trademark owners of the following wordmarks mentioned in this work of fiction:

Pert: Procter & Gamble Company, The
Viper: Daimler Chrysler Corporation
Yukon: General Motors Corporation
Harley: Harley-Davidson Motor Co. Inc.
Baskin-Robbins: Baskin-Robbins Incorporated

Chapter One

Detective Rico Santana knew there was going to be hell to pay. One way or the other, there always was when *she* was involved. If not from Rivera, his captain, then from the unrelenting ache in his cock and the lack of sleep that always followed any encounter with Skye Delano.

¡Carajo! He lusted after her. Maybe if he fucked her, it would get her out of his system.

Rico gritted his teeth against the need he could already feel building, the anticipation. Now he was sorry he'd brought along backup. If he just had some time alone with her he'd…

Shit. He needed saving…from himself. Fucking Skye would be professional suicide—maybe even personal suicide. Rico had a feeling that once would never be enough with her.

He hit the turn signal and eased the unmarked police car toward an empty parking space. Out of the corner of his eye he saw Cia Caldwell's tight disapproving frown. She was the newest member of the department, and as far as he knew, she'd never had any personal contact with Skye. She'd heard the stories though, and read the captain's file.

His mistake was calling Skye from the bullpen. When he'd looked up, Detective Caldwell was standing next to his cubicle. "Rivera is going to ream you," she'd said before the phone had even hit its cradle.

"It'll be dark soon. They're not going to find those kids without Skye's help."

Cia squared her shoulders. "I'm going with you."

A ripple of anger shot through Rico. He didn't need a babysitter.

A flash of sanity followed. Yeah, maybe it'd be better.

The captain was going to be pissed enough. At least this way Rivera would see it was all about finding the kids—not about finding an excuse to see Skye again.

¡Carajo! How could he be so hard when right now the only thing he should be thinking about was two missing kids?

Rico parked the sedan in front of Skye's apartment complex. Caldwell had her door open before he could even turn off the engine. He grimaced and looked down at the bulge in the front of his pants. "Wait here," he said.

Caldwell's mutinous expression let him know what she thought of his order. But he was the senior detective and she was new.

He got out of the car, heart beating and cock throbbing. Every time he saw Skye the lust that rolled through his system made him think of standing in front of a wave of molten lava.

Rico braced himself as he took the stairs up to her apartment and rang the bell. It was going to be worse this time. He knew that. Always before he'd seen her at a crime scene or the station. He'd never been alone with her in a place that might lead to something physical.

The cop in him said he was crazy to go into this situation without backup. The man said he was a fool not to try and fuck her.

When the door swung open, Rico knew he couldn't keep denying what his body was telling him. Shit. Everything about Skye whispered of sex and dark mystery, danger. She was beautiful temptation, silver-blonde hair and jet-black lashes framing hypnotic pale blue eyes.

In that second he didn't care whether the rumors about her were true or not. She was a fantasy. His fantasy.

Rivera had warned him off her after the last search, when the perps responsible for kidnapping a couple of kids had turned up dead. The captain had told him more as a friend than as a commanding officer that a personal relationship with Skye could be the end of his career.

Rico was a cop first. Came from a family of cops. Above everything else, that's what he was, what he'd always wanted to be. A cop.

So he'd kept his distance. Avoided her. Until now.

Now the only thing he could think about was pressing her back into the apartment and taking her against the wall. On the floor. Eventually in the bed.

¡Carajo! The things he wanted to do to her, the things he wanted to let her do to him, actually shocked him.

She half-smiled and it was like a fist around his dick, the ache was so bad. "You came quick," she said and his heart jumped at her choice of words. He wondered if she'd guessed how badly he wanted her. Fuck, he'd be lucky if he lasted one stroke before shooting his load into her.

For a minute all he could do was stare into her eyes. He thought he saw desire in them but he wasn't sure if it was real or imagined. All his cop instincts failed him when he was around her.

He tried to focus on the reason he was here. The kids.

It helped—some. "Are you ready?" he asked.

Skye studied the raven-haired cop standing in front of her. She could feel the lust pouring off of him, could read the fantasies even without delving into his mind.

Her body craved his, had from the first moment they'd met.

It'd be so easy to get involved with him.

So easy but so dangerous.

So very, very dangerous.

She stepped out of the apartment and locked the door behind her. "Ready."

* * * * *

There were still plenty of police cars present when they got to the search site. Without getting out of the car, Skye could sense the frustration and fatigue and worry that hovered over the group of cops.

The search was winding down. If the kids were here, still alive, their chances decreased with another night spent in the woods. If they were somewhere else, the odds of being found alive dropped with every passing hour. Rico had told her that the abandoned rental car was the only lead—so far.

They got out of the unmarked police car and Skye immediately felt Captain Rivera's frown. His hand twitched in an involuntary move to cross himself. He barked out an order to Rico, "Santana, get over here!"

She half-smiled as she watched the female detective stick to Rico's side in an outward show of moral support even though Caldwell's tightly compressed lips let everyone know that she didn't approve of what Rico had done. It had been a chilly ride to the scene.

"What's she doing here?" Rivera demanded. He didn't bother to keep his voice down, to keep the censure out of it. It was no secret that suspicion still burned in his gut from the last time she'd been called in.

Rico answered, "She's here as a volunteer, Captain. The search is shutting down. I'll be off-duty and assisting her."

"I'll also be off-duty and assisting," Detective Caldwell said.

A distraught couple huddled next to Captain Rivera, their eyes swinging from one cop to another. The man was rail-thin, tall, pale as an office worker. He cleared his throat. "We'd appreciate any help we can get." The woman clutched his arm, nodding at the officers. She was much shorter than the man, rounded in a way that suggested comfort, old-fashioned motherhood.

The parents.

Skye pitied them.

Jon and Karen Armstrong had come to Las Vegas on a family vacation, bringing with them their nineteen-year-old niece and their five-year-old daughter. It was supposed to be a win-win situation. The niece was having some family problems, so the trip would give her some time away from her parents. Jon and Karen would get a babysitter. Now the Armstrongs were trapped in an incomprehensible nightmare.

They'd gone out for dinner and gambling last night, left the niece, Brittany, babysitting their daughter, Callie, in the hotel room. When they got back at three in the morning, the kid, the niece, and the rental car were gone.

Shortly after noon, the car had been located about thirty minutes outside of the city limits. The cops had been searching since then.

The Armstrongs' grief and pain rolled over Skye, chased by Rivera's angry frustration. He was in a corner and hated it. There'd be hell to pay if he tried to send her home now. Everybody watching the scene unfold knew it.

"Get on with it," he growled to Rico. "Anything goes wrong and it's your ass on the line." He expanded his glance to include Caldwell. "Both of your asses."

"Yes sir," Caldwell said.

Rico nodded.

A dog and its handler emerged from the woods. "Here's the last team, Captain," one of the cops standing nearby said.

Skye walked over to the rental car, knelt down next to the driver's door, let her senses flare out, flow backward with information. It was all part of her ability to hypnotize, only instead of applying it to others, it was self-directed. For periods of time she could become *other*—human in form but with the skills and instincts of an animal. The more she knew of the chosen animal, of its abilities, the closer the melding.

As the scent washed over her, she briefly let herself become wolfen. Hunter. Tracker. Unashamed predator.

The odor near the car was so strong that it burned her nostrils. Tainted blood. Rancid. Foul-smelling. Unnatural. Like the smell of death, and yet it wasn't.

The scent belonged to someone who'd been in the car. The odor lingered on the door handle, went around the car and headed toward the woods.

There were other scents around the car. A female, young, healthy. Another person whose blood reeked of something horrible. A new drug? A new disease? It wasn't cancer in any one of its numerous forms. It wasn't HIV or AIDS. Skye knew those smells too well.

All of the scents led to the woods. She followed them to the edge, found they were joined by other scents. More tainted blood. Altogether, five different people with it. Skye couldn't tell whether they were male or female. That had never happened before.

She tracked the other smells backward, stopped at the cluster of parked cars. The five people had all been here, had probably left together in another car. The healthy female didn't go with them.

Detective Caldwell moved alongside Skye. "You ready to start now? Everybody is standing around waiting."

"Sure," Skye's voice came out with a hint of humor but the detective didn't notice.

They walked back to the rental car. The parents were there. They looked at Skye with desperate hope.

"Thank you for coming," the woman said. Skye nodded, inhaled, would know which scent belonged to the mother.

The man offered a handshake, "I'm Jon Armstrong, this is my wife Karen." Skye accepted the extended hand, took his scent along with it.

Rico asked, "You ready for the inside of the car? The crime scene guys have already come and gone." Skye nodded and he opened the door.

The smell of tainted blood was even stronger in the closed confines of the car. It almost gagged her. She took a minute to focus, to begin the task of separating out the different scents—Jon Armstrong, Karen, foul blood times two—close in smell but slightly different, the healthy female who went into the woods, another healthy female, this one a child with a hint of shampoo—not baby shampoo but something else. Skye sorted through the scents lodged in her memory until she found the one she was looking for—Pert shampoo. There were other smells, cops, then fainter scents—rental car workers probably, or people who'd rented the car before the Armstrongs.

She stood up, stepped back from the car and nodded to Rico. He closed the door, shifting so he was standing next to the parents and the captain. A small cluster of cops was huddled with them.

The dog and handler stood off to the side. "Need a scent article?" the handler asked, part serious, part joking, in large part frustrated by lack of success. He held up a plastic bag with a stuffed animal in it. Skye's lips tilted up for a second. "No thanks."

She turned to the waiting cops and parents. "The child was never here. The niece was. She went into the woods with five other people. Two came in the car with her. Three arrived in another car. The five probably left together in the other vehicle."

The search-and-rescue dog handler scowled at Rico. "You tipped her off."

Skye looked at Rico and raised an eyebrow in question. He shrugged. "The dogs haven't been able to pick up a trace of Callie, either. They get a start on Brittany but lose it."

The woman began weeping. Her husband pulled her against his shoulder. "Are you sure Callie was never here?"

"Yes. She uses Pert shampoo. Her scent doesn't leave the car here." The woman's weeping grew more intense.

"Mr. Armstrong, is that the shampoo your daughter uses?" Captain Rivera asked.

"Yes. Yes. She's got her own little bottle of it. She's the only one who uses it." Jon Armstrong's voice was strained, tight with emotion.

Rivera sighed and gave the order, "Okay, Santana, get the civilian outfitted with a tracking unit and a radio. I'm considering you and Caldwell officially on duty and in charge of supervising the civilian. I expect you to keep me current on the situation out here. Is that understood?"

The detectives agreed and returned to the unmarked car with Skye. She strapped a leather sheath onto her leg, checking to make sure the knife it held was secure. She could feel the captain's gaze burn into her back. He'd arrest her if he could do a search and find the switchblade she always carried.

"The knife is driving the captain crazy," Rico said, standing so close that Skye could smell his aftershave and feel his body heat. She let it fill her senses, wrap around her like a warm blanket.

Skye half-smiled. "Does he want me to go in unarmed?"

Rico pulled his eyes away from the long knife. His expression was all cop. Against his will he was thinking about the last search, about the men who'd kidnapped a young brother and sister to use in their porn movies.

After the children were found the trail had gone cold…until a couple of cops from another department had stumbled on the perps. They were in a motor home parked in the desert but they weren't alive and hadn't been for days. They'd been knifed and left to rot.

Looking at the knife Rico wondered…and he didn't want to. He knew what the captain thought. Everyone knew what Rivera suspected.

She'd voluntarily surrendered the knife for testing. It didn't match the murder weapon. But she could own other knives.

Rico shook his head to clear the unwelcome speculation from his mind. He didn't want to think she could kill like that.

"You know Rivera would rather you didn't go in at all," he told her.

"You asked me, Rico." Her eyes met his. "Sorry now?" It was barely a whisper, yet it slipped past his guard. His dark eyes locked to hers though she made no effort to pull him into their depths.

Rico couldn't keep his pulse from racing. When this was over… He tried to close his mind against the fantasy, against the need. "No, I'm not sorry."

Caldwell saw the look pass between the two of them. Her lips tightened until they almost disappeared altogether. "Ready?" Her voice came out more strident than she'd intended but it achieved its goal. The heated, unspoken exchange between Rico and Skye ended. Their gazes broke apart.

Skye positioned the camelback full of water onto her back then double-checked the medical supplies and power bars zipped into its pockets. Rico handed her the police tracking unit and radio so that she could slide them onto a belt around her waist.

He knew there was no point in suggesting that someone go with her. Even if she agreed, she'd soon lose them. On the last search she'd traveled miles by foot, run most of it, outdistanced and outlasted the team following her. "Check in at intervals. Okay?"

Already Skye could feel the pull of the hunt, the call to be *other*. "Sure."

Rico saw the way her eyes changed, deepened into bottomless blue pools of color. It was one of the things that bothered the captain so much. Rico cursed himself. He should be spooked by her, not turned on. "Don't use the knife unless it's life or death," he said.

Another half-smile but no reply. She was already hunting. Rico stepped away and Skye went to the edge of the woods, focused on the stench of tainted blood. It was so strong that she didn't have to bend down to smell it. The dogs could have easily tracked it but they had no way to tell their handlers it was there.

Miles passed. Hours passed. She was not aware of either. Her sole focus remained on the stench of tainted blood. Somewhere along the way the scent of healthy female faded, became so faint that it almost disappeared. But not completely.

Occasionally the radio came to life, startling her. The intervals became more frequent as the night wore on.

Midnight came and went.

Her adrenaline began to surge. Had she been an animal she might have lifted her face to the sky and howled. She was close. Instinct told her she was close now.

The woods opened to a clearing. Here she sensed death. Felt it. Smelled it.

It was not the obvious smell of a carcass left in the open.

But more the lingering presence of a life violently taken.

She halted in the clearing. Absorbed her surroundings.

There was a partially erased circle traced in the ground. Tainted blood had been sprinkled along the edges of it. Death had come here. In this circle.

The scent trail led out of the circle, across the clearing, to a pile of rocks in a shallow ravine. The animals had helped themselves to what they could dig out. Part of an arm protruded from the pile of rocks, its skin shredded. An upper leg bone glistened, stripped clean of meat.

Skye didn't need to uncover the face to know it was the niece. Her scent lingered over the body like a disenfranchised spirit.

The radio crackled. This time it was Caldwell. "Anything to report?"

"I found the niece. She's dead."

"Do not touch the body!" Caldwell barked through the radio. "Do not contaminate the scene!" In the darkness Skye shook her head, almost laughing out loud. She'd be glad when this was over, when Caldwell could disappear back into the sea of police blue.

A second later Rico's voice flowed out of the radio. "What's the situation there?"

"I'm in a shallow ravine. The niece is buried under rock. One arm and part of a thigh have been exposed by animals. Actual scene of death took place in a clearing approximately forty yards behind me."

"Stand by while I contact the captain."

Skye knelt next to the body and examined the wrist more closely. The tear there was too smooth to be from an animal and there was very little blood on the ground. She let her senses flare out, flow backward with information. Most of the blood was missing from the body.

The hairs on the back of her neck moved away from her skin. She stood and walked to the clearing, looked at the broken circle, smelled the stench of tainted blood, and knew that whatever had transpired here, it was dark and evil. Something to be avoided.

A coyote song erupted in the distance. Joyous, excited. There was prey nearby, it sang. The hunt was on. The kill was near. Other voices joined the song, filling the night air with their excited cadence.

Skye drank it in, allowed it to flow through her then stilled as thoughts of the missing five year old filled her. Intuition or uncanny ability, it didn't matter which, she knew with certainty that the coyotes had found Callie. And that the little girl was still alive.

Once again the radio came to life. Rico said, "A team is on its way. We've got your coordinates. Stay put. We'll come in as soon as they get here."

Skye lifted the radio to her mouth. "Can you hear the coyotes?"

"Jesus, yes, it's giving me the creeps."

"They've found the little girl. I'm going to cut across land and follow the sound."

"No. Stay put. That's an order." This from Caldwell.

Skye grimaced. "I'll leave the tracking device on a tree near the body, in case you need the signal to find it."

"Stay put!" If Caldwell could have come through the radio and physically restrained Skye, she would have.

Skye ignored her. "Rico, are you there?"

"I'm here."

"I'll keep the radio. But it'll be off. I'll call you when I can. I can't risk the coyotes hearing it before I get close."

She could hear his sigh. Knew he wouldn't argue with her. This was why he'd contacted her and asked her to come to the site. This was why he'd risked pissing off his friend and captain.

"Do you think she's still alive?" he asked.

"At this moment. Yes."

Another song went up in the distance. More excited. More urgent.

"I'll be in touch." Skye turned off the radio before either of the cops could respond. She secured the tracking unit to a tree then let the sound of the coyotes fill her again, let herself sink more deeply into their world. There was little time left now, not if the child was to stay alive.

Chapter Two

The coyote songs never stopped, nor did the animals scatter until she was almost upon them. Their yellow eyes glowed and disappeared, glowed and disappeared. Even when movement and song finally stopped, she knew they were close, watching, waiting, calculating. They were wary but not afraid. Tourists with their careless eating habits and generosity had taught the animals to associate food with humans. There might yet be something for them here. So they stayed near but out of sight.

A whimper came from somewhere above Skye and she spotted the child nestled high in a tree, arms and legs wrapped around the trunk. "Can you climb down?" she asked, her voice gentle, soothing.

The child's voice quivered, "No."

"I'll come get you then."

The limbs were close together but many of them were not strong enough to take Skye's weight. It hindered her progress, slowed it, but didn't deter her. As soon as her body was even with Callie's, she told the little girl, "I'm going to help you turn around. Then I want you to wrap your arms around my neck and your legs around my waist. Can you do that, Callie?"

"Yes."

"Okay, let's do it. Your mom and dad are really anxious for you to get back home."

Skye eased the little girl away from the tree and somehow managed to breathe even as the child locked her arms around her neck in a stranglehold. "Easy now. We'll be down on the ground in a minute."

The child clutched harder. "Dogs. Bad dogs," she whimpered.

"Coyotes. They helped me find you. Now it's okay. They won't bother you."

As soon as Skye's feet touched the ground she knelt. Callie continued to cling, not wanting to release her hold. The child was shaking, cool to the touch even in the mild night air. Skye untied the jacket she'd secured at her waist before leaving the apartment. After she wrapped it around Callie, she asked, "Can you eat something, Callie?"

"Thirsty."

"Okay." There was plenty of water in the camelback. She moved the mouthpiece to the child's mouth. "Suck on this."

Callie drank for a long time.

"I've got something that's banana-flavored and something that's chocolate-flavored. Which one do you want?"

"'Nana."

Skye got out the power bar and peeled back the wrapper. While Callie ate, Skye pulled the radio off her belt, turned it on, and pressed the button to transmit. "This is Skye checking in."

"Where the hell are you!" Captain Rivera was back on scene.

"I've got the child. She's okay."

Rico came on, "You've got her?"

"Wrapped in a jacket right in front of me. She had a big drink of water. Now she's working on a power bar."

Through the radio, Skye could hear a cheer go up.

Rico asked, "Any idea where you are?"

"I'm closer to the road than to where you are. I'll backtrack and go out where Callie came in. Are her parents on site?"

"No. We finally got them to go back to their hotel. We'll send a car to pick them up."

"Good. I'll keep the radio on."

"You do that," Rivera barked.

Any number of responses flashed through Skye's mind. She didn't allow herself to voice any of them.

The child's trail was long and unorganized and often difficult to follow. Callie had been lost and panicky as she'd crashed over and through the terrain.

The closer they got to the road, the easier it was to hear the cars. The traffic had increased since the grim discovery and Callie's rescue.

The little girl had stopped shivering. Now she clung to Skye's back, more asleep than awake.

They kept moving. The trail led out of a thick grove of trees and up a steep incline. Skye could hear a car approaching. She saw its headlights in the distance as she crested the incline and found herself along the road. Automatically she reached for the radio. "I'm on the road. Do you have a cruiser heading back toward town?"

Caldwell jumped in with a familiar order. "Stay put. Hold while I get the captain."

Skye gritted her teeth. She was tired, battling physical and mental exhaustion. It had been a long night. And now she could see the first hint of light at the edges of dark sky.

Before the radio came to life again, Skye had her answer. The car in the distance turned on its flashing lights and siren. The sound cut across the night air and woke Callie with a start.

Rico's deep rich voice came over the radio, "A cruiser is heading back toward town. Do you see it?"

"Yes. It's coming our way."

"Good. Callie's parents are in it. Did you locate her entry point?"

"Yes."

"Okay. I'll be there in a few minutes."

The cruiser picked up speed and closed the distance in record time. It screeched to a halt in front of where Skye and

Callie waited along the road. Within a second, they were engulfed in arms.

"Callie, thank God, oh God, my baby is safe." The woman's grip was strong with emotion. The man's was just slightly less fierce.

Skye stepped away from the hugging as soon as the little girl released her hold and was wrapped in her parents' arms.

A young female cop stood grinning next to the patrol car. "We've been cruising back and forth waiting for you to come out. The timing was almost perfect."

Skye laughed. Happy despite the grisly find earlier. A child lived. Many searches didn't end so well.

Sirens blared in the distance. Skye could see two cars coming their way fast. She moved away from the young cop and the reunited family. Once again she allowed herself to become wolfen.

They'd all been here. The five, the niece, the child. Skye could almost picture it. The rental car had pulled into the turnout at the side of the road. The niece may have already picked up the two strangers, or maybe this is where they joined her. Brittany left the rental car, walked to another spot, where another car had parked. The child hadn't been with her.

All five with the tainted blood had stood here. Only two had gone to or come from where the rental car was parked. Skye went back to where Callie's steps had disappeared down the steep slope. There was the stench of foul blood several feet away from where the child had been—as though the strangers had started to pursue her but given up after a short distance.

Skye turned back as the unmarked car squealed to a halt behind the first cruiser. Caldwell and Rico climbed out. The captain got out of the next vehicle. "Anything?" he barked at Skye, careful to avoid meeting her eyes. From experience, she knew that he was anxious for her to be gone.

Skye doubted the police would find anything here. But she told them what she suspected anyway. When she was done,

Rivera said, "Caldwell will follow up for report purposes. You're free to go. The department thanks you for your help. Caldwell."

The detective opened the back door of the unmarked. A clear sign that Skye was to get in.

"I'll ride along," Rico said. He shot an angry look at his superior officer. If Rivera noticed it, he let it pass.

Skye slipped into the car, not bothered by the captain's attitude. Cops were a complication she didn't need. She'd just as soon not get into bed with them.

Her body tightened in argument as her eyes studied Rico. With one exception. She'd make an exception for him. But even as she admitted it to herself, she doubted that he'd ever cross the line to be with her. He was a cop and she was...a lot of things.

"The department owes you," Rico said as Caldwell started the engine and pulled back onto the road. Despite trying to clamp down on his anger, he couldn't keep the hostility from his voice at the way she'd been dismissed. A child was alive because of her. A murder scene was discovered.

Skye half-smiled. "Think the department will pay if I send a bill?"

Some of the tension left Rico. He laughed. "No. Rivera has been bitching about budget cuts all week."

She slipped the radio off her belt and handed it to him. Their fingers touched briefly and flashed icy heat up Rico's arm. His eyes locked on hers. He could swear he saw a flame deep in their centers.

"Don't want to get charged with theft of departmental property then." Her voice was lazy, soft, amused. It was like velvet against sensitive skin. To Rico it was a siren call that had his cock hardening. Frustration rippled through him. This was why Rivera had ordered Cia to drive Skye home.

¡Carajo! He'd see her all the way to her apartment and finish this. He'd take her as soon as they got out of sight. To hell

with what Caldwell might think. To hell with what the captain might say. He was on personal time now.

Caldwell hit the brake and swerved just enough to break the contact between Rico and Skye. He sent her a dark look. Her lips tightened into that disapproving line he was growing to hate. "Sorry, something ran out in front of the car," she muttered then turned her attention to Skye. "The crew at the murder site found a pentagram carved in a tree near the circle. What do you know about that kind of thing?" Her voice made it clear that she thought Skye had more than a passing acquaintance with black magic.

Skye shivered even though it was warm in the car. She leaned her head back against the seat. Whatever had transpired in the woods last night was dark and evil, something to be avoided. "They drained her of blood. Probably in the circle."

"Shit," Rico muttered. "Shit."

Caldwell whipped her head around. "How do you know that?"

Skye shrugged and didn't attempt an answer. She said, "What do you know about the niece, Rico?"

"Not much," he answered. "Just that Brittany was having some family problems."

"What kind of trouble?"

"Typical stuff. My take on it is teenage rebellion. That your take on it, Cia?"

"Yes. Black clothes. Black fingernails and lipstick. Multiple body piercings—nose, ear, tongue, probably more but that was enough to make me lose my appetite."

Skye laughed, which earned her a dark look from the detective. "Drugs?"

"Not that anyone knows about," Rico answered.

"Friends out here in Vegas?"

"Again, not that anybody knows about. Her parents are supposed to be going through her e-mails to see if she'd made any connections."

Skye looked at Rico. "You have a picture?"

"Yeah." He pulled the visor down, retrieved a picture and passed it to Skye.

She studied the punked-out kid who favored black even for her body jewelry. Brittany looked like a hundred other kids that Skye had seen in ghettos and high-end clubs alike. Lost, searching, sometimes heartbreakingly hopeless. "Okay if I keep this?"

"No," Caldwell said instantly.

"Keep it," Rico said at the same time.

"It's an ongoing police investigation, stay out of it," Caldwell managed through gritted teeth.

"I'll make a note of that," Skye said.

"You'd better."

Rico started to chide the other detective then thought about the last case and wondered if he'd done the right thing in letting Skye keep the picture. "You'll pass on anything you come across, right?"

"Of course. Always." Amusement rippled through her voice.

Rico tensed, sexual frustration making him edgy. He almost asked her to return the picture. Almost.

The radio in the unmarked came to life. Rivera's voice barked out an order for Rico to get back to the station as soon as the civilian was dropped off.

Caldwell visibly relaxed. Rico wanted to howl with frustration. Even for the fuck of his life he couldn't disobey a direct order. Unwillingly, he glanced back at Skye. Her mouth turned up in the half-smile that made him want to take her down to the floor and shove his tongue past her lips while his cock tunneled in and out of her cunt. He wanted to ride her so hard that the only smile she'd give him was soft and contented, not challenging or amused.

Fuck. Why couldn't he fall for one of the "nice" girls that his parents were always inviting over for dinner? Or at least one of the women who liked to hang out in cop bars and put out for guys wearing badges? Why'd his dick crave this particular woman?

Skye had them stop the car several blocks away from her apartment. "It makes the neighbors nervous when they see too many cop cars coming and going," she said as she gracefully slid from the unmarked.

"I'll contact you later today," Caldwell said, "for the report."

"Give me at least twelve hours to sleep."

Caldwell nodded, anxious to get away from Skye…anxious to get Rico away from her.

Skye's eyes met Rico's and darkened slightly. "See you around," she said before shutting the door and heading down the street.

He watched as she walked away. He wanted to follow her home and fuck her, then curl up around her body and sleep for twenty-four hours.

Shit. He couldn't take much more of this.

* * * * *

Skye rolled her shoulders in an effort to relax and let the events of the night fade. Even though she was physically tired, her body was tense, edgy.

She was changing. There was an underlying discontent now, a craving that hadn't been there before.

If she were like other women then she'd say it was her biological clock ticking. But she wasn't like other women. And it wasn't the urge to have children that made her restless, it was the urge to take a mate—or rather, two mates.

Skye wondered again about her origins. But she didn't attempt to search within herself. She'd long since learned that any attempt to explore the dark well of forgotten past sent shards of excruciating pain through her mind.

There were only vague, emotional memories of a happy time spent with a mother and two fathers, followed by the wrenching agony of separation, then later, the driving need to survive.

She'd had a computer hacker retrieve her records from the social services department. But there was nothing that she didn't already remember — she'd been found in a ghetto of Los Angeles at the age of five, a silent child with no history, no name.

Until she'd discovered the ability to hypnotize and sink into a self-induced state of being *other*, any attempt at speech had caused a sharp skull-piercing pain to rip through her mind.

She could speak now without the threat of pain but she still couldn't retrieve the memories. It hadn't mattered for a long time but now she feared that it soon would.

Her body was changing, making demands that her mind argued would be dangerous to her survival.

It had gotten worse since seeing Rico again. And that couldn't be a good sign.

For either of them.

A city bus passed and disappeared around the corner. A dark blue Yukon with tinted windows trailed behind it. Even out of sight, she could follow the progress of the bus. Its brakes squealed in the early morning air as it rolled to a stop. The engine strained when it accelerated again.

Skye rounded the same corner a few minutes later and had only an instant to take in the scene in front of her and react to it. The blue Yukon was alongside the curb. A man had his arm around a woman's neck, his hand over her mouth as he pulled her toward the car. She struggled wildly but without effect — he was three times her size, large and well-muscled.

Without hesitation Skye pulled the knife from its sheath on her leg. The man never saw her coming, only felt the sharp, excruciating pain as a blade cut deeply along his rib cage. He bellowed in rage and released the woman.

Skye crouched, completely focused on the man, ready for his charge. He took a step forward then stopped when the woman he'd been trying to abduct began screaming. Panic replaced the anger. He hesitated only a second longer then jumped into the Yukon. Its driver gunned the engine and took off. The car fishtailed around the corner. There was no time to get a license plate number.

The woman stopped screaming but couldn't seem to take her eyes off the bloody knife in Skye's hand. Skye slipped it back in its sheath as she said, "You okay?"

The woman nodded but she looked like the next loud noise would send her screaming down the street. "Angry boyfriend?" Skye asked.

"No. I didn't know him. I didn't know either of them."

Skye hated to ask, hated to lose the knife again, hated to think about being hauled into the police station for questioning but she offered anyway. "I live close to here. You can come in and call the cops."

The woman shook her head. "No. Please. No cops. I'll tell my boyfriend about it tonight."

Skye shrugged and felt a sliver of amusement creep in. Maybe for some women telling their boyfriends was enough. It wouldn't be for her. "Suit yourself."

When Skye started to walk away, the woman stopped her with a tentative touch on the arm. "Are you Skye Delano?"

Skye studied the woman for a long moment. She was small, petite, delicate, with short black hair and skin so pale it suggested that she didn't see the daylight very often. "Why do you want to know?"

The woman's free hand lifted to her necklace in a nervous gesture. "I was going to try and catch you at home. That's why I took the bus. I need your help. My sister's missing."

"And you are?"

"Haley Warren."

"Let's go to my apartment. You can tell me about your sister over coffee."

The woman offered a tentative smile along with a nod of acceptance and they traveled the short distance to Skye's apartment. There was only one room, with a tiny bathroom carved out of a wall. It was spartan, a place to sleep and eat, but not to live.

"How are you at making coffee?" Skye asked.

Haley smiled. "I've been a bartender, waitress, and short-order cook. Does that qualify me to make coffee for you?"

Skye laughed and felt at ease with her unexpected guest. She'd long ago learned to trust her instincts. "That'll do it. If you don't mind making some, I'd appreciate it. I've been running through the woods all night. I'd like to hit the shower before we talk."

"No problem. Take your time."

"Thanks. Coffee beans are in the freezer. Grinder is next to the coffeemaker." Skye waved her hand in the direction of the kitchen — or what served as the kitchen — a couple of appliances behind an L-shaped counter in one corner of the apartment.

She bypassed the sofa and chair, moved over next to the queen-size bed at the far end of the apartment, snagged some fresh clothes from the dresser before disappearing into the stamp-sized bathroom.

If she'd been alone she would have luxuriated in the hot stream of water then crashed. But those options weren't available to her now. So she took a quick shower, pulled on her clothes and went out to the couch.

A steaming cup of coffee waited for her on an end table, along with sugar and a small container of half-and-half. "You must have been one hell of a waitress," Skye said.

Haley's smile was quick and infectious. "I always made good tips." Then her smile faltered. "I don't know what you charge to look for a missing person, probably more than most waitresses can afford. I just want you to know, whatever you charge I can pay it. My boyfriend gives me money whenever I need it." She nervously touched the pendant on her necklace.

It was old and quite beautiful, the stone in the middle a deep, dark red. For an instant Skye felt pulled toward it—almost like a hypnotist's medallion. But then the sensation faded.

"Go ahead and tell me about your missing sister."

"Where do you want me to begin?"

"How long has she been missing?"

"Two months."

"Did you report it to the police?"

"No." Haley bit down on her lip. "Kyle, my boyfriend, has been looking for her." She began twisting the pendant.

Remembering her visitor's earlier reluctance to call the police, Skye said, "And he doesn't want you to call the cops?"

"It's not like they'd do much anyway." Haley's voice was defensive. But then something inside her seemed to collapse. "You might as well know all of it. Jen is eighteen. My parents live in Florida. She came out here about four months ago. She was hanging out with a friend, Amy Weldon, some hotshot senator's daughter. They were doing the club scene. At first I thought, okay, let her get it out of her system. I mean, I was like that when I was her age—fake IDs, hitting the bars, maybe saying yes to guys I should have said no to. It gets old after a while, especially if you don't have any money. And I knew Jen didn't have any money. I knew her friend Amy had to be paying for everything. So I thought she'd get tired of it and cut Jen loose." Haley stopped and looked at Skye for encouragement to continue.

Skye said, "Only she didn't."

"No, finally I said something to Jen about it. How could she mooch off her friend like that? She got pissed and said it wasn't my business but she'd tell me anyway. Amy's grandfather left her a pile of money and as soon as she turned nineteen she was going to be rolling in it, so Amy didn't care if she cleaned out her checking account now. She was going to be nineteen in a couple of weeks."

"Did your parents know Jen was out here?"

Haley looked like she was going to cry. "Yes. But they're real old-fashioned. I mean, *real* old-fashioned. They read the Bible every night. They go to church more than they go anyplace else. Vegas is Sin City to them. They won't step foot in it and they don't want to have anything to do with Jen or me until we repent and come back home on our own.

"I didn't blame Jen for not wanting to go back. But the more I saw her with Amy, the more worried I got. I thought maybe if Jen went back home, even for a little while, she'd chill out, find a different friend. So I called my parents and begged them to come out here and get her but they just started preaching about hell and damnation and repenting before my soul was lost for good. And then a week later Jen disappeared."

"And you don't think she left town?"

"No. She loved Vegas. And she would have told me if she was leaving."

"Have you talked to the friend?"

"Not since right after Jen disappeared. Amy was totally creepy about it."

"Why did you worry about Jen and Amy being together?"

"Have you ever been to a nightclub called Fangs?" Haley asked.

"No."

"Amy and Jen hung out there. It's for the Goth crowd. You know, Gothic. Vampires. That kind of thing. They were at the club every night. It was okay at first. I mean, that's the club Kyle and I go to. But then they started to get more and more into the scene. Finally Kyle fixed it so the bouncers wouldn't let Amy and Jen in anymore. He told me to stay away from them." Haley was twisting the pendant continuously now. "He's really protective of me."

Skye let the last comment pass. "Why did he want you to stay away from them?"

"Because Amy was really, really into the occult. And Jen started getting into it too."

Chapter Three

The back of Skye's neck tingled in awareness but the hair didn't stand up in alarm as it had in the woods. What were the odds of two teenage girls turning up missing in Vegas, both with some link to the occult? For Haley's sake, Skye hoped Jen didn't end up in the same condition as Brittany Armstrong.

Skye rose from the couch and retrieved the photo of Brittany from the jeans she'd left in the bathroom. When she handed the photo to Haley, she asked, "Does this girl look familiar?"

Haley worried her bottom lip between her teeth as she concentrated on the picture. "Sort of." She gave an apologetic shrug and returned the photo. "So many of the kids that come to Fangs look like that. I'm sorry. I can't be sure. Why?"

Now it was Skye's turn to shrug. "Another missing kid."

"I'm sorry I can't help."

"Do you know where Jen and Amy were living?"

"No. They always came to the club."

"What about other clubs? Any favorites?"

"I don't know."

"Do you have a picture of your sister?"

"Yes." Once again Haley's hand reached up and covered the pendant. "But I don't have it with me. I...I only just decided to try and find you. I didn't want to go back and get it."

"I'll need a photograph of Jen before I can do much to help you."

"I'll get you one." Haley twisted the necklace. "I'd better go. You can find me at the club. At Fangs. Kyle and I are there every night. He doesn't know about this. About me coming here. Please don't say anything in front of him."

"Haley, do you think he had something to do with Jen's disappearance?"

The woman visibly startled. "Oh no. No." Her voice was firm, confident. "It's not that. He's just very protective. That's all. He doesn't want me to get hurt."

Skye stared at the woman. Haley met the stare—a little timidly, but she met it and held it, and for a few seconds fell into the blue pools of Skye's hypnotic eyes. "You're sure he didn't have anything to do with your sister's disappearance?" Skye's voice was whisper-soft, like a warm breeze moving through the other woman's mind.

"Yes, I'm positive," Haley answered. And Skye knew she was telling the truth—or at least what she believed to be the truth.

A blink and Haley was free. She looked at Skye and searched her memory for what they'd been talking about. "I'll get you a photo."

"Okay. I'll swing by the club tonight."

Haley nodded and walked over to the door. "Thanks. I forgot to thank you earlier."

Skye thought about the men in the blue Yukon and took the moment to trap Haley once again. "Have you seen the men who attacked you before?"

Haley's brows pulled together in guileless concentration. Her answer was the same under hypnosis as it had been at the bus stop. She didn't know who her attackers were.

Skye released her and asked, "Do you need a lift somewhere?"

"No. No thanks."

"I'll walk you back to the bus stop then."

Haley's voice was barely a whisper. "If it wouldn't be too much trouble."

* * * * *

The phone rang and woke Skye. She started to get out of bed to answer it then heard Detective Caldwell's chilly, efficient voice as the machine picked up.

She tuned the voice out and snuggled under the covers, letting her mind drift, shuffling and replaying the events of the last twenty-four hours.

Without a picture there wasn't much she could do to help Haley find her sister. Names were meaningless in the club scene. Easy to change. Easy to forget.

Skye had her doubts about being able to locate Jen Warren in the first place. Especially if the boyfriend had been looking for the last two months. That was still a big "if" in her mind. Any number of possibilities flitted through her thoughts. The boyfriend might know where the sister went, or what happened to her. If he was spooked by the interest in the occult, and money was no problem, he may have just paid the sister to disappear from Haley's life.

The simplest thing to do would be to take the answer out of his mind. Skye wondered how easily that could be accomplished. Despite the police rumors, not every one was susceptible to hypnosis, and Skye rarely took a person so deep that they blurted out everything they knew, much less did anything she asked.

About the only lead Skye could follow up on was to find out where the other girl, Amy Weldon, was and go see her. Too bad Haley didn't know where Amy was staying or even if she was still in Vegas.

Caldwell's voice stopped. The answering machine clicked a few times to indicate it was finished recording and was now prepared for the next call. Skye got out of bed, dug around in the dresser and selected black jeans and a pale blue tank top then wandered over to the phone.

It was a long shot, but worth a try. She looked through the government pages and found a listing for the U.S. Senate. A call later and she knew there were two Senator Weldons. One from Florida, one from New York.

Haley and Jen were from Florida. Skye called that senator first and left a message explaining that she was trying to locate Amy in connection with a missing person's case. Then she redialed and left a message for the other senator.

That done, she retrieved her switchblade and slipped it into her pocket along with the picture of Brittany Armstrong, then laced on black boots and snagged her Harley jacket. She would just as soon eat at Fangs than linger at home and risk Detective Caldwell getting impatient and doing a drive-by.

It was three flights of steps down to the parking garage. The Harley waiting for her was the only thing Skye had ever splurged on. Its black paint and silver chrome shone in the dimness. Its engine surged to life at a touch, promising freedom and power, reminding Skye of how it felt to run unchallenged in remote woods and across open desert.

Fangs was on the outskirts of town in an almost isolated area. The parking lot was full and a long line of people waited to get into the club.

Skye wandered over to join the crowd. Most of them seemed young, female, and covered with body piercings and perfume. The smell of pot and booze and Ecstasy permeated the air around them.

She slipped her Harley jacket off. The evening air was warm and relaxing. Skye let it fill her, soak into her, refresh her.

As the last of the sun disappeared, the door to the nightclub opened. A man stepped out. Like the crowd waiting to get in, he wore black. A ripple of excitement moved down the line as the bouncer began checking IDs and letting people inside.

Skye studied the crowd around her and was amused by how many sported hickeys. Not just one, but multiple bite marks, as though they'd been the main course at a ten-person meal.

A thin kid with a bad case of acne sidled up to her. Made bold by alcohol and a sense of being in his element, he flashed a fanged smile and asked, "You alone?"

Skye blinked in surprise. The boy's smile widened to show her his filed, pointed teeth. "Meeting somebody," she told him.

He looked back to the end of the line where a couple of girls his age were standing and watching him. "Okay if I hang here?"

She studied him. He was just barely twenty-one, physically, younger emotionally and intellectually—a world apart from her in experience. "Sure. It's a free country."

"I'm Mike," he said, flashing his fangs.

"I'm Skye."

"I haven't seen you here before."

"First time." She smiled at him. He fell into her eyes without urging. Skye blinked and turned her head slightly, releasing him, surprised at how susceptible he was to hypnosis. She hadn't accidentally trapped someone since she was a child learning how to deal with her strange ability. "You look like you're a regular here," she said.

"I come here pretty much every night."

"Are most of these people regulars?"

"Yeah. A lot of them are."

A groan went up among the people standing in line as forward movement stopped. The bouncer disappeared into the club for a second then stepped back out, closing the door behind him.

Mike sighed. "I thought for sure they wouldn't cut it off until you got in. The vamps like women with long hair."

Skye examined his face. She didn't need to hypnotize him to know that he was serious. "Vamps?"

He was startled by her question, momentarily unsure of himself. "Uh, sure. Isn't that why you're here, to uh, to be with a vamp?" He flashed his fangs again, but with less confidence.

Skye wanted to laugh. She wondered if maybe she'd been staring at herself in the mirror and had somehow fallen into a weird subconscious reality. "I'm just getting into this whole Goth scene," she said, remembering Haley's term.

Mike straightened. "Oh, so, like, you don't have any experience with vampires yet."

She studied him and knew from years of experience that he wasn't jiving her, he was serious about this. "No."

He looked up as the girls from the end of the line joined them. "Guess we're not going to get in," one of them said. Her voice was heavy with disappointment.

The other girl slipped her arm through Mike's. Her eyes flashed with jealousy. The boy looked uncomfortable. He muttered, "That's my sister Candy and this is Dawn."

Dawn glared. "I'm his girlfriend."

Candy offered a shy smile. "We were hoping they'd let us in with you. The vamps *always* go for people that look like you."

It amused Skye that they'd thought to use her as their ticket into Fangs. She didn't bother to contain her laugh. It was soft, unconsciously seductive, as warm as the night breeze.

Candy's eyes widened and she clutched her brother's arm, jumped in place a few times. "He's coming this way. Oh my god, he's coming this way."

The bouncer was moving along the line of people. As he passed, some of the women flirted outrageously with him. He stopped briefly, sent several up to wait for him at the entrance then continued on.

Skye followed him with her eyes. Felt the excitement of the three people next to her as the dark-haired man stopped in front of them. His gaze met hers boldly before moving to encompass the other three then returning to Skye. "They're with you?"

"Yes."

The bouncer gave a small nod of acknowledgment. "You're in," he said before turning around and going back to the club door.

Candy and Dawn both squealed. Mike flashed his fangs at Skye.

"Let's go before he changes his mind!" Candy grabbed her brother and Dawn. The three of them hustled after the bouncer.

Skye followed her new companions, amusing herself with the thought that they might ditch her once they got inside. But they didn't.

The club was packed but they found a table against the wall furthest from the dance floor. "We're in," Mike breathed as he sank into a chair. "This is SO RAD."

"Don't you come here every night?" Skye asked.

He flushed. "Uh, sure, but we don't get in that often."

"So you just hang out all night in line?"

Candy giggled. "It's not so bad. The waiters come out and take drink orders. We've made friends with some of them. When they're working they can usually get us inside once it gets late."

"And you come here because you want to meet a vampire?" Skye couldn't keep the hint of disbelief out of her voice.

"Well sure." Dawn gave Skye a strange look. "I mean, this is where you come if you want to, like, meet a vampire. Isn't that why you're here?"

Mike broke into the conversation, "She's just getting into the Goth scene."

Dawn and Candy both nodded, like that explained everything. Dawn said, "So you're a vampire virgin."

Skye laughed. Despite the black clothes, pierced noses and lips, these kids were so much simpler than most of the runaways she hunted. She was enjoying them. "Maybe you guys could clue me in."

Candy almost bounded out of her seat in excitement. "Sure. Oh yeah. I mean, it's the least we can do. We've never gotten into the club this early before."

"I'll go get us some beers," Mike volunteered.

Skye reached into a pocket and handed him some bills. "Whatever's on tap is fine. First round's on me."

"Hey, thanks." He pocketed the money and hurried toward the bar. Skye was surprised that Dawn hadn't gone with him so she could guard her territory. But the girl had a bigger plan. She leaned over and said, "The whole thing about being with a vampire is the sex. It's incredible. I mean, mind-blowing. It's because they take your blood while they're doing it, not that you remember that part, but you just *know* it was one of the things that made the sex so great. I mean, don't get me wrong, Mike is great and all, but not like a vampire. Somebody who looks like you doesn't have to settle for a vampire wannabe."

"So you've done it with a vampire?" Skye asked.

"Before Mike and I hooked up," Dawn said then added dramatically, "now I have to live on the memories."

"What about you?" Skye asked Candy.

The older girl ducked her head. "I've just been bitten a couple of times." She fingered the hickeys on her neck. "Most of them were just wannabes, I could tell after it was over, but one of them was the real thing…I mean, wow, I thought I was going to faint when his mouth was on my neck, only his girlfriend got pissed and he stopped before he actually bit me."

"Was she a vamp, too?"

"She wishes," Candy muttered. "No. She works over at the MGM. She's a maid like me. We both work the day shift."

"Guess she can't be a vampire then." Skye looked around the club. The dance floor was overflowing. People were packed around every table and along the bar. She retrieved the picture of Brittany and put it on the table. "Do you remember seeing this girl at Fangs?"

The two girls exchanged glances. Skye hoped they'd answer willingly, not force her to hypnotize them. "Are you like a cop or something?" Candy asked.

"Or something." Skye shrugged. "It's no big deal if you can't help."

Dawn picked the picture up and studied it. "I think she was here last week." Candy took the picture from her. "Yeah. She didn't get in though. At least, not that I know of."

"Was she alone?"

Candy shrugged. "I don't know."

"I didn't notice," Dawn said.

Mike returned with the drinks. His sister showed him the picture. "Skye wants to know if we've seen this girl."

He swallowed. "Uh, you're not a cop or anything, are you?"

"No." She let her senses flow out momentarily. There was just the barest trace of pot in his system. The girls had none in theirs.

"Uh—" he looked back down at the picture, "—yeah, I think she was here one night last week. She hung out in the line but she was behind us. None of the waiters we know were working that night, so we didn't get in the club."

"Did you notice if she was with anybody?"

"Is she in trouble or something?" Mike asked.

"No." For an instant she let him slide into the blue pools of her eyes. "Did you notice if she was with anyone?"

He concentrated, frowned. "I don't think so. She left before we did. Only she walked. Yeah, I remember that now. I mean, it's not like we're even close to a bus stop or anything."

Skye blinked and released him. "How late do you guys stay when you can't get in?"

"Three or four in the morning, usually," Candy answered. "I mean, most of the vamps are probably gone by then. They've only got until the sun comes up to do whatever they do."

"Makes sense." Skye put the picture back in her pocket then took a long sip of beer. "So how do you tell the real thing?"

"You get a rush just by looking at one of them," Mike answered. "I mean, if you hadn't shown up before the sun went down, I would've thought you were a vampire."

Dawn moved closer to her boyfriend, dismayed by his answer. Candy said, "Oh my god, there's one. He's got to be one. Look at him."

Edgy awareness and need rippled through Skye as soon as she glanced up. Pure sex. That's what she thought when she saw him.

He was tall, filled out with well-defined muscles, his stomach flat. There was nothing underneath the black vest but smooth skin. Matching black pants hugged his body like a sensual embrace as he skirted the dance floor. Long black hair was held away from his face by a leather strap. A deep red ruby glinted from a single earring stud. He had the face of a dark angel.

A mate, her body claimed, sending a pulse of heat to Skye's cunt, the primitive, internal voice inside of her getting harder to ignore.

"Wow," Candy breathed when the man disappeared out of sight around one end of the bar.

"Yeah, wow," Dawn echoed. This time it was Mike who moved closer in a jealous gesture.

"Definitely a vamp," Candy said.

"Yeah, definitely," Dawn agreed.

Their comments eased some of the tension in Skye's body. She hid a smile in her beer mug before taking another sip. Except for the flashes of fang and the uniform all-black clothing that the patrons wore, this club was like a lot of nightspots Skye had been in. "So how'd you find this place, anyway?" she asked idly.

"On the Internet," Mike answered.

Dawn giggled. "Believe it or not, Mike's a real computer geek. His boss is *always* asking him to fix stuff on the computer."

Skye smiled at the boy. These kids were a surprise. She had a laptop and knew how to do searches, but mainly she used it to research locations when she was out of town and hunting.

"Really?" she asked. "What'd you do, search for vampire hangouts?"

Mike grinned at her. "No, there are a lot of newsgroups on the web. We joined some of them. Then found out about a private chat room. Somebody in it mentioned this place and we decided to check it out."

Candy chimed in, "The Internet is, like, so cool. There are people from all over the country in the chat room. The person who told us about this club was from San Francisco. But they'd been in Vegas with a friend who knew about Fangs."

"So mainly you just chat about vampire hangouts?"

Dawn giggled. "You must not hang out in any chat rooms."

"You're right. So what do people talk about?"

"EVERYTHING," Candy said dramatically then grinned, "but mainly sex."

A slow song started to play. Dawn tugged at Mike's hand. "Let's dance." He gulped a swallow of beer to fortify himself and followed her to the dance floor.

Skye watched them dance. The girl next to her sighed. "They're so cute together."

"You don't have a boyfriend?" Skye gently probed.

"No."

Skye studied the girl. Like her brother, she was battling a case of acne, though hers wasn't as bad and she'd done a good job with her makeup. Her brown hair was short and spiky, and left her ears with their collection of studs and rings showing. Unlike Dawn and Mike, Candy didn't have jewelry in her nose or lip. But even with less jewelry and longer hair, she'd always be average-looking.

"This place doesn't seem like it'd be very good for meeting guys," Skye finally said. "It looks like there are about five women for every man."

Candy slowly spun her beer mug on the table. "I know Dawn said the whole thing about being with a vampire is sex and all, but if one of them gives you some of his blood then it'd make you, uh, you know, like, way more attractive to the opposite sex." The girl ducked her head, embarrassed to reveal so much about herself.

Skye tried to lighten the mood. "I thought you ended up a vampire if they made you drink their blood."

"Well, yeah, that can happen, too. But they've got to, like, totally drain you of blood then give it back to you. It'd be cool to have all that vampire power. That's what Mike wants. I mean, the cool thing about being a computer geek, you can do that anytime. You don't have to be up during the day. But I like going out in the sun and stuff. I don't really want to become a vampire, just maybe have one for a boyfriend, or at least make friends with one."

Skye stroked her finger down the length of the beer mug. She could feel the pieces of the puzzle beginning to slip into place. "Do you guys talk about dark magic and occult rituals in your chat room?"

Candy gave a dramatic shudder. "Sometimes. But only about how creepy that kind of stuff is and how people who don't really *know* about vampires sometimes think it's all the same."

Skye finished her beer and wondered if this was what Haley meant when she said Jen and Amy were really getting into the Goth scene. Had they come here night after night trying to meet vampires and perhaps become one? Had Brittany Armstrong been looking for the same thing?

It couldn't be a coincidence that Brittany Armstrong had been totally drained of blood. Had she thought she'd rise with vampiric power, only to end up very, very dead?

Mike and Dawn returned, flushed and sexually stimulated, both with new hickeys on their necks. Dawn giggled and told Candy, "Tom from work just walked in. Go ask him to dance."

Skye thought again how refreshing these kids were, despite their vampire fantasies. She stood and decided to see if Haley was here with Jen's picture. "I'll be back. Keep an eye on the jacket, okay?"

"Hey, sure, no problem," Mike said.

Skye slipped through the crowd easily and found an opening at the bar so that she could look around. Haley was at a corner table. It was set apart from the other tables in a way that hinted this area was reserved, private, and trespassers wouldn't be welcomed.

There was another woman at the table and three men. Skye studied them all. She'd assumed Haley's boyfriend Kyle would be big and muscled, not short and wiry. But there was no doubt in Skye's mind that the red-haired guy sitting so close to the small woman was her very protective boyfriend. His arm was draped possessively over the back of her chair, his hand covered hers where it rested on the table.

The other woman was tall and beautiful. And like Haley, she also wore a necklace with an old, beautiful pendant on it. Her pale skin and blonde hair were a perfect contrast to the ebony-skinned man next to her. The third man at the table was the gorgeous "vampire." As soon as Skye focused on him, the edginess returned full-force. She looked away and met Haley's startled glance.

Consciously or unconsciously, Haley's free hand began worrying her pendant. Skye turned her head slightly in response to the bartender's presence and ordered another beer, leaving it to Haley to make the first move.

A few minutes later Haley passed the bar, disappearing down a short hallway and into the woman's bathroom. Skye paid for the beer, took several sips then followed Haley into the bathroom.

The other woman was nervous but she gave Skye a hesitant smile and retrieved a photograph from the small black purse she was carrying. "Here's the picture."

Skye took it, glancing at it briefly. Jen was a younger version of Haley. They could almost have passed for twins, though Jen favored body piercing and Haley apparently didn't.

The bathroom door opened and the blonde who'd been sitting at Haley's table walked in. Haley turned quickly, leaned into the mirror as though she was checking her makeup. Skye slipped the photo into her pocket and left the bathroom to reclaim her spot at the bar.

She was halfway through her beer when a familiar scent drifted over her, causing her womb to ripple and her vulva to swell and grow slick. She looked up as Rico stopped next to her. "What are you doing here, Skye?"

Chapter Four

His voice and eyes were all cop, but it didn't matter to her body. The danger he represented didn't stop her heart from beating more rapidly, from sending lava-hot blood through her veins, from making her want to rub her body against his and entice him to mate with her.

Skye fought the need and answered, "Just out for a night on the town, Rico."

He moved closer, unable to stop himself from doing it. His cock was rock-hard, visions of taking her here, now, of pushing her onto the bar and standing between her legs, thrusting into her until she screamed in release washed over him, dampening his chest with sweat. *¡Carajo!* When had he ever wanted to claim a woman in front of witnesses?

Rico forced his mind away from the vivid fantasies. He was on the job. He had to know that she wasn't here hunting Brittany Armstrong's killers.

"This doesn't seem like your kind of place," he said.

"It doesn't seem like yours either."

"Just checking something out for a case."

She took a swallow of beer, watching him closely as she asked, "So how does this place link to Brittany Armstrong?"

He was good, there was just the briefest hesitation, but she knew she'd guessed correctly. Rico tried to change the subject. "Caldwell said you didn't call her back."

Skye laughed, but didn't bother to deny knowing about the detective's call. Rico frowned at her. "Cia's a good cop. Rivera wants her to tie up the loose ends with you. Don't give her a hard time."

"I'm not on the police payroll," Skye reminded him. "But I'll make you a deal. Tell me what you've got that ties Brittany to this club and I'll go quietly to the police station and help your detective with her paperwork."

He gritted his teeth as frustrated lust shifted to anger. She always played it the way she wanted. Screw the rules. Screw the law or duty or anything else.

"It's an open police investigation," he reminded her.

"Yes, I think Caldwell told me that." Skye looked down at her watch and noticed that it was well after midnight. "Yesterday, I believe."

"Why do you want to know about Brittany Armstrong?"

Skye shrugged as though none of it really mattered. "Curiosity, Rico. You're here, I'm here. Why not ask?"

He watched her sip the beer and idly look around the club. His earlier suspicions seemed like paranoia. She was the best at what she did, had found kids when there was no hope of finding them. A hunter, a tracker. But not a killer. There was no hard evidence to prove she was a killer. The information she wanted wasn't sensitive, she'd guessed the most important thing anyway. "You'll go to the station?"

The corner of her mouth twitched. "Anything to help the police."

Rico ignored the comment and said, "Brittany's parents came up with the name of this place. She'd printed out a posting from some site on the internet about a cool place in Vegas." He shrugged. "There's no real tie but I figured it'd be worth checking out. The kid was nuts, living in a fantasy world. The local police pulled in the computer. All they've got so far is that Brittany spent a lot of time online visiting vampire sites and hanging out in chat rooms with other kids just as crazy."

"Like these kids?" Skye suggested with a slight smile. From where they stood next to the bar, Skye could see at least four kids sporting filed, fang-like teeth.

"Yeah." His tone said he'd already made a judgment about the kids at Fangs. "Do you have Brittany's picture with you?"

Skye thought about the picture zipped in her Harley jacket. She knew she shouldn't play with him this way, but she couldn't stop herself. "Want to frisk me and see, Rico." Her voice was low, soft, purposefully seductive. It stroked him like a lover's caress.

His eyes dilated. Fantasies merged and burned through him. He knew that he shouldn't touch her. He did anyway as a slow song began playing.

She went willingly into his arms as he guided her onto the dance floor. Their bodies rubbed, pressed, melded. He unbraided her hair and ran his fingers through it. He stopped thinking about being a cop and just let himself feel. He was rock-hard, a constant state when he was around her.

His hands skimmed down her back, pulling the tank top out of her jeans so he could run his palms over the warm skin of her sides. "God," he groaned, burying his face into her hair.

She pressed against his hardness, enjoying the friction of the slow dance. Her nipples were tight and hard. Her sex already swollen and wet, prepared for him. She could smell her own arousal—and his. He smelled right. The primitive part of her recognized him for what he could be—what he was. A mate.

Skye hadn't been with anyone for so long. Hadn't wanted to be, though there was always a hint of need tingling through her.

Now, as she took his scent into her lungs, a shiver of fear raced along her spine. If she slept with him, there might not be an escape for either of them.

Self-preservation warred with urges unfamiliar in their intensity but Skye couldn't stop herself from playing in the fire of lust. She nuzzled into his chest and used her teeth to take a small playful hold on his shirt-covered nipple.

Rico groaned and pulled her more tightly against his body. Waves of lust shot from his nipple to his already engorged cock.

He was desperate for her. So desperate that he was tempted to forget that he was on the job, that Caldwell—his newly assigned partner and guard dog—was going to be here any minute. He was so desperate that he wanted to pull Skye out to his car and fuck her there. He couldn't stand the thought of another day spent like today, so horny that he couldn't get to sleep, jerking off only to be hard again and again. Shit, it was worse than when he was a teenager.

Skye wound her arms around his neck and brushed her fingers against the hair where it touched his collar. She let herself sink into the heat of him.

She wanted to trail kisses up his neck, along his jaw, cover his lips with hers and absorb him like a sensual feast while their tongues slid against each other and mated in the dark wet heat of their mouths.

She wanted to, but she didn't.

Her mind overrode what her body desired.

Rico would be a dangerous mate.

He was a cop.

And for her, the hunt and the kill were sometimes inexorably tied together.

The music changed, picking up in pace. Rico stiffened and stepped away. Out of the corner of her eye, she saw Detective Caldwell approaching the bar. The phone on his belt began to hum. Rico pulled it off and checked the number. "I've got to go."

Their eyes met and locked. Heat simmered between them. He stepped back. "Return Caldwell's call, okay?"

Aroused. Torn. Edgy with need, Skye nodded and watched him leave.

"Who was *he*?" Candy asked when Skye returned to the table. "I mean, he was like, *so hot!*"

"A friend," Skye said as she pulled the picture of Jen out of her pocket. "What about this girl? Ever seen her here?"

Mike flashed his fangs. "Is it worth a round of beers?"

"Sure."

"Okay." He scooted closer and glanced at the picture. "Yeah, she used to come here every night."

Dawn leaned forward. "I remember her. She *always* got in. And she *never* had to wait in line. But I haven't seen her in like, maybe a couple of months."

"She come alone or with a friend?"

"With another girl I think. You remember, Candy?"

Candy studied the picture. "Yeah, I think she had a friend with her. They cut in line every time." She shrugged. "They were probably friends with a vamp and that's why they always got in."

"You ever see them with a vamp?" The kids all shook their head "no". "And you haven't seen them lately?" Once again the kids all indicated they hadn't.

"Thanks." Skye zipped the photo into the same jacket pocket that held Brittany's picture then pulled some bills from her jeans and began to count out the beer money.

"Oh my god," Candy breathed, "oh my god. Vamp alert! Vamp alert!"

Dawn and Mike both twisted in their seats. Skye looked up. The gorgeous "vampire" who'd been sitting with Haley was gliding toward them.

"May I join you?" he asked as he stopped next to the table. His voice was velvet seduction, but it was his eyes that drew her as he sat down without waiting for an answer.

They were as black as a starless night. Yet deep within them a flame burned, tempted, promised ecstasy to anyone who could reach it and bathe in its heat. Skye leaned forward, let the darkness surround her as she moved toward the flame. The lust that had been riding her when she was with Rico returned with a vengeance. She wanted relief. She wanted what the deep flame offered. But the promise remained elusive, just out of reach, encouraging the seeker to move further and further into the darkness.

Without conscious thought, Skye slipped into another world. Into being *other*. And as soon as she did, she saw the flame for what it was. Understood the power of the hunter in front of her.

A jolt of surprise ripped through her. She'd never met anyone else who could hypnotize as she did.

He was very good at it. And very powerful. But her strength had been forged in hell. With a blink and a slight twist of her head she easily escaped the trap of his eyes.

His face registered shock before it changed into an emotionless mask. The midnight-colored eyes never left her face as he murmured, "I am Giovanni Banderali. Gian to my friends."

His voice was silky-soft, tempting and beautiful. Yet he was dangerous, deadly — as she was.

Adrenaline whipped through Skye's body along with desire. "Skye Delano," she said, letting her voice duel with his, move over him like an erotic fantasy.

The flame in the dark centers of his eyes flared even as the look of a hungry predator flickered across his face.

Skye turned to her companions. They sat around the table in eager disbelief. Transfixed. Unable to believe their good fortune or speak. Unable to take their eyes off the man they thought was a vampire.

"Candy, Dawn, and Mike," she introduced them.

Gian acknowledged each of them, staring briefly into their eyes as he did so. A waitress appeared at the table unsummoned. "Were you about to order something?" Gian asked.

"Beers," Mike managed. "We were getting a round of beers."

Without a word the waitress disappeared. She returned within moments with four beers and a wineglass full of dark red wine.

"Oh, wow," Candy breathed. "You're the real thing. I just know you're the real thing."

Skye only barely managed to contain a laugh. Gian gave a slight smile and shook his head when Skye started to hand the waitress some money. "It's on the house."

"This is your place?" she asked.

"Along with some partners."

"At the private table?"

"You're very observant."

Skye half-smiled as she let her eyes move over his features, linger. He was unforgettable. Like no man she'd ever encountered before. He was pure sex. Life and death rolled into the same coin.

Her body recognized him, just as it did Rico.

A mate.

"You're hard to miss," she said without inflection and let her eyes wander from Gian over to the kids.

His eyes lingered on her for a second longer then he too shifted his focus to include the others in his comment. "I don't think I've seen you here before."

"Oh," Dawn was finally able to speak, "we're here every night."

Candy added, "But mainly we're waiting outside."

"Your club is like so totally rad," Mike said.

Gian gave a small smile. "I'll tell the doorkeeper that you may come into the club any time it's open. There's no need to wait in line."

"Oh my god, oh my god," Candy breathed. "I can't believe this. It's like the best night in my life."

"Perhaps mine as well," Gian murmured. His dark eyes moved over Skye. "I can't believe you've also been waiting outside."

"This is Skye's first night here," Mike volunteered before she could answer. "She's just getting into the scene."

Dawn giggled and added, "Yeah, she's a vampire virgin still."

Something burned deep in Gian's eyes. He studied Skye. "Is that why you're here? You're trying to find a vampire?"

Skye felt the pull of his eyes, as though once again he was trying to draw her into their darkness. Her lips tilted up in an amused smile. "That's not high on my list tonight."

His eyes lingered on her face for a long moment before moving back and focusing on Mike. "The DJ is doing a good job. Wouldn't you agree, Mike? It makes you want to get out on the dance floor."

Without hesitation, Mike stood. "You're right. Come on, Dawn. The music is too good to miss. Let's dance." He didn't stop to take a fortifying gulp of beer as he had before the last dance, this time he practically dragged his girlfriend to the dance floor.

Skye picked up her own beer and took a swallow as she waited to see what Gian would do next. He turned slightly in his chair. Several tables over four young men sat. Like Mike, they were completely dressed in black. Three of them had canine teeth elongated and filed into sharp points. They were animated, high or drunk. The fourth sported silver studs and chains, but was quieter than his companions. There was no obvious contact between Gian and the young man, no point at which Skye knew Gian had used hypnosis, and yet the young man looked over at where Candy sat and got to his feet.

He was hesitant, almost shy in his approach. But soon he stood next to the table, his attention on Candy. "Uh. Hi. You want to, uh, dance?"

"Yeah," Candy answered, breathless.

Skye watched as the two young people moved through the crowd and got to the dance floor. Then she turned to Gian. "You're very good. I'm impressed."

"And yet you can elude me."

Her heart began racing in anticipation as he moved so close that she could feel his warm breath across her lips. "Can I?"

"Who were you dancing with earlier?" His voice was a seductive whisper.

"A friend."

"A lover?"

She smiled slightly, but didn't answer.

He reached up and gently stroked her cheek then cupped the side of her face in his hand, trapping her so that their eyes met, so that she couldn't break his hold, couldn't look away.

Skye laughed. It was low, sensual, excited. It held no fear.

She stroked the line of skin bared by the vest he wore and slipped her hand under the smooth fabric so that it rested on his heart. Then without warning, her eyes became the endless blue of a summer sky. She felt him fall into them and beckoned him to come deeper, to rejoice in the sensation of being a hawk flying high over the desert. To embrace the warmth of the sun. The power of the breeze.

He stayed with her, though she knew he was not yet trapped in the illusion. Underneath her palm his heart began beating faster. And then his mind pulled away, took hers with it, dropping them into night-darkened woods. Into the sensation of running as a wolf runs, effortlessly, powerfully. The smell of the earth was intense, familiar to Skye. So many times this was what she'd become when she searched. A hunter, a predator rejoicing in the movement of body, in being alive.

His voice whispered across her. Commanding, compelling, his voice a smooth trap. "Come with me."

It was a dangerous game they played.

She let the illusion go, escaping from his mind and letting him escape from hers. "Where to?" she asked and once again saw shock register on his face at being unable to trap her.

"To my table."

Skye laughed, amused. Perhaps she'd have asked this same thing of him if she'd been able to hold him in her eyes. "Okay."

They stood. Skye pulled her jacket off the back of the chair and followed Gian.

As soon as Haley saw Skye, her hand flew to the pendant in an agitated gesture. The man next to her noticed the reaction. His eyes sharpened, moving from Skye to Haley and back again. His posture screamed possessiveness, a willingness to do anything to protect what was his. And once again Skye wondered if he was responsible for the disappearance of Haley's sister.

Gian indicated the empty seat next to Haley. Skye sat down. He followed her, introducing the pale blonde as Kisha, her boyfriend as Nahir before saying, "I think you've already met Haley."

"If you call sharing a sink in the ladies' bathroom an introduction," Skye said easily, naturally. She smiled at the other woman and added, "I'm Skye Delano."

Haley's hand never left the pendant. "I'm Haley Warren." Her eyes flit nervously to the man beside her. "This is my boyfriend, Kyle."

Syke met his eyes and knew instantly that he too could use them to hypnotize. There was little doubt in her mind that by the end of the night he'd know about Haley's visit to her apartment. If the other woman didn't lose her nerve and confess, her boyfriend would simply pull it out of her mind.

They played cat and mouse. Parried with questions and answers until dawn approached and the club began to clear of people.

Emboldened by the events of the evening, Mike and Candy and Dawn dared to stop by the private table. Candy impulsively hugged Skye and whispered, "Thanks for everything."

As they left, Skye wondered how many hours of sleep she'd get before having to face the music and visit Detective Caldwell. "I'd better get going, too," she murmured.

Kyle stood, helping Haley to her feet. Skye watched them closely and saw no fear in the other woman's face.

Gian also stood, offered his hand to Skye. She let him pull her up.

"We'll meet again, I'm sure," Kyle said.

"Yes, I'm sure of that, too."

Haley's glance flew from her boyfriend to Skye and back. Her hand reached up and began worrying the pendant. But she followed Kyle willingly as he led her away.

Gian kept a hand on Skye's arm as they walked out to where the Harley was parked. "Nice bike," he said.

She turned and leaned against it. "Yeah. I love it. Maybe I'll take you for a ride on it sometime."

He moved into her, slid his arms around her waist and pulled her against his body. She put her arms around his neck, did what she'd been aching to do since she first saw him. She slipped the band out of his long black hair and ran her fingers though it.

Gian groaned and covered her lips with his. She opened her mouth so that their tongues could touch, slide against each other, send desire shimmering through them.

His hand moved up, cupping her breast through the thin tank top and equally thin bra. Need shot through her. Hot, fierce. She moaned. Their lower bodies shifted, rubbed, strained to mimic what their tongues were doing.

When the kiss ended, both of them were breathing hard. Gian stepped back. Skye's body screamed in protest, in frustrated need.

"Come back to the club when it opens tonight," he said.

The survival instinct that had kept her alive warned that playing with him would be addicting, all-consuming, too dangerous. "Maybe," she answered.

Gian moved in to her again, capturing her face with his hand. He was all predator now. His body so completely motionless that it melted into the night.

She watched him. As silent and still as he was. Two dangerous hunters sizing each other up.

Then he lowered his head again, brushing soft kisses along her throat, stopping over her rapidly beating pulse. He bit down gently, laved the spot with his tongue, and bit again. Heat burned through her, racing through every artery, every vein like a roaring fire.

"Come to the club tonight," he whispered against her neck.

"Maybe," she repeated.

He bit again, harder this time then moved upward, covering her mouth with his, making thought and conversation impossible. When the kiss ended, Gian said, "I've got to go back in now. I'll see you tonight."

A soft laugh escaped her. Yes, her body demanded. Maybe, her instincts cautioned. But she didn't say anything as he moved away from her, blending with the night before disappearing into the dark interior of the club.

She brought the Harley's powerful engine to life and headed home.

* * * * *

Inside the club, Gian tapped out a code and the door securing the private chambers opened. Kyle stood in the hallway, waiting.

"She lied about not knowing Haley," Kyle said without preamble. "Haley sought her out and asked her to look for Jen."

"Then I owe your companion a reward for luring Skye here."

Kyle's face tightened. "You take this too lightly, Gian. Skye is dangerous to us. She reeks of the Angelini bloodline. I could feel her touch on Haley's mind."

"And did your companion betray us?"

Kyle hissed, flashing needle-sharp fangs to show his displeasure. "You know she didn't. You know my blocks will hold."

"Then let me worry about Skye. She's my problem now."

Amazement flashed across Kyle's features. "You plan to bind her?" This time when he spoke his fangs were sheathed.

Fire raced along Gian's veins. In all the centuries he'd been alive, he'd never desired any woman enough to bind her to him as a companion. But tonight that had changed. He smiled in anticipation of the hunt to come. "Yes. She will belong to me."

"And you will share her with another? A shifter? A human?" Kyle asked, disbelief sounding in his voice.

"She is not bound to another."

"Yet." Kyle's face grew somber. "The Angelini have always taken two mates in order to make their hunting easier, in order to better protect themselves. You know that as well as I do."

"She has their blood in her, but she is not completely one of them."

"And I say again—yet. Have you ever known one of their bloodline to be anything but a hunter?" Kyle shook his head. "You take unnecessary chances. What of her family? They may well declare you rogue for binding her to you. Then they would claim it as their right to kill you."

Gian flashed a smile, allowing a hint of fangs to show. "I do not fear the Angelini. And they can make no claim on her. Perhaps she is not even known to them. She doesn't bear their mark."

"But she reeks of them. She's dangerous, as they are. She was born to kill our kind." Kyle's fangs glistened as he spat the words, "Vampire hunter."

"She will be my companion."

"And if you can't control her then you'll be forced to kill her."

Gian's eyes flashed to red, his lips pulled back, exposing his fangs. "She will be mine."

* * * * *

The first rays of the sun had broken over the horizon as Skye pulled into the parking garage. Rico was waiting for her there.

He pushed himself away from the hood of his car. His face was taut with desire. The front of his pants stretched tight over his erection.

His eyes darkened with furious need when he looked at Skye's neck. "You let one of those punks bite you."

She half-smiled at the memory of Gian. At the thought of him being called a punk. The smile triggered a deep growl from Rico. In two steps he had her pressed against one of the columns in the garage. His lips covered hers as his tongue demanded entry.

Skye opened for him, knowing that this time her mind wouldn't be able to suppress the demands of her body. Her clit was already swollen and throbbing. She was wet and aching with need. Their earlier encounter, and the moments spent with Gian had only fueled the desire.

As soon as Rico's tongue slid over hers, she whimpered. He growled in response and lifted her so that his erection was perfectly aligned to her cunt.

Even through their clothing, Skye could feel the raging heat of him. She wrapped her legs around his waist and he rewarded her by grinding into her, rubbing his thick jeans-covered erection against her in the same rhythm as his tongue mated with hers.

Skye had never felt so out of control. So ready to be mounted—mated. Always before, sex had been a recreational activity, a casual coming together.

But not now. Not with Rico. Her body was making that clear.

Rico's hand pushed her tank top up and freed her breasts to the early-morning air. Skye's already hard nipples tightened further. She arched into his palms when they covered her breasts and rubbed against the sensitive peaks.

Her womb spasmed and sent a flood of desire to her already soaking passage. Another whimper escaped. She pulled her mouth away from Rico's and pleaded. "Suck me. Bite me."

Lust roared through every pore in Rico's body. He'd dreamed of this, of having her beg for his touch.

He lowered his head and licked his way down her breast until he got to the pale pink nipple. It was stiff and engorged, a juicy berry waiting for him to take it in his mouth.

When she whimpered again and tried to close the distance, masculine satisfaction whipped through him. With a groan, Rico latched on to the tender flesh, lashing it with his tongue then suckling it as Skye writhed against him.

He couldn't think beyond the ache in his cock. The scent of her was driving him crazy. The need like nothing he'd ever experienced. He freed one hand and used it to open the front of her jeans.

Skye instantly shifted so that he could slip his hand inside her panties. She was swollen, wet, on fire.

With a groan Rico pulled his mouth away from her breast and looked down at where his hand disappeared into her pants. He was panting, barely able to pull enough air into his lungs and breathe, barely able to think. "You make me forget I'm a cop. I could take you right here, right now."

Skye laughed, a small husky sound that ran along Rico's spine. "That'd be hell on your career if someone came along and reported you." She let her legs slip from around his hips, but stood so that his hand was still trapped against her wet cunt. She leaned forward and whispered against his mouth, "Do you want to come upstairs and finish this?"

He thrust his tongue into her mouth as his fingers echoed the movement, tunneling into her tight, wet sheath and fucking her until she cried out, flooding his hand with her juices as she climaxed around his fingers. Only then did he pull away long enough for her to straighten her clothes and lead him to her apartment.

As soon as the front door closed, he was on her. Some part of his mind was shocked at the rough way he stripped her of her clothes, but he couldn't stop himself, couldn't control the need—and she didn't fight him. She let him take her to the floor, helped him get his own clothes off then wrapped her body around his.

A red haze filled Rico's mind as he plunged his cock into her. Skye screamed and pressed against him. Her arms wound around him, holding him to her as he pounded in and out of her until she came.

Her whimpers sent fingers of hot ecstasy along his spine and through his cock. He couldn't hang on, couldn't make it last. With a groan he shot his seed into her. And even then, the need wasn't sated. As if reading his mind, his fantasies, Skye rolled to her hands and knees, spreading her legs, and lowering her upper body so that he could see the glistening, swollen slit and the small triangle of black pubic hair.

She needed him to mount her, to prove that he was dominant enough to be with her. To be one of her mates.

The thoughts were foreign to Skye but her body ruled. She'd come twice, but she needed more—craved more.

She shivered as Rico's hard body covered hers, as his thick cock plunged into her vagina and his balls came to a rest against her wet, swollen labia and sensitive clit. He allowed just enough of his weight to rest on her so that she knew he was the stronger one physically.

"I've fantasized about this," he whispered against her neck as his hands moved to her wrists, holding them to the carpet. "I've jerked off imagining doing this to you."

Skye arched into him and begged, "Please, Rico."

His mouth latched on to her neck, covering the place where she'd allowed some punk to bite her. The need to dominate rushed over him like molten lava. She was his and when he was finished with her, she'd know it. He bit down hard, replacing the mark with his own as he pumped his hungry cock in and out of her tight sheath.

She moved into him, crying out each time the tip of his penis slammed into her cervix, but the pain was welcome, the nearness to her womb only drove her higher. She wanted to scream, to howl, to scratch and bite like an animal in heat. She wanted to clamp down and hold him inside of her—actually felt as though there was a hidden place inside of her that was created for this, for locking her mate to her.

Instinct ruled where rational thought had always dominated before. Skye opened herself wider, pressed more of her upper body to the carpet and angled her cock-filled channel higher so that he could plunge into her deeper, harder.

The slap of his balls against her clit only fed the hunger, the need. She would take his seed, bind him to her. He would be her mate.

Sweat poured off of Rico's body. His heart felt like it was about to explode in his chest. His breath heaved in and out of his body.

He'd never been so rough with a lover, he'd never let himself lose control. But the feel of her, the smell of her, the sounds she was making had pushed him beyond any limit, had filled his cock so full that every stroke was exquisite agony.

His balls swung tight and heavy against her slick flesh, sending waves of sharp, hot pleasure through his cock along with the urge to pound into her, to shove himself deeper than any man had ever been.

Fuck! What had she done to him?

He couldn't fight the frantic need. His head went back, his body arched violently, giving him the extra depth he sought.

Beneath him she cried out, opening herself deeper then closing around the tip of his penis, trapping him inside her, forcing him to come with each jerk of his hips, each involuntary attempt at escape.

Over and over again he came, each release making him cry out, each release triggering an answering cry in her. The pleasure was hot and fierce, overwhelming, consuming. He would never get enough of this.

Chapter Five

Skye came awake slowly, luxuriating in the warm male chest pressed against her back, in the arms that circled her waist and held her tight. Rico.

She'd never brought a lover to her apartment, never slept all night with one and woken this way. Some instinct had prevented her from doing it. Now she recognized it for what it was—an intimacy only to be shared with a mate, not with a recreational sex partner.

The complications would begin soon enough.

The questions.

About the mating.

About the way he'd been locked deep inside her.

How he'd orgasmed—how they'd both orgasmed each time the head of his penis had tried to escape.

She'd searched for answers herself, but there were none.

Like so many things in her life, she could only accept that it was natural.

Nothing had changed and yet everything had changed. They were bound together. She knew it on a gut level. Knew from experience that it was useless to fight whatever it was that made her *other*.

But he would fight it. She knew that, too.

She snuggled deeper into Rico and felt his cock begin to stiffen against the cleft of her ass. He nuzzled her neck and Skye's nipples tightened. An ache began to build between her thighs. They'd have to face the day soon enough. Before that happened she needed him again.

Skye rolled over slowly and smiled as she took in Rico's dark good looks. Gone was the fierce lover who'd mounted her repeatedly in the living room then one last time as they'd showered before crawling into bed. Now his face was relaxed, almost boyish. She used her body to roll him to his back. He frowned in his sleep but didn't wake up.

Pleasure roared through her—a primal satisfaction unlike any she'd ever known—at the sight of the bite marks she'd left on his neck, over his heart, on his inner thigh. She moved over him and pressed her lips against his lips, then nibbled down the tanned column of his throat until she got to a small brown nipple. She laved it with her tongue then lightly bit it before moving to its twin. Rico woke and immediately laced his fingers through her hair. She continued along his ribs and across his tight abdomen.

His body tensed when she stopped. She could feel the heat of his cock against her cheek. She looked up at him then. "Have you fantasized about this, Rico?"

His fingers tightened in her hair. She ran her tongue along his cock. "*¡Carajo!* You're going to kill me!" he said as his hips pumped upward.

Skye moved so that she could wrap her hands around his hungry cock. Rico's nostrils flared, his face flushed. His hips pumped again. Power and pleasure flooded through Skye. He was hers.

She took the head of him into her mouth and began sucking as she stroked his shaft. His eyes closed, his ass flexed and he arched off the bed. She let him move in and out of her mouth, taking more of him each time and using her lips and tongue to love him.

The fingers buried in her hair tightened as he groaned and panted. A sharp hunger built in Skye. She moved so that she could straddle his face.

Rico's hands went to her hips. His mouth latched on to her clit. She gasped and pressed downward as he stroked her with his tongue then sucked her until fingers of pleasure shot through her body, demanding release. She took his cock to the back of her throat and swallowed. He tightened his grip on her hips and continued his assault on her engorged clit. The heat and need built until they were both writhing and clutching and gasping, then crying out in ecstasy.

Skye moved so that she could wrap her arms around him and rest with her face against his warm chest. Rico pulled the covers up over their sweat-slick bodies as they both shivered from the aftermath of pleasure.

"It's never been like this before," he said and Skye could hear a hint of fear in his voice. She could feel the struggle taking place inside him. Finally the cop won. "I've got to get to the station. You coming by to see Caldwell?" There was worry in his voice this time.

Skye smiled against his chest. "If I have to. Or you can just tell her that you'll see to it personally."

Rico stiffened against her. She let him retreat. What was done, was done. They were bound together. She accepted it as she'd learned to accept so many things that couldn't be easily understood, but that didn't mean she could explain it to him.

"Shit," he muttered under his breath before rolling away and retrieving his clothing from where it'd been thrown in his haste to take her last night. He didn't dare look toward the bed until he was dressed. He still wanted her.

His heart did a triple beat in his chest. Fuck. What had he done? What had she done? The sex last night couldn't have been real. Had she hypnotized him? Let him play out the erotic fantasy of being locked deep in a woman's body? What was he supposed to do now?

There'd be hell to pay if Rivera and the rest of the department found out about this. But his cock was already telling him to forget about calling this a one-time event.

Rico went over to the bed and sat down on the edge, careful to avoid the trap of her eyes. She sat up and pressed her lips to his. "This is between us," she surprised him by saying.

He couldn't stop himself from meeting her gaze, from studying her expression. There was no hint of the amusement he usually found there. If anything, her face looked almost…gentle. "I'll call you later," he heard himself say, wishing he could say the compulsion was hers, but honest enough with himself to admit it was his.

The familiar half-smile appeared and with it the urge to wipe it off her face. He couldn't stop himself from pushing her down to the mattress and kissing her. But as soon as his body was on top of hers, it demanded something else.

His thighs spread hers. Then with one hand holding hers to the mattress, he used his other hand to unzip his pants and guide his cock into the wet heat of her. She whimpered into his mouth as he took her hard and fast.

* * * * *

Skye lay in bed until the blinking light of the answering machine caught her attention. There were two messages. She deleted the first one as soon as Detective Caldwell's voice began speaking. The second message was from Senator Skip Weldon. It was unexpected, simple and to the point.

He had caught a red-eye to Las Vegas and was staying at the Tropicana. Would she please contact him as soon as possible. It was extremely urgent. He'd like to discuss his sister, Amy Weldon. Three weeks ago they had buried her. But now there were reports that she was alive. Skye returned the call and thirty minutes later she walked into the hotel restaurant and was led to a table where two men waited.

Skip Weldon rose from his chair and shook her hand. The senator was handsome. Skye would give him that. But he had the easy polished charm of a politician. And underneath the expensive cologne, he smelled of cocaine and paid-for sex.

The second man was the senator's aide, Martin. He was shorter than his boss, whipcord-thin with wire-rimmed glasses. But like Senator Weldon, the odor of cocaine permeated Martin's skin.

"Thank you for meeting me on such short notice," Senator Weldon said as the three of them sat down.

Skye offered a charming smile of her own. "I've got to thank you, Senator. I'm just getting started on a case and you're my best hope for a lead."

"Please, call me Skip." The senator gave her an assessing look, as though he was wondering whether or not he could mix business with pleasure. Skye decided to turn down the charm.

"Why don't you start first, Skip, and tell me about your sister, Amy."

The waitress returned to take their orders. The men knew what they wanted. Without looking at a menu, Skye ordered a hamburger and French fries with a side order of salad.

When the waitress left, Martin spoke, "I've been in touch with the local police department. You have quite a reputation."

She didn't respond to the comment, choosing instead to let silence settle around the table. Skip and his aide exchanged glances, the senator asked, "Do you follow politics?"

"No. It's never been an interest of mine."

"Then you're probably not aware that the other Senator Weldon is my father. I contacted him after I got your message. He told me that you'd also tried to reach him."

"Yes. I did. Which Senator are you? Florida or New York?"

"Florida." The arrogance of power rang through the single word.

Skye nodded, encouraging him to go on.

"My father has been approached by a large number of influential party members. They're convinced that he'd have a good shot at the presidency should he run. Of course, it's too early now for serious public discussion, but I believe he could take the party's nomination and win in a national election."

"He's what the country needs," Martin interjected. "Exactly what the country needs."

Skye could sense where this was heading. She supplied the, "But…"

Skip offered the charming smile again, pausing long enough for the waitress to set their food on the table and leave. "But if my sister is alive then we need to find her and get her into rehab before some liberal newspaper latches onto her and totally destroys my father's hope for a nomination."

"It's absolutely essential." Martin's eyes burned with the conviction of a zealot.

"What kind of rehab does Amy need?" Skye asked.

"Rehab probably isn't the correct word for it." Skip exchanged another glance with his aide and nodded.

Martin opened the folder sitting on the table next to him and handed Skye an envelope. "There's two thousand dollars in the envelope. The information Senator Weldon is about to disclose is extremely sensitive. By accepting the money, you would be expected to keep this information confidential. Initially the Senator wants a low-profile search done in order to determine if there is any reason to believe that Amy is alive. We'll negotiate additional fees if your preliminary search suggests she's not dead."

Skye studied the senator and his aide, but even as she did so, she knew she'd agree. The search for Amy was the search for Jen. And there was little doubt in her mind after seeing Haley and Kyle together last night that the next time she saw Haley, Jen's sister would have changed her mind about asking Skye to help.

"Do you have a photo of Amy?" Skye asked as she folded the envelope and slipped it into her pocket.

Skip smiled. Confident, almost pompous. "Welcome to the team."

Martin pulled a picture out of his folder and handed it to Skye. The photograph was professionally done. The girl in it was posed and made up to look all-American. She had short black hair and was slightly overweight. Pretty in a normal way. She wouldn't stand out in a crowd. Skye doubted that Amy looked like this at Fangs. "Is this a current picture?"

"It was taken a year ago," Skip answered. He grimaced in distaste. "The last time I encountered my sister she was dressed in black and looked like a corpse."

Martin said, "Skye, what the senator is having a hard time telling you is that before his sister's supposed death, she became very interested in the occult. Through private investigators we were able to determine that she'd attended several black magic ceremonies and over the last couple of years has become obsessed with the notion of becoming a vampire. Obviously the family's first concern is to get their daughter into a facility where she can be treated and hopefully cured — again, if she is in fact alive. In addition, getting help for Amy needs to be done with haste and complete secrecy. And I can't stress this need for secrecy strongly enough. The senator's father is a devout man and his followers are very conservative values-oriented people."

"Why do you think Amy might be alive?"

The senator answered, "Several friends of mine have contacted me in the last month swearing that they saw a girl resembling Amy in Las Vegas. One of them said Amy responded when he called her name, but he couldn't find her when he followed her into a club."

"What club was it?"

"A place called Bangers."

"I've never heard of it."

"It's a strip club."

Skye had been in her share of them. In one form or another, runaway kids usually ended up in the sex trade.

"Where else was she seen?"

"The other times were both here on the main drag. Nowhere in particular."

"Now tell me why you think she's dead."

Martin answered, "Six weeks ago Amy flew to Las Vegas. She arrived on a Thursday night. The following Sunday she supposedly died in a car fire. There was one eyewitness, the driver of the truck she ran into. His description of the person driving her car matched Amy, but the fire burned so intensely that police weren't able to retrieve any identifiable body parts. Everyone assumed she had died in the fire."

"What happened to her money?"

Both the senator and his aide stiffened. Martin opened his mouth to say something, a slight movement of Skip's hand halted him.

"I assume you mean Amy's inheritance."

Skye was watching them as closely as they were watching her. She weighed her options, decided to give them something. "I contacted you because a friend of Amy's has been missing for about two months. While they were together in Vegas, Amy was paying for everything and making it known that she didn't care if she wiped out her checking account. If she's alive then she's probably going to need money soon."

The senator's jaw twitched. "A good point. Unfortunately, Amy turned nineteen the Wednesday before she came to Vegas. She appeared at the bank near closing time on Thursday and had them wire the funds to a casino here. The casino has cashed out the account."

"How much money?"

"Five hundred thousand dollars."

"And there's no trace of it."

"None."

"How often did Amy come to Vegas?"

Skip shook his head. "I don't have any idea. Her mother maintains a separate house in Los Angeles and only travels to

Washington or New York when politics make it necessary. My stepmother and I aren't close. In my opinion, she has always been overprotective of Amy and bears some responsibility for Amy's interest in the occult.

"My father hired a private investigator to try and reconstruct Amy's movements from the time she took the money until the time of her death. Unfortunately the detective came up with absolutely nothing and did not get any cooperation from Amy's mother."

"Were Amy and her mother close?"

"I assume so, but I can't answer that question definitively. I was sixteen when Amy was born and already away at school most of the time."

"I'll probably need to talk to her mother."

Skip nodded to Martin. The ever-efficient aide pulled a piece of paper bearing a name, address and phone number out of the folder and handed it to Skye. "Please remember that what's been said here is in confidence. The senator's stepmother is not entitled to know anything about the investigation, including the proposed step of placing Amy in a rehab should she be located."

Both men were watching her closely again. Without inflection, Skye said, "I'll remember that."

Martin pulled one final item out of the folder before closing it, signaling that Skye was now in possession of all the information they were prepared to give her. "Here's the senator's card. His private number is on the back. My private number is also listed there. Contact us immediately if you find her alive. Again, we can't stress how sensitive this matter is."

Skye accepted the card without comment.

* * * * *

The police station was swarming with cops and criminals. Skye's talk with Detective Caldwell was brief and to the point, done at her cubicle with chilly efficiency.

"Wait here while your statement's printing," Caldwell said as she rose from her chair and left. Rico wandered around the corner while she was gone.

He'd showered since he left Skye's apartment, just as she'd showered, but she could still smell herself on him, could smell him on her. It filled her with primitive satisfaction.

"Cia didn't tell me you'd called," he said as he stepped into the cubicle. His eyes went dark as they traveled over her body and lingered on her pebble-hard nipples.

The bullpen around them suddenly seemed quieter. Skye said, "I didn't call."

"Where's Cia?" he asked.

"Waiting for my statement to be printed." Her voice was unintentionally husky. Inviting.

Rico's face tightened. His pants stretched over his growing erection. Skye's clit responded, throbbing as it stood at attention. She couldn't stop herself from running her fingers along the front of her jeans.

"Fuck!" Rico said. It came out a strangled plea.

Caldwell returned. When she saw them together her lips disappeared in a disapproving frown. Rico stiffened and his cop-mask fell back into place though his face remained slightly flushed.

"Here's your statement," Caldwell said as she thrust a small handful of papers into Skye's hand.

Skye read the statement and signed it then dropped it to Caldwell's desk.

A uniformed officer stepped into view. Jon and Karen Armstrong trailed behind him. Callie clung to her mother with her head buried in the curve of Karen's neck.

"Detective Santana," the officer said. "The Armstrongs wanted to speak with you before they left."

Karen's eyes teared up when she spotted Skye. "I never thanked you," she said and surprised Skye by wrapping her in a hug. Callie whimpered, but didn't respond otherwise.

"How's she doing?" Skye asked when the embrace ended.

Callie's mother shook her head wordlessly. Jon answered, "We're leaving for home in a couple of hours. The psychiatrist we've consulted thinks that once we get her back in familiar surroundings she'll come out of this withdrawal."

Karen murmured softly, "Callie, do you remember Skye? She found you in the woods." The small girl's only response was to tighten her grip on her mother.

Jon rubbed a hand over his face in emotional exhaustion. "We might as well go to the airport and wait for our flight." He smiled at Skye. "Thank you. It seems so inadequate, but thank you."

Skye studied the family. Sorrow moved through her at the child's withdrawal. This wasn't the same child she'd found in the woods. "Can I have a few minutes with her?"

Caldwell spoke instantly. "That wouldn't be advisable."

The Armstrongs' faces showed their confusion at the detective's quick objection. "Can you help her?" Karen's voice was tentative, painfully hopeful.

"Maybe," Skye said.

"You've had to deal with a lot of traumatized children, haven't you?" Jon asked.

"Yes."

He took only a second to think it over before nodding decisively. "Could you suggest a place? We've already checked out of our hotel room."

Rico spoke up, "You can use a room here. Follow me."

He led them to an interrogation room. At the door he took Skye's arm. Next to him Detective Caldwell stiffened. Rico said, "I'd like to be present for this." His eyes touched hers, then moved over to the one-way window at the end of the room.

Skye hesitated briefly then said, "Just you." Rico nodded and she followed the Armstrongs into the room.

Skye pulled three chairs away from the table. She positioned hers so that her back was to the room she knew Rico would be watching from. The Armstrongs sat facing her.

Karen tried to pry Callie away from her body and turn her to face Skye. The little girl whimpered and clutched harder. "Leave her. She's fine," Skye said.

Then she waited.

She let the silence fill the room.

She let the silence fill herself.

She waited for some of the silence to fill the child, saw it in the slight loosening of Callie's arms. When she saw that subtle hint, Skye reached over and began stroking the girl's baby-fine hair.

Her voice was whisper-soft, gentle like a night breeze. "Do you remember who I am, Callie?"

The girl nodded "yes" against her mother's shoulder.

"Are you afraid of me?"

The girl shook her head "no".

Skye laughed. It was soft and inviting, reassuring. "Are you sure you're not afraid?"

Callie's head turned slightly so she could see Skye out of the corner of one eye. It was all Skye needed. Without hesitation she let the little girl fall into the endless blue of her eyes.

Chapter Six

"Did someone come to your hotel room and go with you and Brittany?" Skye asked.

"No."

"What were you and Brittany doing before you left in the car?"

"I was watching TV. Brittany was talking on the phone."

"Do you know who she was talking to?"

"No." The child gave an exaggerated frown. "Brittany *always* whispered when she was on the phone."

"What happened after Brittany stopped talking on the phone?"

"She watched TV with me. But then she said we were going to leave the hotel room. She said we'd get ice cream."

"What was on TV?"

"A movie."

"What movie?"

"Harry Potter."

"Did you go get ice cream when you left?"

Callie pouted. "No. We went to a place with lots of cars and Brittany told me to wait while she went inside for a few minutes. She said we'd get ice cream after she came back out. Only she was gone a long time and I got scared waiting in the car all by myself. So I got out and went to look for her. Only I couldn't because the man at the door said this wasn't a good place for little girls and I needed to go back to the car and get inside and lock the doors."

"Do you remember the name of the place you were at?"

"No. But there were naked people inside. Somebody opened the door and I saw naked ladies inside."

"Were they naked all over? Or were they just naked on the top?"

The little girl frowned. "Some were just naked on top. But the ones dancing were *all* naked."

"Was everybody inside naked, or just some people?"

"Just some people."

"Can you picture it and tell me what it looks like?"

Callie scrunched up her face. "It was like a house only you couldn't see inside it. They had music playing. I heard people yelling. But that's all I remember. It was dark."

"Did the people yelling sound like they were fighting?"

"No. They sounded like Daddy when he's watching football."

"Okay. Did you go back to the car and lock the doors?"

"Yes."

"Then what happened?"

"Brittany came back out to the car. There was a man with her. He scared me."

"What did the man look like?"

Callie struggled with an answer. "He just looked like a man. Only he scared me. When he got in the car I got down on the floor in the back. I didn't want him to look at me. And Brittany didn't tell me to get up and put my seat belt on."

"Did the man know you were in the car?"

"I think so."

"Did he scare Brittany?"

"No. She talked to him while she was driving."

"What did she say?"

"That she couldn't do it tonight. She had to baby-sit me." Callie frowned again. "I'm not a baby."

"Did Brittany say anything else?"

"No."

"Where did you go in the car?"

"To the woods."

"Where you got lost?"

"Yes."

"What happened there?"

"We stopped and there was another car. Brittany told me to stay in the car, but I didn't. She and the man walked over to where the people were standing."

"How many people did you see?"

"I saw a girl and another girl and another girl and another man. The tallest girl and Brittany started talking."

"Could you see the other people's faces?"

"No."

"What color clothes were they wearing?"

"Black. Everybody had black clothes on."

"Did they have their bodies pierced like Brittany did?"

"I think the girls did."

"Could you hear what they were talking about?"

"Not at first. But then Brittany said she couldn't because she was babysitting. The other girl said it didn't matter that I could come with them. She said if they used me in the ceremony it might even make the magic stronger. The other girl knew my name. She said for me to come over to the car. Only I was too scared to move."

"What happened next?"

"The man started back to the car. And Brittany screamed for me to run as fast as I could." Tears began trailing down Callie's cheeks. "I didn't want to leave Brittany. But she kept screaming for me to run. I started running. Then when I looked back, I saw horrible red eyes chasing after me. So I ran even faster."

"And you got lost?" Skye's voice was gentle, soothing.

"Yes."

"Did anything bad happen to you when you were lost?"

"No." The voice was small. "But I was scared. I thought they'd find me. All night long I saw eyes staring at me, only they were yellow instead of red. I ran as far as I could. Then I climbed a tree."

"And now you're back with your mom and dad who love you very much. Right?"

"Yes." Callie added in a whisper. "But I'm scared."

"Of what?"

"Brittany's friends. They'll take all my blood and kill me."

"Why do you think that might happen?"

"Because that's what they did to Brittany. They took all her blood and killed her."

"How do you know that?"

"Mom and Dad were talking about it."

"Did they talk about anything else that scares you?"

Callie took a minute before answering the question. "No."

Once again Skye let the silence fill the room.

Waited for it fill the child.

Skye's voice became a promise of help, a musical sound so beautiful that it couldn't be denied. "Callie, something scary happened when you went on vacation with your mom and dad and Brittany. Your cousin, Brittany, got killed because she made some very bad friends. But she kept you safe, Callie. And you were brave and tried to help the police find the people who killed your cousin. Now it's okay to let the scary memories go away. Are you ready to let them go?"

"Yes."

Skye sunk further into that other world. She took Callie into the endless blue again. Then with the gracefulness of a deer, they moved through the woods, heard the calming voice of the trees as wind moved through their leaves. She could feel the little girl's joy as nature wrapped its arms around her.

"Are you afraid of the woods now?" Skye asked.

"No."

The sunlight faded and darkness surrounded them. They flew as an owl does. Saw the forest in all its nighttime glory. The little girl's eyes got wider as she saw the night as she'd never seen it before.

"Are you afraid of the dark now?" Skye gently asked.

"No."

They circled the woods one more time. Night faded to day. And the illusion dissolved as Skye let little girl thoughts of dolls and balloons and bubblegum-flavored ice cream fill her mind. Then with a blink, it was done.

"Can we go to Baskin-Robbins now?" Callie asked in the carefree voice of childhood. "I want an ice-cream cone."

* * * * *

Rico and a stone-faced Detective Caldwell were waiting for them as they stepped out of the police interrogation room. Callie never stopped talking as they walked out to the family's rental car.

Once again Karen hugged Skye. When she was done, Jon offered his hand. "If there's anything we can ever do for you, let us know. We're in Richmond, Virginia. We're in the phone book."

"I'll remember," Skye told him, then stood with the two detectives as the Armstrongs climbed into their car and left.

"Do you know anything about a strip club named Bangers?" Skye asked Rico.

He shook his head. "Not my beat. But I don't remember hearing they've been raided. Why?"

"A kid I'm looking for may have been seen there. Want me to flash Brittany's picture around when I hit the strip club scene tonight?" Skye joked.

Caldwell's reaction was immediate and predictable. Her entire body stiffened while her lips almost disappeared from being pressed so tightly together. Rico put his cop face on. "Do you have the picture with you?"

"No."

The look he gave Skye told her that he didn't believe her. But he let the subject drop. "Are you going to Bangers?"

"It's my first stop."

"I'll meet you there."

Remembered intimacy simmered between them as their eyes met and held. It wasn't a good idea for them to be together in a place that existed for sex.

He knew it. She knew it. Yet neither of them voiced the thought.

* * * * *

As soon as Skye walked into Bangers she knew that if Amy and Brittany had frequented strip clubs, this was probably one of them. The clientele was diverse, everything from bikers to out-of-town tourists. Scattered in among them were more women than you'd expect, all of whom seemed to favor the solid-black, silver-studded, heavily body-pierced, Goth look. One of them sported fangs.

Rico and Caldwell were already there. They sat at the bar, backs turned away from the action taking place on stage as they talked to the bartender. Everything about them screamed cops.

A thick-necked black man with bulging arms covered by tattoos approached Skye. When he got to her he jerked his head in the direction of a table near the stage and said, "Big Daddy wants to talk to you."

Skye nodded and followed the muscleman. Another black man was sitting at the table, his hair a mass of dreadlocks. As soon as Skye got to him, he turned to the four women sitting with him and said, "Get scarce." They left without a word.

"Must be my lucky day. Big Daddy was just sitting here thinking about conducting some business with his friend, Skye." The man stood and offered his hand. She took it and they went through a series of intricate moves before the handshake was done and they both sat down.

"What kind of business?"

Big Daddy laughed. "Can't do no business without being a good host." He snapped his fingers. A bare-chested waitress came over immediately. "Baby, get a beer for my friend."

The waitress disappeared. When she returned and sat the beer down on the table, Big Daddy pushed a couple of bills into her green g-string. There was barely enough fabric to cover the money.

Skye put the bottle to her mouth and took a swallow as she waited for him to begin. He eyeballed her. "A couple of Big Daddy's girls got hurt real bad. Big Daddy is trying to find the motherfucker who did it."

"What happened to them?"

"Got their faces beat in. Then got *whore* carved on their stomachs."

"They live?"

"Yeah. But they ain't gonna look the same and their value to Big Daddy has been greatly reduced. They was good-lookin' girls. Now I'm gonna have to send them where the clientele ain't so picky."

"When'd it happen?"

"One a little while back. One two days ago."

"The cops have any leads?"

Big Daddy slapped the table and laughed so loudly that heads turned in their direction. Then with a mercurial change he stopped laughing and looked straight at Skye. "I got my own kind of justice. And it don't involve cops."

Skye shrugged. "Can the girls describe the guy?"

"No. Nothing besides the fact that he's a vicious motherfucker."

"There're a lot of those around."

Big Daddy laughed again. Then he snapped his fingers and the muscleman reached into his pocket and pulled out a collection of pictures. He dropped them on the table in front of Skye. She studied them. The faces barely looked human. The carved-up stomachs a further testament to how vicious the attacks had been.

She looked closely at the picture that had both girls standing side by side before they'd been attacked. They were young, underage or just barely legal. Both were white with a drugged-out runaway look to them. Both had stringy brown hair and green eyes.

"They related?" Skye asked.

"No."

"Looks like he goes for the same type."

"Yeah. Big Daddy thought so too. Big Daddy's got protection on some of his girls just in case."

Skye separated out the picture taken before the attack. "This one for me?"

Big Daddy flashed pearly-white teeth. "If you think you're gonna need it to help Big Daddy with his problem."

"What're their names?"

"The piece on the right is Tia. The other one's Angel."

"They staying with your other girls, down by the biker bar?"

"That's the place."

"I'll need to talk to them."

"Big Daddy will tell all his people they can talk to you about this."

"I'm working a couple of cases right now. I'll fit it in when I can." Skye pulled the pictures of Jen, Brittany, and Amy out of her pocket and laid them side by side in front of Big Daddy.

"Mmm, mmm. These two wouldn't bring in much money." He pointed at Brittany and Jen, garbed in black and covered in body-piercings. "Big Daddy don't let his girls do themselves like this."

Skye tapped the picture of Amy. "She probably has the same look. This is an old picture. They may have come around here."

"Big Daddy can't be everywhere at once. He doesn't personally keep an eye on the girls at this club." He studied the pictures a moment longer then looked at his bodyguard and nodded.

The other man leaned forward and flipped the picture of Brittany over. "Used to see these two every night."

"They hustling?"

"No. I may have seen them once or twice with a couple of guys. But they weren't working girls." He flipped the picture of Amy over, leaving Jen's picture faceup. "Another dude's been around here a couple of times looking for this one."

"Red hair, short, wiry?"

"That'd be the dude."

So Kyle had been looking for Haley's sister. It answered one of Skye's questions, but opened the door to another question—whether or not he'd ever found Jen.

"A friend of the family," Skye said as she scooped up the three photos plus the picture of Tia and Angel and put them in her pocket. Then she turned to Big Daddy. "I've got to go visit with my friends at the bar about these other girls. The sooner I find out what happened to them, the sooner I can turn my attention to your—" she gave a half-smile, " —quest for justice. Maybe to help things along, your friend here could call me if he sees my girls. And maybe you'd let your girls know it's okay for them to look at my pictures and tell me what they know."

"So Big Daddy helps you find your girls and you help Big Daddy find the motherfucker who damaged his girls."

"Something like that."

"Big Daddy will let his people know."

Skye finished the rest of the beer then put the bottle back on the table. "Thanks for the drink," she said as she stood. "I'll stop by and visit the girls as soon as I can."

"Big Daddy'll be in touch."

For once Rico and Caldwell wore identical frowns when Skye joined them. "How can you sit at the table with that scum?" Rico asked. A muscle twitched in his cheek.

"Think of it as being undercover," Skye answered.

His frown deepened. "It looked like you were doing business with him."

"My business, Rico. And I'm not a cop."

The bartender came over and asked her if she wanted something. She ordered another beer. "Get anywhere flashing Brittany's picture?"

"You'd better not be carrying it." Caldwell's voice was hostile.

Skye grimaced. "This is getting old. For the record, the kids I'm looking for disappeared before Brittany did."

"Who are they?" Caldwell asked.

"That's privileged information," Skye answered and the detective's lips pressed together in annoyance.

"But they were into this vampire shit, right?" Rico asked. His expression was all-cop.

"Yeah," Skye agreed. "They were." She knew he'd run a check for missing persons when he got back to the station. She also knew he wouldn't find anything. "Don't guess you'd want to exchange information," she ventured.

Caldwell's frown was immediate. Rico's eyes narrowed.

"Stay out of the Armstrong investigation. It's an open case." Rico's voice was terse.

Skye studied him, wondered if he was uptight because he'd seen her with the pimp or because Caldwell was with him. She paid the bartender and took a swallow of beer. Rico's phone hummed and he walked away without a word.

"Thanks to your stunt with the kid, the captain reamed his ass this afternoon." Caldwell's voice was hostile.

"And I thought aiding citizens was supposed to be a police priority." Skye looked over at the detective, amused at how quickly Caldwell averted her eyes.

"Doesn't it bother you that Rico got in trouble because of something you did?"

"Would it have been better if I talked to the kid somewhere else, privately?"

Caldwell looked like her head might explode any minute. "You don't have any respect for authority at all, do you?"

"I play it the way I see it."

"And you don't care what happens or who gets hurt?"

Skye shrugged, growing tired of the conversation and the company.

"One step over the line and I'll see that you spend time locked up."

"I'm sure you will."

Rico walked back over to the bar. By now Caldwell's face was flushed and angry. "I read the transcripts. You had no right to tell that child to forget what she saw. You destroyed any chance we had of getting her to ID someone or provide a description for an artist's drawing. You should have had one of us in the room with you."

Skye shrugged. She'd held Callie's mind in hers and knew with certainty that the child had given them what she could. She was tired of cops with their rules and regulations. The session with Callie had worn her down, lowered her resistance. She didn't use her skills in that manner very often. It was difficult to go so deeply, to maintain control and hold another's mind for such a long period of time.

Right now she felt some of her usual control slipping. She wanted to rip the sanctimonious Caldwell off the barstool and kick her ass. Only the knowledge that it would complicate things with Rico kept her from doing it.

"Nothing's free, Caldwell. The price for the information you got is what you had to let go to get it. Callie would never have been able to ID anybody."

"You don't know that," the detective argued.

"Cia, just drop it," Rico said.

"It's not right, Rico, you got your ass chewed because of this."

"Just drop it," he repeated and Skye could read the struggle in his face, the conflict, the need that echoed in her own body.

"Are you working all night?" she asked and saw Caldwell's lips tighten in the too-familiar disapproving line.

Rico's body tensed. "Yeah, Cia and I have a few more places to hit."

Need made Skye edgy. Unpredictable. She felt like a bitch in heat.

Her nipples were rock-hard, her panties wet. Fuzzy images from the past washed over her and she knew that this was why her mother had two mates. Fuck. Of all the men to want, of all the men to bind to her, why did it have to be him? "I'm out of here," she said and walked away from the bar without looking back.

When Rico didn't follow her out to the parking lot, Skye considered going to Fangs, to Gian. But instinct warned that he was just as dangerous to her as Rico was.

With a grimace she thought maybe it was time to buy a vibrator. She'd never needed one before. But the edginess that rippled over her skin, the hunger that had her nipples so tight that it was painful, was distracting, dangerous in its own way.

She went home instead. Only to find Gian waiting in the hallway outside of her apartment.

The flame in the midnight centers of his eyes promised something she didn't want to resist. His voice was pure seduction. "Invite me in."

Chapter Seven

She'd wanted him and here he was. Without a word Skye unlocked the apartment and opened the door. But when she went to step inside, Gian caught her arm. "Say the words, Skye. Invite me in."

She gave him a small half-smile. "Come inside, Gian."

The door closed behind him decisively, triumphantly. His expression was fierce predator and aroused man. She wouldn't deny him.

Skye took the Harley jacket off and dropped it over the back of a chair. His eyes traveled along her body, taking satisfaction in the beaded nipples, in the need he could see rippling over her skin. It wouldn't be an easy hunt, but in the end she would accept his binding. She wouldn't be able to fight the demands of her body, of her Angelini bloodline.

Gian's eyes settled on the mark he'd given her in the parking lot and for an instant he could only stare in disbelief. She'd allowed some other man to touch her, to cover his mark with their own.

His mind instantly flashed to the man he'd seen her dancing with at the club. "Who is he?" Gian growled as he closed the short distance, crowding into Skye's space, wanting her to fear his retribution.

She didn't back up, didn't back down. "Who?"

"You've been with someone else."

"And you're a virgin?" Her lips tipped up in a half-smile that sent heat roaring through his veins along with possessive rage.

His nostrils flared. There was no remorse in her. No fear.

She was strong, but he was stronger. She had some of The Bloodline in her, but he was full-vampire and had been for centuries. A flick of his wrist and he could snap her neck. A quick strike and he could bleed her to death, or to the point where she was so weak that he could overcome her defenses and make her a puppet, a servant whose only desire was to please her master.

His gums tingled. His fangs threatened to slip from their sheaths, itched to sink into her neck, into the hot, thick, rich blood that flowed there.

Skye stilled and he could see wariness replace her earlier amusement. "Should I tell you to leave?" she asked.

Gian stepped back and forced a calmness into his body. Few laws applied to him, but he could not be here if she denied him access. There would be time to deal with this other man later—unless she'd taken him as a mate.

Kyle's words came back to haunt him. *And you will share her with another? A shifter? A human? The Angelini have always taken two mates in order to make their hunting easier, in order to better protect themselves. You know that as well as I do.*

The thoughts stilled Gian. He had shared women in the past, though he'd never thought to share his companion. But if she had truly bound another man to her then there would be no choice. To destroy her mate would mean that he'd have to destroy her as well. She would never be completely safe otherwise.

Gian's eyes narrowed. Perhaps she would never be completely safe anyway.

He cursed himself. He should have taken her last night, should have bound her to him first. The call of her blood was a siren song, a melody that had resonated in his soul from the first moment he'd seen her.

She moved away, toward the kitchen. "Do you want something to drink?"

Now it was his turn to half-smile. Oh yes, he wanted something to drink. But until her defenses were lowered, until her senses were clouded with passion, he would have to wait to take what he wanted.

"Red wine if you have it."

"What about white zinfandel?"

"A little sweet for my taste, but I'll share a glass with you."

She took him literally, pouring wine into a single glass before taking a seat on the couch. Gian joined her, once again pushing into her space, but this time as a lover would. "You didn't join your friends at the club tonight," he said, taking the wineglass from her fingers and pressing his lips over the spot hers had been.

"I stopped by a place called Bangers instead. Have you heard of it?"

A small laugh escaped him. So she had been out hunting tonight, as he was out hunting now, only the prey was different. "I know it."

She took the glass from him, brushing his fingers with hers and sending a pulse of fire to his cock. Her eyes never left his as she said, "Haley's sister was seen there."

He threaded his hands through her hair, tilting her head so that her neck was slightly arched. The bite mark pulsed with the beat of her heart. "Let's not talk about Jen."

She set the wineglass down on the coffee table. "Or anything else?"

"Or anything else," he agreed, leaning forward so that his lips hovered above hers.

Skye pressed her hands to his chest, feeling the smoothness of his shirt and the hardness of the body it covered. The need to be with him was a compulsion that was impossible to fight, just as it had been impossible to fight the need to be with Rico. Her body was like a separate entity. It wanted both men, needed them both, would settle for nothing less than having them.

Gian's fingers undid her braid, freeing the hair to cover her shoulders and arms. His hands traveled to her sides and guided Skye so that she straddled him on the couch. She slipped the band out of his long black hair and plunged her fingers into thick silkiness.

Desire whipped through Skye with an intensity that had her cunt tightening painfully. She rubbed her lower body against him. Felt him pump into her involuntarily. He was rock-hard.

Their mouths met, tongues mated in heated, wet, darkness. Bodies strained for as much contact as possible, trying to melt into each other.

Gian ended the kiss, pulling away just far enough so that he could slip the tank top out of her jeans and over her head. It dropped soundlessly to the floor.

The bra she wore was pale blue, almost transparent. When he would have reached for it she denied him in a low, husky voice. "Not yet."

Skye's hands moved to the buttons on his shirt. One by one she freed them. When she was done, she leaned forward and ran her tongue along his breastbone, in a line over to his heart then up across the small nipple. Gian panted. His lower body pumped into hers again and he grabbed her head, forcing her mouth to linger over the dark brown nipple. "Bite me," he whispered, fighting the urge to open a wound on his chest and make her take his blood.

Skye teased him instead.

Her tongue scraped over the nipple and sent a bolt of fire to his cock.

He arched into her, pressing his nipple against the seam of her lips. "Bite me."

She grasped it between her lips, sucking it and striking it with her tongue, sending him spiraling higher and higher.

The desire to mark him, to claim him, whipped through Skye with the same urgency she'd experienced with Rico. She clamped down on his nipple and bit, reveling in the way he cried out, in the way his cloth-covered cock rose to press itself against her cunt.

The beat of his heart drew her attention. She rubbed her lips and tongue along fevered skin until she was above it, until it felt as though it pulsed in her mouth. Once again she bit, clamping down on him hard, marking his skin with her teeth.

Fire roared through her blood, through his. They were both panting when she released her grip on him and leaned away, pushing his shirt aside so that bare skin could touch bare skin.

Gian's hands removed the bra without protest then returned to cover her breasts, squeezing her nipples in a rhythm that alternated between exquisite pain and unbearable pleasure. This time it was Skye who panted and moved her lower body against his.

Her hands released the snap on his jeans and pulled the zipper down. She could feel him hard and thick against her. His lips left hers and moved along her neck, made the fire in her veins burn even hotter. He trailed kisses along her collarbone then back over the throbbing pulse in her neck. She arched into him, freeing his cock so that it burned against the palms of her hands. He was huge, ready.

Gian's hand slid along her side, rested briefly on her hip before slipping inside her panties and cupping her in his hand, rubbing her clit and teasing along the edges of her wet, swollen slit.

Skye arched above him, tempting him with her pebbled nipples, the beat of her heart, the smell of her arousal. Gian's tongue lashed out across her areola and she moved in, offered herself to him, pleading as she'd made him plead. "Bite me."

The need to sink his fangs into her, to have her blood spill over her nipple as he suckled was almost unbearable. His hiss was deep and primal as he clamped onto her breast, taking as much of her into his mouth as he could and reveling in the way she writhed and panted above him.

Her thumb teased the engorged head of his penis as he sucked, as she pressed herself against him in demand. His lips moved to the spot above her heart and he bit her, as she'd bitten him, only harder, so that the hot rush of her blood flowed over his tongue, intoxicating him, binding him.

Skye thrashed above him, the primitiveness of his bite filling her with feral pleasure. She was slick and swollen, consumed by dark need. She wanted him to drink her down.

The animal instinct to mate was overwhelming, overpowering. She pulled away from him and stood, stripping the clothing from her body.

He reached for her, pulling her to him and burying his face in her cunt, spearing his hot, greedy tongue into her channel. Her fingers dug into his hair, to steady herself, to hold him to her body. She spread her legs wider, offering more even as she demanded more. Again and again his tongue laved her clit, the inside of her thigh, her slick channel as though he was bathing in her scent, marking himself in it. When she orgasmed he tumbled them to the floor and hungrily ate everything she had to offer then locked his teeth on the inside of her thigh, biting her, marking her.

It sent her up again. Made the blood in her veins burn.

She pushed him to his back and stripped him of his jeans, biting his neck, the place over his heart, his inner thigh before running her tongue along the thick veins and ridges of his cock.

He was huge, hungry, hers.

She took him into her mouth and sucked, thrilling in the groan that was torn from his throat, at the violent way his body moved underneath hers. She cupped his balls, reveling in their size, in the way they tightened at her touch.

Desire tore through Gian, a feral hunger unlike any he'd ever known. He wanted to fill her mouth with his cum, to cover her body with it.

He'd thought to bind her to him, but instead she was binding him to her.

There was no fighting it, no turning back.

His body already craved hers as it had never craved another — as it would never crave another. This was an Angelini mating, not the making of a vampire companion.

Another wave of fire ripped through Gian's body as her hands squeezed his balls, as her fingers explored the smooth skin behind them. The need to dominate whipped through him, the urge to fuck her.

A growl tore from his throat as he pulled her away from his cock. She struggled, her eyes flashing wild and hungry, but she was no match for his strength as he forced her to her back and covered her with his body, slamming his cock into her at the same time his fangs found the pulse in her throat.

Her heart thrilled. Her soul rejoiced.

Pleasure commanded Skye's body. She arched into him, offered herself even as she took him deep within her, locking him to her, claiming him.

Ecstasy flooded her mind with each hot wave of orgasm, until finally there was only darkness.

Gian shuddered as his fangs slid back into their sheaths.

His cock was still buried in her hot, wet channel, but he couldn't bring himself to pull out.

Her eyelids flickered then opened. "Did you bind him to you?" Gian asked.

She stilled underneath him. "Yes."

"Does he understand what it means? Is he willing to share you?"

Skye's heart raced, her mind whirled with questions. Gian was the first person she'd ever met who could hypnotize as she did. She'd thought them alike at Fangs, but now her instincts screamed caution. To admit that she knew so little about her origins — about what she was — would be dangerous.

She countered with a question. "Are you willing to share?"

His face tightened marginally, deep in his eyes a flame flared and danced. "Is there any choice?"

"No."

"Then we will both have you." *But I will command you. I will own you for all eternity. You will be my companion.*

Gian dropped his head and whispered a soft kiss over the mark on her neck.

Sharp, painful need surged through Skye, from bite mark to bite mark to bite mark, from nipples to clit to womb. She arched against him, crying out.

He pulled his mouth away from her fevered skin and stared into her passion-clouded eyes. "Merge with me," he whispered.

Skye felt his mind pressing down on hers as his body was, offering unparalleled ecstasy. She accepted the offer, embraced the dark promise in his eyes.

Chapter Eight

Rico was pissed, tired, and edgy as hell. The extra shifts, the constant presence of Caldwell, and the never-ending hard-on had finally gotten to him. For the first time since he was a rookie, he'd almost crossed the line and used excessive force on a perp.

Now he waited in Rivera's office, like a kid sent to the principal's office. He shifted in his seat, trying to relieve some of the pressure in his dick, and praying that somehow he could make it out of here without getting on the captain's shit list.

¡Carajo! He needed Skye. He needed to shove his cock in her and make her scream. He needed her like he needed to breathe. And that didn't sit well either.

He'd known better than to fuck her. He'd known better, and yet he'd do it all over again. He closed his eyes, remembering the taste of her, reliving the moment she'd positioned herself on her hands and knees and spread her legs so that all he could think about was her wet, glistening slit.

Somehow he had to unload Caldwell, had to convince Rivera that he didn't need Cia dogging his every step. Shit! If Caldwell hadn't been with him last night, he'd have dragged Skye into one of the private booths at Bangers and fucked some sense into her. It had pissed him off to see her drinking beer and making deals with a lowlife like Big Daddy.

Rico shifted again, using his hand this time to try and reposition his cock so that the ache wasn't so acute. Fuck, he just wanted to get this meeting with Rivera over with so he could find Skye.

* * * * *

Skye woke to sunlight streaming across her eyelids. Her neck throbbed where the two men in her life had bitten her.

She sat up, feeling lightheaded. When the sensation passed, she got out of bed and went into the bathroom. The mark on her neck was darker today, an erogenous zone aching to be touched.

She couldn't remember when Gian had left or when she'd climbed into bed. She couldn't remember anything past that moment their minds and bodies had merged in shared ecstasy.

He was pure sex. Dangerous. Life and death rolled into the same coin. And yet she craved him, knew that she would have to fight both herself and him the next time around. He would own her if she allowed it.

She stepped into the shower, luxuriating in the hot water that caressed her body. She felt different today, satisfied, well loved. Complete. She stilled at the thought and let herself sink inward.

The need to be with Rico and Gian was still with her, but the edginess was gone. Skye traced the bite on her neck and her nipples tightened at the touch, like a thousand erotic shockwaves were going through her—all originating from the spot where Gian and Rico had both marked her.

Her body pulsed with remembered pleasure and she ran her hand over the mark above her heart then massaged her nipples, pulling and squeezing, imagining what it would be like to be with both men at the same time, to have them licking and suckling her before moving down to her cunt, and then filling her with their cocks.

One hand traveled lower, brushing against the mark inside her thigh before moving to tease her clit, circling and stroking until it stood at attention so that the hot water could lash across it like a fiery tongue. Ripples of pleasure pulsed through Skye, but they were pale imitations of what she'd experienced with Rico and Gian. She covered her clit with her palm and slipped her fingers into her cunt, moving in and out until a small burst of satisfaction eased her.

As the last of the pleasure faded, Skye felt the hint of compulsion left in her mind by Gian. The need to come to him. To obey him. To give him whatever he wanted.

She laughed out loud. Amused now. Challenged. Alive. Seduced by the very danger of him.

As she stood under the hot spray of the shower, she put away the heated memories of their night together and erased the compulsions from her mind.

The pounding on the door came as she stepped out of the shower.

"Skye, let me in!" Rico yelled.

She grabbed a robe before moving to the door and opening it for him. His lust rolled across her body in a molten wave, reminding her of a large alpha male, a dark wolf that wanted to mate. His nostrils flared as he devoured her with his eyes.

Rico's eyes went unerringly to the spot on her neck. "You were with him again." There was anger in his expression, but pain, too. Skye's heart rebelled against the sight of it. She moved into Rico, wrapping her arms around his waist and pressing against his body. He stiffened, but didn't push her away. She needed this, needed the warm press of his skin against hers. It had never been like this before.

"I need you both," she said. "It's not something I can control."

"And I'm supposed to be happy about that?"

"Not any happier than he is."

"That's it? I don't like it. He doesn't like it. But you expect us to be okay that you're fucking us both?"

Skye pulled away. An unfamiliar guilt rippled through her. She should have fought the demands of her body, should never have bound him to her.

"Do you want me to hypnotize you? Make you forget about being with me? Make the cravings go away, or at least fade?"

Rico's face tightened. "You'd do it if I said yes?"

She searched inside herself and found what it would cost her to let him go, saw the gaping hole it would leave. "I'll try if you want me to."

A muscle twitched along his jawline. "So I can share you or do without, those are my options?"

Solemn eyes studied him. "Can you go to someone else?"

Rico's nostrils flared. He tried to remember the last woman he'd fucked, tried to picture shoving his cock into someone else. It didn't work. The fire that had his balls ready to explode didn't want anyone else. It only wanted Skye—here, now.

Dark desire rushed over him along with fantasies he'd never allowed himself to explore. He pulled her to him and covered her mouth with his, devoured her as he stripped off her robe and pushed his fingers into her already slippery cunt, gathering her juices and spreading them backward, along the cleft of her buttocks, the pucker of her anus.

Satisfaction ripped through him when she tensed, when he felt the resistance as his finger slid into her back entrance. He opened his jeans and freed his cock. It was rock-hard, the head flushed and dripping with excitement.

She didn't fight him as he forced her down onto her hands and knees and covered her body with his. When she opened herself as she'd done before, it was all that Rico could do not to shove himself deep into her cunt.

"Oh no," he growled as he ran his penis along her slit, bathing it in her juices. "You want both of us then you're going to learn to take it this way, too." He pressed his cock against the tight rosette of her anus.

She started to fight him then, but the whimpers she made weren't the sounds of fear. He held her wrists to the floor and thrust, burying the head of his penis in her.

Fire breathed across Skye's nerve endings. Pain and pleasure rushed up her spine as the short digs of his cock pushed him deeper and deeper. She tightened on him, fought him, even as she reveled in his dominance, in his savage demand, in the way he panted and groaned above her.

Rico pushed against the fierce squeeze of her muscles. Her whimpers and screams and sobs drove him, had him pumping in and out of her, fighting his own release. He freed one of his hands and used it on her clit, nearly screaming himself when she clamped down on him, when her shuddering orgasm caused his testicles to tighten mercilessly before erupting and sending waves of white-hot seed through his cock.

Chapter Nine

The evening sky was in full bloom when Skye crossed the railroad tracks and stopped in front of the house where Big Daddy's girls stayed. She should have done it earlier but she'd slept late into the day and then Rico had stopped by.

An unfamiliar lightness moved through her body along with the heat of her memories. It shocked her to realize that she was actually happy, content.

She turned off the engine and sat, her mind still circling her unexpected feelings, examining them.

It took a few seconds for the emotions to fade and awareness to settle in. Someone was watching her.

She scanned the area as she got off the bike then relaxed when she found the interest was coming from within Big Daddy's house.

That was to be expected.

She looped her helmet over the handlebars and went to the front door. It was opened before she could signal her arrival.

"Girls are all working a gig," the woman said, her bulk blocking the doorway but not concealing the man who stood behind her.

Shocked awareness rippled through Skye at the sight of him. He could have been her twin.

Her eyes were drawn to his neck. To the strangely compelling tattoo of a winged creature. An unfamiliar word whispered though her mind. *Angelini.*

He moved toward her, swamping her instincts with contradictory impulses — run, fight, stay, question. She stepped back, giving herself more room to maneuver, but he didn't cross the threshold.

She could feel the power in him as he tried to trap her in his eyes, but the force of his will was too much like her own. She should know him, it was there in the deepest well of her memories, but when she reached for it she was met with the same searing mind-pain she'd experienced as a child. "Who are you?" Skye asked.

There was just the barest flicker of surprise. Then his gaze hardened, his lips parted in a silent snarl when his eyes zeroed in on the mark on her neck.

As though given a silent command, the woman closed the door before Skye could ask her question again.

* * * * *

The sun was just setting when Skye pulled the Harley into the parking lot of Fangs. Once again the line was long, the entrance guarded by a heavily muscled bouncer.

Candy, Mike and Dawn stood apart from the line, up near the door. Skye could see that their enthusiasm for the nightclub hadn't diminished. As she joined them, Candy spotted the bite on her neck and squealed. "Oh my god, oh my god. He did you, didn't he?"

Skye laughed and felt lighthearted. Not for the first time, she wondered what it was about these kids that drew her, amused her. Made her feel like an indulgent older sister. She shrugged, didn't see any point in denying it. "Yeah, he did me."

"Oh my god. Oh my god," Candy breathed. "Was it like, totally awesome?"

Behind them the door opened and Gian stepped out. He found her instantly. His eyes locked to hers. Skye's laugh was husky this time. "Yeah, he was totally awesome," she murmured.

Gian stepped over to them, cupped her face in his hand. "I'm glad you think so."

She brushed her lips against his, teased him with the tip of her tongue but didn't let him take control of the kiss. His eyes bored into hers. A predator's hunger lurked in them. She saw the exact moment when he discovered that the compulsions he left in her mind were gone. "Nice try," she whispered before pulling away from him.

Something unfathomable moved behind his eyes, causing her survival instinct to shimmer along her nervous system. His mouth moved to cover the mark on her neck. He bit down, sending a wave of pain-coated desire through her system before he let her go.

"I'll be back," he told her. It was a promise. A threat. His words whispered over her skin and made her shiver even as he strode past the parking lot and disappeared in the pitch-black night.

"Oh my god," Candy breathed once again, awed. "Oh my god."

The line began moving. The bouncer stepped aside and let them in without comment. They found a table near the dance floor.

"This is so rad," Mike told Skye. "I mean, totally rad. We don't even have to pay for drinks anymore. We tried to last night but Gian said no way, we were his guests. He's like, totally cool."

A waitress brought beer to their table. She looked at Skye to see if she wanted anything. Skye shook her head no. She was only here long enough to talk to the kids.

"I think he was kind of pissed when you didn't show last night," Dawn ventured. "But I guess he must have found you later."

"I was at a place called Bangers." She watched them closely to see if they knew the place. All three of them grimaced. "You've been there?"

"Yeah, totally sleazy," Dawn answered.

Candy wrinkled her nose. "We only went once."

"How'd you find out about it?" Skye asked.

Dawn shrugged. "Somebody else in line. One night it was pretty obvious that we weren't going to get in here. A couple of girls behind us started talking about this other place that vamps sometimes go to. So we figured what the hell, why not go there."

Candy picked up the story. "We saw a couple of vamps, but not that many, not like here. It's a lot rougher crowd over there. We only hung out for a little while."

"Have you heard of any other good places to look for vamps?" Skye asked. It was difficult to keep a straight face.

Candy frowned at her. "Why don't you just ask Gian about it? I mean, it's so totally obvious that he's a vamp. And now you've got the proof and everything." She grinned. "What'd it feel like when he bit you?"

Skye wanted to bury her face in her hands and laugh. Or scream. Instead she answered, "It was totally erotic. But I think maybe it's just a hickey, Candy. There aren't any fang marks."

The girl giggled. "Vamps aren't that stupid. They're not going to actually leave puncture marks."

There was no winning with these kids. Skye shook her head. "Have you heard of any other places, like Fangs and Bangers, where people go to hook up with vamps?"

Mike answered, "There's a place called Toppers. I went with a couple of guys one night. It was okay. Lots of action, but same as Bangers, not that much vamp action."

His girlfriend frowned. "Is it a strip club?"

"Yeah."

"Who'd you go with?" Dawn demanded and Mike looked decidedly uncomfortable.

Skye rose from the table. She touched Dawn lightly on the shoulder so that the girl turned away from Mike. The instant their eyes met, Skye said, "Please let it go. Mike did me a favor by talking to me." When the girl nodded, Skye blinked and released her.

"I'm sure I'll see you guys again," Skye told them as she stepped away from the table. "Don't let the vampires bite you."

The kids laughed.

* * * * *

Bangers was packed, full of sweaty bodies and the stink of paid-for sex. Skye pushed her way to the bar and ordered a beer. The guy sitting next to her leered and offered to pay. She passed.

Tonight there were more kids here from the vampire crowd. Skye watched them. It was a rougher crowd than Fangs. There were fewer kids looking for a way to belong and more kids looking for a way to act out violently.

The mood was ugly.

A drunk staggered over to Skye. He was beefy, barrel-chested, his head attached to his shoulders with no sign of a neck. "Hey baby, let's you and me go to a room and have a private dance."

"I don't think so."

He gave a nasty laugh and Skye slipped the switchblade out of her back pocket.

"What's wrong, bitch, too good to give some to Leon?"

"Something like that."

Leon snarled and lunged for her. She swung her leg up and kicked him in the balls. When he screamed and doubled over, Skye leaned close enough to press the blade against his chest. He wasn't too drunk to be afraid. "That was a friendly warning, Leon." The blade pressed harder into his chest, made a cut in his shirt. "The next one won't be so friendly."

"Bitch," he muttered and backed away. When he felt safe, he yelled, "Dikey bitch."

Skye pocketed the knife and turned back to her beer.

"Smooth," the bartender told her. "So smooth I didn't even see the blade, but I know you must have one."

"Practice makes perfect."

The bartender laughed. "Wouldn't have thought you were the type."

Skye studied the man. He was around fifty maybe, with a flattop military haircut and a ring in one ear. The muscles on his arms and chest said he was no stranger to exercise. Probably a weightlifter. "You work here most nights?" she asked him.

Caution flickered in his eyes. "Yeah. It's a pretty good gig. Wouldn't want to do anything to lose it."

"I can appreciate that. Guess you didn't know anything when the cops flashed you a picture last night."

The bartender chuckled. "That's right." He cocked his head. "I don't quite know what to make of you, pretty thing. Last night I saw you doing some business with Big Daddy over at his table. Then I saw you sitting at my bar casual as can be with a couple of cops. Tonight I see for myself that you wouldn't have any problem knifing somebody. And on top of that, I wouldn't have figured this was your kind of place."

"People are complex beings."

Her reply got a belly laugh in response. "You're sure a piece of work, pretty thing."

"Skye." She held out her hand. "Skye Delano."

"Now there's a name I've heard." He shook her hand. "Nelson, but most folks call me Sarge."

"Nice to meet you, Sarge."

"Same here, pretty thing."

Skye took a swallow of beer. "You have an eye for faces, Sarge?"

He chuckled. "Depends on who's doing the asking."

"I've got three faces I'd like you to take a look at."

"I can't make any promises without seeing them."

Skye pulled the photos out and laid them side by side on the bar. Sarge chuckled and tapped his finger on Brittany's face. "Could have sworn I heard that cop last night say something about staying out of a police investigation."

"I have a problem with authority."

"Think I heard that last night, too."

She laughed. "You've got good ears."

"It always pays to know what's going on around you."

Skye took another swallow of beer and waited. The bartender made a pretense of studying the pictures. She knew he was deciding how much to tell her.

He moved Amy's picture so that it was next to Jen's. "Used to see these two almost every night." He flipped the picture of Jen over. "Another guy's been around looking for her. Gave me his private number in case I see her. I don't want any trouble with him." Sarge reached up and touched his neck in the exact spot where Gian had bitten Skye. "I figure you already know something about that guy."

"Yeah, I do."

Sarge nodded. He slid the pictures of Amy and Brittany away from Jen's photo. Then he tapped the picture of Amy. "Saw her just last week. She was sitting right over there in front of the stage. Seems to me she was sitting with a group of guys, including the one who's at the table now." Skye followed his glance, saw a big guy who could have passed for a football player. From the back he looked familiar. But she couldn't be sure from where she was sitting. "Guy with the skinhead and the neck tattoos?"

"Yeah, he's been a regular lately. Usually here with two buddies." Sarge flipped the picture of Amy over and touched a finger to Brittany's picture. "This one came in the other night. I can't swear to it, but I think one of that guy's buddies talked to her." Sarge shrugged. "Next time I looked somebody else had the table. Didn't see where they went or if they left together. Now I'm thinking that with the cops interested and you interested, this girl must be dead."

"It'd be a good guess."

Sarge flipped the picture of Brittany over. "Then whoever killed her better hope the cops find them first."

Skye gave a half-smile but didn't comment. Sarge moved away to fix drinks. She watched the table, watched the man who might link Amy and Brittany together. He lingered longer than necessary when he shoved a tip into the waitress's g-string then he drank slowly, repeatedly checked his watch.

Skye knew that she had to get close enough so that she'd recognize him by smell, know him by sight. If she could hypnotize him, it would be even better. She slipped away from the bar, but as she drew near, he sensed her approach and swung his head around.

A feral, ugly look flashed behind his eyes and Skye didn't need to hypnotize him to know his murderous thoughts. She recognized him immediately, had sliced him with her knife to keep him from pulling Haley into the blue Yukon.

Chapter Ten

Black fury whirled in the man's eyes. "Bitch," he snarled and Skye slid the knife from her pocket and moved back, ready for his attack. His entire body tensed. The need to hurt, to kill, shimmered over him like a second skin. His eyes flickered once again to his watch. He stood, his fist opening and closing in frustrated rage. "Later, bitch. We'll settle this later."

Skye watched him leave. Though his back was turned, she knew that his awareness was centered on her. She was tempted to follow, but let him go. There'd be another chance. She was sure of it.

Minutes passed. Skye went to the door, spoke briefly to the bouncer. Haley's assailant had left in a dark blue Yukon. Alone.

She returned the bar. Took a few minutes to question some of Big Daddy's girls. They were all high and none of them knew anything.

"See you around," she told Sarge.

"Watch your back."

"Always."

Skye timed it so that she walked out with a group of people. Every one of her senses was alert to danger, but there was none—or at least no danger that didn't always exist for a woman in the parking lot of a strip joint.

The Harley was parked next to the building, under a light. She checked it over quickly, let her senses flare out to see if it had been tampered with. The bike smelled as it always did—of metal, gas, and leather.

She'd wanted to check out Toppers, but now that she knew there was a connection between Brittany, Amy, Jen and the attack on Haley, it seemed more important to go to Fangs and talk to Haley, probably Kyle, as well. The Harley roared to life and a few minutes later, she made the turn into Fangs.

A long line of people still waited, hoping to get inside. The parking lot was crowded and overflowing. She rode back into the street and down along the row of cars until she found a spot and stopped the bike.

The attack came suddenly. Unexpectedly.

A dark car pulled away from the curb just a few feet from where Skye had parked. It sped up and hit her as she was taking her helmet off. She was thrown into the Harley and bounced back to the pavement. A door opened and the man she'd seen earlier at Bangers jumped out. The stench of tainted blood from inside the car reached her before the end of the heavy pipe he was carrying crashed into her ribs with such force that she couldn't move. Vaguely she heard screams and running footsteps. Somehow she managed to bring her arm up in an effort to deflect the next blow. The pipe struck with a killer's determination. There was a sickening sound as her bone broke. Waves of pain and nausea rushed over her.

"Finish it!" the driver of the car yelled.

The man with the pipe aimed for her head but she managed to move so that it struck her chest again. It became hard to breathe, as though her lungs were rapidly filling with blood. There was the sound of a loud pop and a thud. Through hazy vision she thought she saw her assailant's body land in a heap several feet away. The eyes open in startled death. She was only vaguely aware of tires squealing as a car sped away. Then Gian was crouched over her, his black eyes filled with demon fury and raw power.

Skye felt like she was underwater. Everything around her was moving out of focus. Even the pain was starting to fade. She coughed and her mouth filled with blood. She could smell death. Could feel it. Knew it surrounded her, waited to embrace her.

Death's shadow had trailed her for most of her life. Not as an old friend, but not a foe either.

Gian's eyes burned into hers, tried to pull her into their dark centers. His voice whispered in her mind. *Trust me. Come to me willingly.*

She fought the compulsion instinctively, habitually — would choose death over powerlessness. But even as she was willing to accept death, the need to survive rose up, brought with it the strength and confidence that had been forged in hell. Wherever this choice led, she would face the challenge and win.

Skye let herself fall into his eyes. Let the blackness of them surround her, flow in and fill her so that there was no thought, no sensation, no existence other than Gian.

* * * * *

Gian could sense Kyle's presence even before the other man knocked. He pulled the sheet over Skye's naked body and called for Kyle to enter the bedroom.

"There was a cop here asking about her," Kyle said, his eyes darkening at the sight of Skye feeding. "He reeked of her."

Gian's face tightened. "Did he leave his name?"

Kyle slipped a business card from his pocket and tossed it on the dresser. "Rico Santana. Detective. He's a dangerous second mate."

"I take responsibility for him."

"Good. We don't need the attention of the police." Kyle's eyes flickered back to Skye. There was a hint of censure in his voice when he said, "You could have easily healed her in one night. Surely you don't think to convert her."

Gian's fangs flashed as he shifted Skye in his arms, pulling her away from the small gash in his chest. She stirred slightly, an instinctive protest, then faded away. "I do what's necessary to keep us all safe, but I am not so foolish as to try and make an Angelini one of us."

Kyle nodded and turned to leave. "You'll come out and replenish yourself?"

"I'll join you shortly."

Kyle hesitated. "My companion worries that you hold her responsible for this. Skye was at Bangers asking about Jen and the other girls."

"I hold Haley harmless. But it would be best if Skye did not pursue this matter further. She is not fully in our world, not fully in my control. Until she is, it would be unwise to forget that Angelini blood flows through her veins. If she finds Jen before we do, she might well kill her."

Kyle nodded. "I will command Haley to stop searching for her sister."

* * * * *

Skye woke slowly. She was naked but not alone, in a room she'd never been in before.

There were no windows and for a terrifying second she flashed back to the part of her childhood that she remembered, to the closets she'd been locked in, to the strange houses she'd been left at, and the people who'd abused her when she was helpless.

But even as her heart sped up in remembered terror, the body next to her shifted and Gian said, "You're awake."

He rose on his elbow and leaned over her. It was pitch-black in the room and yet she could see his outline. That only happened when she hunted, when she allowed herself to become *other*.

"Can you turn on the light?"

Gian leaned down, brushed his lips along her neck and murmured, "Of course," against her soft skin as he reached past her and turned on a small nightstand light. Its soft glow didn't extend much further than the bed.

She looked up at him. Met his eyes. There was no compulsion in them. No pull. His dark hair formed a silky curtain on either side of his face. His naked chest looked smooth and polished in the soft light, unmarred except for where she'd bitten him. The mark hadn't faded, if anything, it seemed darker. A flicker of memory made her think she'd bitten him again, but she couldn't hold on to the image.

"Your place?" she whispered.

"Yes." Gian lowered his face and pressed his lips against hers. His tongue stroked against the seam of her mouth and she opened for him, welcoming him.

The kiss was gentle, soft. There was no frantic need, just a coming together. A merging of two into one.

When the kiss ended, Skye asked, "How long have I been here?"

"Three days."

She couldn't remember any of it.

She slid away from him and sat up, taking inventory of her body.

There was no pain though her arm was bruised from the wrist to the elbow, the color more yellow now than black.

Her chest was the same.

She ran her hand over her ribs and tried to remember what had been damaged.

Broken arm. Broken ribs. A punctured lung.

Death had been close. She was too familiar with it not to recognize its presence. And yet now there was nothing broken. No pain. And even the bruising was faint. She should have felt weak. And yet she didn't.

"This is amazing. What did you do?"

Amusement flashed briefly in Gian's eyes. His laugh was soft and brushed along her spine like a feather. He moved closer, his chest pressing against her shoulder, his tongue tracing the shape of her ear. "What answer do you want?" He eased her back down onto the bed, trailed kisses to her mouth and stopped, his lips hovering over hers. "The mind is a powerful tool. Maybe that's the best answer for you."

She stared into his dark eyes, tried for a memory of the last three days. There were vague impressions of being awakened, of staring into Gian's eyes as he hovered over her, of hearing his soothing voice as he stroked her throat and forced her to drink something hot and metallic. But there were no concrete memories.

Gian smiled slightly and began stroking her hair. It smelled clean and freshly shampooed. She inhaled, took in the scents around her. There was nothing alarming. Nothing that hinted at death.

Skye thought about the attack. Tried to recover time from that point forward. "What happened to the man who jumped me?"

"I killed him." If there was regret in his voice, it was only because her attacker's death had been quick.

"And the driver?"

"He got away. Did you recognize either of them?"

Gian was watching her intently now, as though her answer was important to him. She wondered if he had been in her mind, knew already what she knew, and was testing her somehow.

"I didn't see the driver's face," she answered cautiously. "I've seen the guy with the pipe before."

Gian continued to study her. She felt it then, a gentle compulsion, a probing, an unheard whisper to share everything with him.

She didn't take her eyes off of him. She needed to understand what price she'd paid for his help.

His expression gave nothing away. The gentle compulsion remained, but was easily ignored. She said, "I need to go back to my apartment."

"Later," he whispered. Then his mouth covered hers in a demanding kiss, a kiss that claimed she belonged to him.

She met his kiss. Ran her hands through his hair and down his sleek, muscled back. Her body arched into his, opened to him, accepted him.

He was forceful, dominant, yet careful to bring only pleasure.

Afterward they showered. He'd been to her apartment and gotten her clothes. She slipped into them before he led her to the door. Skye watched as he keyed in a code, noting the numbers instinctively. The door slid open and exposed a hallway. The sound of music and voices rushed over her and she immediately knew where she was. Fangs.

"You live here?"

"I keep a room here. But I have other places as well."

They walked to the end of the hallway and through another door with a keypad. When this one slid open, they were only a few feet away from where the bartender was busy mixing drinks.

Skye looked at the scene in front of her. As usual, the club was packed.

She spotted her young friends at a table near the dance floor. Mike looked up and motioned her over. Gian grabbed her arm as she started to step away. "Join us after you talk to them." He nodded toward the table where Haley and Kyle already sat.

It was more of an order than a request. Skye hesitated before she answered, mentally balancing what she owed him for saving her life against what she'd tolerate in a relationship with him. "I'll stop by before I head home," she promised casually.

Gian's eyes darkened and the flame in their centers flared up. She braced herself, waiting to see if he'd try and press his mind on her, force his will on her. He went still, studying her as though he was contemplating a chess move. Finally his lips quirked up and he leaned down to brush his lips against hers. "See you in a little while, then."

Skye relaxed. "Okay."

"Hey, where've you been?" Mike asked as soon as Skye joined them at their table. "There's been this rumor going around in one of the chat rooms about some vamp's girlfriend getting attacked right outside the club."

"Only nobody we've talked to actually saw anything and nobody knows any details," Dawn added. "And Mike even looked for it in the newspaper. There wasn't anything about it."

Candy joined in. "But we were starting to get a little freaked. I mean, nobody's seen you or Gian in, like, days." She giggled, "I guess there wasn't anything to worry about. I mean, it looks like you guys have just been into each other and that's why we haven't seen you."

A waitress arrived at the table with a drink for Skye. "It's just orange juice. Straight-up. Gian sent it over."

"Thanks." Skye took the glass, suddenly feeling very thirsty. The waitress moved on to another table.

"So do you know anything about a girl getting attacked?" Mike continued.

Dawn leaned forward and almost whispered. "And what happened to the guy who attacked her? I mean, we all know he's dead. No vamp is going to let someone attack his companion and live."

Candy chimed in, "They took a poll in one of the chat rooms. It was almost a tie. Half the people said that if it happened, the vamp was probably so pissed that he killed the guy by breaking his neck or something. The other half said the vamp would have sucked all the guy's blood and killed him that way. That's what I thought. I mean, they probably don't like to waste blood."

Skye was so surprised by the conversation that all she could think to say was, "I'll ask Gian about it."

"That'd be rad," Mike said. "It's, like, totally awesome to have an inside source."

Candy rolled her eyes and told her brother, "Don't let it go to your head."

"Yeah," Dawn agreed. "Since we've been getting into Fangs every night, Mike's, like, become king of the chat room, or something."

"Or something," Dawn said. "It's more like he's become the vampire action reporter. People all over have their computers set up so that when he goes online, they know it. Then they start e-mailing and asking him about the action in the club."

Skye shook her head. "What action?"

Candy giggled. "Well, like how many vamps were here the last time we were here. Which ones look like they've already got regular human companions. Which ones are new. Stuff like that."

"Oh, hey, I almost forgot," Mike said. "We think we saw one of those girls you were asking about. She was in a dark blue car. It came by the other night before they opened the door."

"What day was it?" Skye asked.

"Two or three days ago." Mike shrugged, "I can't remember exactly."

"It was the day after the girl supposedly got attacked," Dawn said. "Remember, we were talking about it with those two girls that *always* get in. The ones right at the front of the line."

"Oh yeah. You're right," Mike said.

"Do you remember what kind of a car it was?" Skye asked.

"Dark blue. Some kind of SUV. It had tinted windows. They drove by a couple of times. Then they stopped and rolled down a window. One of the girls that's here a lot walked over to the car and started talking. I guess that's why I noticed it at all. I think a guy was driving, but I didn't really pay that much attention to him. And I can't be totally sure it was one of those girls you were asking about."

"It was," Candy said. "Once Mike said something, I thought right away that he was right and she was one of them."

Skye turned in her seat and got the pictures out of her jacket pocket. As soon as she put Amy's picture on the table, both Mike and Candy said, "That's her. Only she's more Goth-looking than in the picture."

"Thanks." Skye slipped the pictures back into her pocket and looked around. "Is the girl she was talking to here?"

They looked around the room. Candy answered, "She wasn't in line earlier. I don't see her. Usually she's here when the door opens. She's a regular. But not like an everyday regular."

Skye sat at the table with them for a while longer, then made her way to Gian's table. As soon as Haley saw her, she nervously clutched at the medallion. Her eyes flicked from Kyle to Skye and back again.

"Did you have a productive visit with your young friends?" Gian asked as Skye slid into the chair next to him.

She took note of the way he worded his question but shrugged and answered casually, "We had a good visit. I'm supposed to ask you if it's true that some vamp's girlfriend got attacked three days ago outside the club. And while I'm at it, they want to know whether the vamp killed the guy outright with physical force or if he drained the blood and killed the guy that way. The poll in their chat room was split about fifty-fifty."

Haley gasped and bit down on her lip. Alarm radiated from her. Gian and Kyle were motionless. Utterly still. Skye sensed that somehow the two men were communicating with each other.

Finally Gian rose to his feet and said, "I need to talk to your young friends." Kyle rose also. "I'll start checking to see how many other people have heard the rumor."

As soon as they walked away, Haley said, "I had to tell Kyle about asking you to find Jen. You've got to stop now. Please."

Skye gave a half-smile. She'd expected this, but she asked anyway. "Why?"

Haley twisted her necklace. "Gian has forbidden it."

"He doesn't have any say in it."

"You don't understand. Please. Stop looking for Jen. If you get hurt again…or killed… Please. Forget I asked you to help."

Skye saw that Haley meant what she said.

"Has Kyle already found Jen?"

"No. No. He'd tell me if he had. He'll keep looking for her."

"I will, too, Haley."

"Gian…"

Skye raised her hand to halt the flow of words. "Doesn't own me. I owe him for saving my life. But he doesn't own me."

Doubt and disbelief warred in Haley's eyes, but she didn't argue.

"I guess you don't have any information to share with me," Skye said.

"No."

"Would you if you did?"

Haley hesitated. Skye could see her struggle for an answer. Finally she whispered, "No. I couldn't. They'd know if I did."

Chapter Eleven

The tape on Skye's message machine was full. There were a couple of messages from Senator Weldon's aide. Almost all of the rest were from Rico. The earlier ones were frustrated, angry, the later ones held fear. *Call me. Just call me and let me know you're okay. Leave a message. Fuck, I can't shake this feeling that something's gone bad. Here are my numbers again. The cell phone is always on.*

She picked up the phone and called his cell. "Where have you been?" he demanded as soon as he heard her voice.

"Out of commission."

"I'm coming over." He hung up before she could say anything.

She called Senator Weldon's aide. Martin answered the phone promptly and immediately sailed into a rant.

"We haven't had a single report from you! The Senator expects to be kept up to date!"

"As soon as I finish talking to you, I'm calling Amy's mother. I need to talk to her—in person. If I can arrange it, it'll happen tomorrow. You can tell the senator that."

"Do you think his sister is alive?"

"Yes."

"I'll inform the senator. He'll expect a progress report after you talk to his stepmother."

Irritation slithered along Skye's spine. "I'll call when there's something to report."

The silence on the other end of the line was heavy with suspicion. "Getting this matter taken care of is a priority with the senator. I'll fly in tonight in order to be on hand when you find Amy."

Skye laughed silently at the thought of taking Weldon's pompous aide on a hunt. "That's a little premature."

"I'll be at the Tropicana, but I'm never without my cell. Call me when you find Amy."

Patrice Weldon answered the phone herself and surprised Skye by saying, "My husband told me that someone had been hired to look for Amy. Of course I'll see you. Do you have the address?"

"Yes."

"When you know what flight you're coming in on, let me know. I'll have a driver waiting for you."

"I'll call you tomorrow morning," Skye said, the knock on her door telling her that Rico had arrived.

As soon as she opened the door he pressed her against his body in a hug that threatened to re-break her ribs. "What happened?" he asked.

"One of my cases went a little sideways and I got hurt."

He pulled back. "You're okay now?"

Skye's lips quirked up. Except for a few hidden compulsions that she probably needed to find and get rid of. "Yeah."

"Let me see." Rico didn't wait for her to show him. He stripped the shirt from her body, his face a hard mask as soon as he saw the bruising. "You didn't go to the hospital. I checked. That's how crazy I got."

"No, a friend took care of me."

"What happened to the guy who did this to you?"

"Do you really want to know?" Her nipples tightened as Rico smoothed his hand over her body.

"You killed him?"

"No."

There was a flash of relief in Rico's eyes. He moved into her and trailed kisses along her eyelids, down her cheek. "Fuck, I was scared." He gave a shaky laugh against her neck. "Cia and I were just getting ready to check out a place called Toppers when you called. I took off like a bat out of hell and left her standing next to my desk."

"You're on duty?"

He crushed her to his body once again, this time burying his face in the silk of her hair. His cock was throbbing, but he didn't dare fuck her. If he started he'd never be able to stop. "I had to know that you were okay."

Soft pleasure raced through Skye's heart at his words, at the emotion behind them. She turned her head and covered his mouth with hers, teasing his lips open with a kiss meant to convey her own feelings. He cupped her face with his hands and drank in everything she had to offer.

When the kiss ended, he muttered, "If Rivera gets wind of this… Fuck…if it happens, I'll deal with it. I can't give this up." Rico shuddered and once again pressed his face into her hair. "I wish I didn't have to leave."

Skye brushed her fingers along the front of his jeans, along the heavy ridge of his erection. "Let me ease you."

He bucked into her hand and groaned. Without a word he opened his pants and freed his cock. It jutted upward—full and ready, proud.

She slid down his body and took the tip of his penis into her mouth, sucking as she explored the slit at its tip with her tongue. He arched and her hands joined in the torment, one circling and pumping his shaft while the other cupped and squeezed his balls.

"*¡Carajo!*" The fierce need to come was already swamping him. His hands buried into her hair, holding her to him, unable to stop himself from thrusting, trying to get more of himself into her mouth.

Her hands tightened on his shaft, sending a wave of desire up his spine. His buttocks clenched. "Swallow me!"

She teased him for several seconds longer, then loosened her hand so that he could slide to the back of her throat. Even then, she didn't do as he'd commanded until he was shaking with need, ready to beg. With a strangled cry, Rico came when the muscles in her throat clamped down on him as she swallowed.

He was panting and dizzy when she pulled back, first cleaning his cock with delicate swirls of her tongue then moving over and covering the mark she'd left on his inner thigh, biting down hard and sharp and sending a fresh wave of desire through him.

Rico closed his eyes, fighting to regain control of his body. Fighting the fantasy of her. As soon as the Armstrong case had cooled down, he was going to take some time off and do nothing but fuck her day after day.

"I've got to get back to work," he groaned, his body radiating reluctance as he tucked his cock back into his pants and zipped up.

She stood then and stepped away from him. "I'm going to LA tomorrow. I don't know how long I'll be gone."

Something tightened in his gut. "Alone?"

"Alone."

Rico drew in a deep breath. Taking her to her knees and fucking her ass had opened a Pandora's Box of curiosity. Once he would have been satisfied to ram a dildo into her cunt while he pumped in and out of her tight little back entrance. Now he wondered what it would be like to have another man fucking her at the same time, to feel her tighten and stretch, to hear her scream and see her submit as two hot cocks filled her.

Blood rushed to his penis at the images flooding his mind. He couldn't stop the question from escaping. "What does he look like?"

"Gian? Dark, like you. But more…aquiline. Midnight eyes and hair that's long enough to wear in a ponytail. Seductive. Powerful. Addictive. Like you."

Rico's nostrils flared at the description, at the picture of her blonde beauty pressed between two dark lovers. He clenched his jaw, wondering if she was seeing the fantasy playing out in his mind, wondering if she shared the fantasy.

She half-smiled and sent more blood racing to his cock. "Do you want to meet him?" she asked.

¡Carajo! He wasn't ready to answer that question, to consider all it implied.

* * * * *

Los Angeles.

Skye had never thought of it as home, even when she lived there.

It was a cesspool that only the strongest, the most ruthless, could climb out of. It was a battlefield where souls were destroyed long before the body was left for dead.

It was a world of metal detectors and armed guards at school entrances.

Of streets filled with voices and music at all hours of the night and day.

Of gang colors and gang wars.

Of hopelessness and savagery and ugliness.

That was Skye's LA.

Amy's world was far different. It was one of quiet luxury and privilege.

Skye was picked up at the airport by a limousine and driven to a house in Pacific Palisades. A maid in uniform showed her to a cozy, private room overlooking the ocean then left after saying, "Mrs. Weldon will be down shortly."

The walls of the room were lined with shelves. Most contained books on the occult, but an entire section contained a collection of tarot cards.

An elegant woman entered. Her deep red hair was pulled back into a stylish bun. Behind her was an older woman.

Something about the second woman caused Skye to still and reach out with her senses. A strong psychic presence surrounded the woman.

It gave Skye pause. She trusted herself completely, but never before had her senses touched upon psychic ability.

The elegant woman extended a hand. "I'm Patrice Weldon. Why don't we have a seat?"

Skye shook the hand. It was warm, firm, the hand of a confident woman.

Caution flared in Skye even as Amy's mother made the introductions. "This is High Priestess Duvier."

There was only the briefest hesitation on Skye's part, an instant where she allowed her instinct for self-preservation to rule, her psyche to recede into a protected space before accepting the Priestess' hand.

The woman smiled with secret knowledge even as she said, "Your energy is strong. Powerful forces bind you to them."

A fleeting image of Gian moved through Skye's mind, but she offered no comment. Releasing the other woman's hand, Skye sat down on one of the chairs.

Patrice and the woman took their places on the sofa. A beautiful mahogany coffee table separated them from Skye.

Silently the maid returned with coffee. "May I?" Patrice asked.

Skye nodded and watched as graceful hands poured coffee for each of them. When a cup was sitting in front of her, she helped herself to sugar and cream. Afterward her eyes strayed to the tarot decks on their tilted display shelves.

"Are you a believer in the Tarot?" Patrice asked.

"It depends on the practitioner."

A small smile formed of Patrice's lips. "That's a cautious answer from someone who has unusual skills of their own." When Skye didn't rise to the bait, Amy's mother continued.

"Your reputation preceded you here. Is everything they say about you true?"

Skye smiled slightly. "I never listen to what they say."

"Do you think my daughter is alive?" Patrice asked.

"Yes. I also believe that it's possible there's someone in Las Vegas that looks like her. What do you think?"

"Did you know that both my husband and my stepson have hired other detectives to try and find Amy?"

Skye shrugged. "I know other detectives have been involved. They reported that Amy attended black magic ceremonies and became obsessed with the notion of becoming a vampire."

Patrice snorted inelegantly. "Skip and his father believe anything from the tarot to devil worship is the occult. They don't make any distinction between spiritual enlightenment and good magic versus supernatural evil."

"You do?"

Patrice stood and walked to the shelf housing the tarot card collection. After a brief pause, she picked up a deck and returned to the sofa. "I believe powerful forces swirl around us, unseen and untapped. On occasion, I read for myself, but it's more meditative than true ability. When I seek guidance and help then I look to more knowledgeable practitioners." She nodded in the direction of the High Priestess.

"And Amy?"

"She was also open to mystical teaching and experiences. But like me, she didn't have a strong psychic talent."

"Did you ever talk to Amy about her interest in vampires?"

"Yes. We had many spirited debates about it. For the last several years she's been interested in legends about shape shifters and vampires. Amy viewed the legends as alternative histories, a variation of reality that most humans weren't able to experience or comprehend. She believed in a more literal translation while I believe that vampires and shape shifters are figurative—symbols in our psychic journeys."

Skye's mouth twisted into a smile as she thought about the vampire seekers at Fangs. "Did she ever mention vampire cults or visiting vampire chat rooms on the Internet?"

Patrice chucked. "God forbid! Vampires on the Internet!"

"Did she have friends with the same interest?"

Amy's mother hesitated, just long enough to give lie to her words. "Not that I'm aware of."

"So she never mentioned a girl by the name of Jennifer Warren or Brittany Armstrong?"

"No." The answer was firmer, surer. She might have known there were friends, but she didn't know their names.

"Did you know about Amy's plans to empty her trust account and go to Las Vegas?"

"My husband and stepson seem to think so. Several of their detectives have asked me that question. The answer is unimportant, though. The trust fund was Amy's to do with as she pleased. Compared to the money my husband has access to, and to the funds in my stepson's various trust accounts, Amy and I are both poor relations."

"So you had no idea what she was up to in Las Vegas?"

Again, the slightest hesitation before answering. "No."

"I gather her relationship with both her father and half-brother is strained."

Once again Patrice gave an inelegant snort. "There is no relationship."

"But you and Amy are close?"

"Yes."

"I assume that she's been in contact with you since she disappeared."

"That's certainly your prerogative. You may believe what you wish."

Skye shifted through her thoughts but found nothing else to ask. Another time, another place, she would have attempted to reach into Patrice's mind. But instinct warned her against it today. Not with Patrice's high priestess serving as a psychic mind-guard.

"Thanks for seeing me," Skye said as she leaned forward in her seat and prepared to stand.

Patrice halted her with a question. "Do you think that you can find my daughter?"

"Yes." There was nothing but certainty in Skye's voice.

Patrice's lips twisted bitterly. "And then what? Amy disappears again—only this time into some facility that will have no record of who she is and no authority to ever let her out again? Or perhaps you've already been paid to simply kill her. My husband and stepson have always used money to pay for silence and convenience."

Skye smiled only slightly. The hell of her own childhood had created a flame in her soul that burned mercilessly. "I can't tell you what's going to happen to your daughter—not until I find her."

When Patrice would have risen to show Skye out, the High Priestess stopped her with a brief touch to her arm. "If I may?"

Amy's mother said, "Of course. This is more your realm than mine."

The High Priestess nodded then turned her attention to Skye. "You shield yourself well. But even without the mark of one dedicated to the hunt, I know you as Angelini. Be warned, to kill one who gives life to others through black magic may be to kill those enthralled, whether they are good or evil. The Angelini have always prided themselves on being dispensers of justice."

Angelini. The word whispered through Skye, echoing from the deepest part of her soul, resonating with innate truth. Unbidden, the image of the man she'd encountered at Big Daddy's house—the man who could be her twin—came to mind. The word had stirred through her mind when she saw the tattoo on his neck.

He'd been as wary of her as she'd been of him. He'd evaded her question and the moment had not been right to pursue an answer. But after this hunt was over, she would seek him out.

To the High Priestess she said, "And if there is no time to sort the good from the bad?"

"If they are truly vampire, truly animated through black magic, then a blade to the heart will suspend judgment."

Patrice gasped and clutched her throat with an elegant hand.

Skye stilled as images of the child molesters, rapists—the vicious predators that she'd hunted—flooded her mind. From the very beginning it had seemed natural to kill them with a knife, to drive it through their hearts in order to ensure they ceased to exist.

On top of those memories came snippets of conversations that she'd had with Dawn, Candy and Mike, along with a collage of images featuring the Goth-clad patrons at Fangs.

They melded and juxtaposed with the elegant sophistication and power of the High Priestess, blended with images of Haley twisting her ancient pendant and ceding control to Kyle.

And superimposed over all of them were vague memories of Gian healing her body, bringing her back when she'd felt death's familiar presence.

Skye had known from an early age that she was not like other people. Was it so much of a stretch to think that other creatures existed?

But even as she asked the question and sought answers within herself, she felt the warning tendrils of pain deep in her mind and pulled away from the thoughts.

"I will consider what you've said," she told the High Priestess.

The High Priestess held out her hand to Patrice. "The deck please."

Patrice passed the tarot deck to the other woman. The back of the cards bore no pattern but shone like onyx.

"Please, cut the deck," the High Priestess said to Skye.

Skye studied the deck and the two women in front of her. "For the answer to a question."

Without looking at Patrice, the High Priestess answered, "Of course."

Skye asked Patrice, "Have you been in contact with Amy since she supposedly died?"

Patrice glanced at the High Priestess for confirmation. The other woman nodded.

"Yes."

"When?"

"Later that night. Not since then."

Skye reached over and cut the deck.

The High Priestess turned the top card.

The deck was old. Hand-drawn with pen and ink. Unique.

A vampire deck.

Patrice sobbed when she saw the Death card.

Chapter Twelve

Gian watched as Kyle stroked a hand down Haley's neck, pausing briefly at her pulse before settling over the ancient medallion that she wore. She turned her body into Kyle's, silently communicating acceptance of his ownership.

On the other couch, Kisha's pale white skin gleamed in contrast to Nahir's onyx flesh. The scent of sex still clinging heavily to both of them. The ruby stone of her companion medallion glittered and winked.

Gian's cock stirred and the medallion he wore around his neck burned against his flesh. His eyes closed briefly in relived pleasure, his cock hardening as he remembered the pull of Skye's lips on his skin as she'd drunk what he'd offered. Perhaps he should have offered the medallion to her when she was weak, when he'd held her enthralled as her body accepted his blood in order to survive, but she was so strong, much stronger than his companions guessed, and he wasn't positive that the bond would hold if she wasn't completely willing.

The walls muffled the sound of the music being played in the public section of Fangs, but the throb of its beat moved through the floor. Nahir broke the silence in the room by saying, "We have watchers at all of the places where Skye might go. When you have her in your possession again, then you must bind her."

Gian flashed his lethal fangs. "I will bind her when I choose and not before."

"You risk much, Gian," Nahir said.

"And I have much to gain."

Gian closed his eyes against the waves of restlessness that assailed him. He hadn't thought to tie Skye to the city, hadn't anticipated that she'd go to LA. But if the High Priestess Duvier was to be trusted, then Skye had been back in Las Vegas since the afternoon, and should be here, should have been here when the sun set. He'd locked the compulsion deep within her, so deep that she shouldn't have been able to fight it. In all the centuries of his existence, Gian had never used such mental force on another being—human or otherwise.

Kyle spoke for the first time, his features serious, his words careful. "You have called her to you?"

Gian rose from the chair and paced the room. "Yes." He felt like a million fire ants were crawling over his body.

"You are bound to her in the way of the Angelini?"

Gian hissed, his fangs extending. "You know I am."

Kyle's features grew troubled. "Perhaps it is not her disobedience that has you growing more dangerous by the moment. Perhaps something has happened to her."

Gian stilled as Kyle's words took root and grew within him. Alarm radiated through every cell in recognition of the truth.

* * * * *

The first thing Skye was aware of was the cold. Her body shivered violently, as though it had been put in a freezer, but she couldn't see where she was. Her eyelids were so heavy that she couldn't open them. Nausea filled her senses next and for several seconds the desire to vomit was overwhelming. When it passed, the shivering also passed, her body returning to normal.

Memory followed. The meeting with Patrice. The flight back to Las Vegas. Getting on the Harley. The sharp sting in her thigh, only a second to see the dart before everything had gone fuzzy then dark.

She recognized the effects now.

One of the places she'd been as a child, as a ward of the state, had been a foster home that relied heavily on illegal tranquilizers—to keep the children controlled, to keep them from fighting when various "uncles" stopped in to "visit".

An old rage poured into Skye at the memory. Hot like the flames of hell. But satisfaction came with it. It was the first time she'd ever killed—the first time she'd meted out justice.

It wasn't the last.

The hunter that lived in her skin was awake now, aware that she lay naked on the floor. Like a chant in her blood, with each beat of her heart, she could feel the call to be *other*, to survive.

The smell of foul, tainted blood filled her nostrils and once again she had to fight the urge to vomit. Carefully she opened her senses.

There were people in the room with her. Two of them, sitting close, radiating excitement, anticipation…lust. The smell of their musk made Skye think they were men, but like the scents she'd encountered when she tracked Brittany Armstrong, they weren't clearly men or women, but something perverted, unwholesome.

She opened her eyes slightly and saw the coffins first. There were three of them lined up against the wall.

A marble table stood waist-high in the center of the room, on the floor beneath it a pentagram was drawn inside a circle full of strange symbols. A jolt of horror rushed through Skye, a fear so primal she had to fight the desire to lunge to her feet and attack whoever was in the room with her.

Only the patience she'd honed after years of hunting and tracking allowed her to bring the fear under control.

Once again she focused on her surroundings, this time noting that there was no source of light other than the black candles. She could see clearly though, and was glad that whatever Gian had done to heal her, had also given her this ability.

There was only one door and as Skye watched through slitted eyes, it opened and a woman came in. The candlelight flickered off the gold chalice she held in her hand, off the blade she wore in her belt.

Athame.

The strange word whispered through Skye's mind along with a vague awareness of knowledge just out of reach.

The woman stopped in front of the altar, her black robes pooling around her feet. She did not smell of tainted blood and yet just like the psychic at Patrice Weldon's home, a strong otherworldly presence hung around her. Skye was careful not to brush against it with her own aura.

The beings on either side of Skye rose to their feet and she knew that she'd been right in thinking that they were men. Like the woman, they were dressed in black robes that pooled around them.

Neither spoke as the woman set the chalice and athame down on the altar before moving over to the wall and opening a wooden panel that Skye had mistaken for a piece of art.

Light from the full moon poured in, bathing the altar in its glow. The woman turned, this time moving to where Skye and the two men waited. "Help her to her feet," she told them.

Skye forced her limbs to go limp, weak, her eyes to appear fuzzy, drugged, as the two men lifted and held her standing between them. "Who are you?" she asked, making sure her voice came out slurred.

"Even now you ask questions." There was amusement in the woman's voice as she reached over and stroked her hand along Skye's cheek.

Skye tried to evade the touch, but couldn't without giving away the fact that she was not as weak as she appeared.

The woman's hand glided lower, pausing like a lover's caress on the place where Skye's pulse beat in her neck, on the place both Gian and Rico had left their marks, then moving lower, to the bite that Gian had left over her heart, and then lower still, to the spot on her inner thigh where both men had also bitten.

"I can feel the power in you. Your blood will feed my children for many weeks."

"Your vampire wannabes?"

Like a lover who didn't want to leave, the woman pulled her attention from the bite on Skye's inner thigh and moved upward, touching the bite over Skye's heart and the one on her neck again before she focused on Skye's face. "Amazing. The world is full of people who would sell their souls to possess what you have the opportunity to possess, and yet even now, you don't believe."

"In vampires?"

The woman's hand stroked the bite mark over Skye's heart. "Your lover is a vampire. He has marked you as his human companion."

Skye couldn't contain the small bark of laughter. "Are you so bored with regular hocus-pocus that you need this? Or are you just power-mad?"

Anger flashed across the woman's features in the instant before she brought her hand across Skye's face in a slap that sent Skye's head snapping backward and left her lips bleeding.

"Bring her," the woman ordered as she wheeled away and stalked to where the coffins waited like soldiers in repose.

Skye let herself be half-carried, half-dragged to where the woman stood. Satisfaction rippled through her in a heady undercurrent at the careless way she was being held, at the knowledge that she'd bought enough time for the last of the tranquilizer to leave her system.

The woman pulled back the lid of one coffin with a strength born of rage and Skye immediately recognized the girl inside. Amy Weldon.

There was no sign of life, yet no stink of decay.

"Force her head down," the woman ordered.

Skye struggled, but not enough to show her true strength, as the men forced her down so that her mouth hovered only inches above Amy's.

Within seconds the first drop from her bleeding lip fell onto Amy's mouth. Another followed then another, until Amy's lips were coated.

With a hiss, Amy's lips parted, exposing fangs. And then the girl's eyes flew open, burning hungry and red, void of everything but the need to feed.

At an order from the woman, Skye's face was pulled away just as Amy surged forward, aiming for Skye's neck. Amy hissed in frustration and struggled to rise from the coffin.

The woman said, "Go to sleep. You'll feed soon," and Amy lay back down, all life leeching out of her.

For a long, disorienting moment, Skye felt trapped, torn between past and present as the reality of the vampire in front of her ripped apart the invisible veil deep in Skye's subconscious — freeing the knowledge that had been hidden there, that had roamed on the edge of her consciousness when she spoke with the High Priestess. Vampires existed. They had always existed. She was born to hunt them down, kill them. Pain seared through her head at the thought, clearer memories followed when the pain subsided. No, she didn't need to kill all of them, only some of them.

Gian was vampire, able to blur the reality of his bite when she was aroused, to meld his own need for blood with her feral desire to claim a mate. She had taken a vampire as a mate, just as her Angelini mother had.

Skye remembered it now, saw the eyes as her mother's vampire mate trapped and held her, commanding her to silence, to forget her origins if she was ever lost to them. She'd been too young to understand what he meant by silence and so the compulsion had lodged in her mind in its broadest context, had caused her to suffer needlessly.

The memories made her nauseous, made it hard to focus. But then the woman's smug voice called Skye back into the present. "My children always wake so hungry. Eventually they'll be able to feed on their own. But for now they rely on me to provide for them. I didn't realize your value when I told my servant that he could kill you. I thought only to stop you from making any more annoying inquires. When my servant died and you survived, I was tempted by the thought of making you one of my children. But it would be too dangerous. I would never be completely sure whose power you would obey—mine or your vampire lover's." She looked toward the altar. Skye's gaze followed the woman's.

At the sight of the pentagram on the altar's surface, the silver chains anchored to each corner, a fresh jolt of horror rushed through Skye, and once again she had to overcome a fear so primal that she knew she would die fighting before she allowed herself to be placed on the smooth, cursed marble surface.

"It's almost midnight," the woman said, anticipation rising in her voice. "We must prepare for the ceremony."

Skye played for more time. "I assume my part is the sacrificial virgin."

The woman laughed. "My servants have probably never been with a virgin. It would have been a novel experience. But I suspect they'll enjoy you even more. You'll be a challenge to them—a test to see if they can do the job of three men since your vampire lover killed their companion. I imagine they're looking forward to worshipping at the altar until your body is drained of blood."

Skye mentally gathered herself, readying herself to fight when the odds could be shifted in her favor, when she was close enough to grab the athame. "You mean fucking at the altar."

The woman shrugged. "Call it what you will." She turned slightly, as though her mind was already on the upcoming ceremony. "Put her on the altar."

Skye struggled slightly as the two men half-dragged her toward the altar. With each step it became more of a challenge to wait, to hold off.

Out of the corner of her eye she saw the woman open the other two coffins, heard her murmur, "Soon my children, soon you'll awaken and share the night with me."

Deep inside of Skye something uncurled, something familiar, yet different, a power stronger than what she usually felt when she allowed herself to become *other*—a power that whispered of Gian.

But there was no time to think, to analyze. As she drew close to the altar there was only time to act, to lurch forward and use the momentum of her upper body to swing the man on her right into the marble altar, to feel a brief satisfaction when he released her and she grabbed the knife. Then her hand streaked in an unerring arch and ripped through robe and flesh as she gutted the second man.

The stench of his tainted blood filled the room along with his screams and the witch's shrill chant, "Up my children! There's blood! Up!"

Skye could not risk a look toward the coffins. Instead she drove her foot into the remaining man's groin. His screams echoed those of his companion as he too curled into a ball on the floor.

"Hurry, children, hurry!" the woman's voice urged, but Skye had already grabbed the chalice and used it to break the window. Waves of evil poured over her as she climbed through broken glass, the athame still locked in her grip. The stench of foul, tainted blood hit her just as sharp claws grabbed one of her calves, raking into her skin and holding her suspended for a brief moment between freedom and horror.

Skye wrenched her leg free and dropped to the other side of the window, turning as she did in preparation for the attack she knew was coming.

The girl who came after her wasn't Amy or Jen, but would have fit in at Fangs. Vampire eyes glowed red and feral, ferociously hungry, as she launched herself toward Skye.

There was no time to think, no time to do anything but meet the attack. Skye lunged forward, driving the powerful blade of the athame straight into the girl's heart. There was a moment of shocked disbelief as the vampire recoiled, raking Skye's shoulders before collapsing.

With ancient knowledge and strength born of power, Skye removed the heart and started running, shredding it with the knife and leaving it scattered until there was nothing left.

Chapter Thirteen

She only stopped running when her instincts urged caution.

Slowly Skye became aware of her surroundings, of the blood that trickled down her body where the broken glass had cut her and the vampire had dug needle-sharp nails into her flesh.

Music blared from a shabby trailer court, male voices yelled back and forth — rowdy, drunk — and she knew that it wouldn't be safe to appear before them in her naked state.

She recognized this place. It was close to Bangers.

A half-smile formed. Except for the blood, she'd fit right in at the strip-club.

Skye made her way around the trailer court, stopping long enough to rinse the blood from her skin and the athame when she encountered a child's small toy-filled swimming pool, and then she moved on, hugging what shadows she could find.

As she moved, she thought about what she'd seen, what she now remembered of her Angelini mother and her mother's two mates — one werewolf, the other vampire.

Flesh of one father's flesh.

Blood of the other father's blood.

Bound together by Angelini magic.

Skye finally understood who and what she was.

If she'd been born male, she would have been able to shift to wolf form, just as any son that she gave birth to might be able to do. If she'd made her first kill under the direction of her family unit, then she'd wear the tattoo of a dedicated hunter — as her mother did, as the man she'd encountered at Big Daddy's did, though she could not place him in her childhood memories.

Her thoughts shifted into the present, to Gian, her own vampire mate. She could feel his compulsion, his call, buried deep within her mind, tearing at the barriers that had always protected her.

There was no other choice but to involve him. She couldn't return to the dark-magic house alone and there was no time to seek out the hunter she'd encountered at Big Daddy's.

The occult priestess had to be destroyed before others like Brittany Armstrong were sacrificed. Judgment needed to be rendered on the newly made vampires. If not tonight, then later.

Skye paused as she neared Bangers, considered her options, then skirted through the car-jammed parking lot in search of a second, more private entrance. A small measure of relief washed through her when she found it, when she saw that the bartender from the other night stood outside, smoking a cigarette.

She moved toward Sarge, glad that she hadn't been forced to use the front door. If he was surprised by her nakedness, at the knife she held at her side, he didn't show it.

Sarge dropped his cigarette to the asphalt and stubbed it out with the toe of his boot as he stripped off his shirt and handed it to her.

"Thanks," Skye said.

"The shirt's all I can do to help you. Word's out to call if you show up here."

Skye stilled. "Whose word?"

Sarge touched a spot on his neck. "Same guy who's been around before."

"Kyle?"

The bartender nodded.

Skye relaxed. "Call him."

Sarge nodded. "Come on in, there's an office here that doesn't get used much. You can wait in there."

* * * * *

As he watched Gian pace back and forth, Kyle stroked his hand along Haley's smooth flesh and rejoiced in his choice of a companion. She'd only been with him a short time, but he knew a satisfaction that hadn't been present in centuries. Until Haley, he'd never been tempted to bind a human to him, to face the decisions that such a selection demanded.

Kyle caressed her silky hair, unable to contemplate that she might not choose to spend eternity with him — that one day she would turn away from his blood, aging and dying as a human would — or worse, that she would elect to become vampire and not survive the change.

There was an innate purity in Haley, a goodness that shone like a candle in a mineshaft. She hadn't sought him out, hadn't sought his kind out. She'd merely wandered into Fangs one night with some friends from work.

He'd seen her and kept her.

Kyle traced the companion medallion and felt its power against his fingertips. The blood-red stone and engraved symbols combined to amplify his will, to make it impossible for Haley to resist his compulsion, though in truth, he'd never used it for that purpose, never needed to. Instead the medallion served other purposes.

It let others know that he had claimed her. And more importantly, it magnified the safeguards he'd constructed in her mind. She could not kill him as he slept, nor could she betray him — intentionally or otherwise — by leading someone else to his sleeping place.

Kyle feared for Gian. He wished now that he'd tried harder to dissuade his friend from wanting Skye as a companion. But the damage was already done. Now there was no choice but for Gian to try and bind her to him.

The cell phone in Kyle's pocket rang and Haley tensed under his hand. He whispered a kiss across her forehead as he reached for the phone. It amused him to carry it, to embrace this modern technology. He and Gian and Nahir had been fledgling vampires when messages where sent by runners or by word of mouth as peddlers traveled from one small cluster of human settlement to another.

"This is Kyle."

"She's here at Bangers. Waiting in the backroom for you."

Kyle recognized the bartender's voice. "This is Sarge?"

"Yeah."

Kyle could feel Gian's impatient presence standing over him. "She is unharmed?"

"She's got some vicious-looking scratches…and some bites. Neck, chest, inner thigh. No clothes. Gave her my shirt but didn't ask her any questions. Like I said, she's here waiting for you."

"Your assistance is appreciated." Kyle closed the small cell phone and said, "She's at Bangers."

* * * * *

Gian could smell the stink of black magic around her, but he didn't hesitate to reach for Skye and pull her to him. His fangs ached with the need to pierce through her skin and take her blood, his cock strained to escape his pants and plunge into her slick channel, even as wild rage rushed through him at the damage that had been done to her.

He tightened his grip on her, using one hand to tilt her face upward. "You are safe now," he said before lowering his mouth to hers in a kiss that both punished and reassured.

Skye's heart lightened. In all the years she'd hunted, there had never been anyone to hold her afterward, to care for her. She met his kiss and pressed into his body, wanting to feel him inside her, to celebrate the fact that she still lived. She was wet, aching by the time their lips separated.

Kyle and Nahir came into the office, closing the door behind them. In the close confines of the small space, Skye could feel the combined power, the combined menace, radiating off them.

When she would have pulled away, instinctively preparing to defend herself, Gian tightened his grip on her. "Where have you been?" he asked.

She'd had little time to think about what she would say, how much knowledge it was safe to reveal. She had only a child's vague awareness of the supernatural laws that governed those not human.

Vampires existed. The Angelini hunted them down and killed them—sometimes.

"I found Amy Weldon—or rather, her 'handler' found me," she said, her mind flitting back to the visit with Patrice, to Patrice's anguished sob at the sight of the Death card. It was too much of a coincidence that she'd been taken as soon as she got back to Las Vegas. Somehow Patrice had managed to warn Amy that she was being hunted.

"Where?" Kyle demanded, moving forward and earning a hissed warning from Gian.

"In a house not far from here." There'd been no time to look for an address, but she could find the house again. "There's a trailer park close by. I'll have to backtrack." There was no question that they would go with her.

"How many were at the house?" Gian asked.

One vampire was dead, but Skye didn't know if the man she'd gutted could be healed. "Four, maybe five."

"Let's go," Gian said, moving her toward the doorway.

She allowed herself to be herded to a dark SUV. Kyle took the driver's seat with Nahir next to him. Gian and Skye got in the back.

"Do you know where the trailer park is?" she asked.

"We know this area well," Kyle answered, and she wondered if this was a well-used hunting ground.

When they reached the broken and torn fence that ran along the back of the trailer park, she said, "I'll need to get out and track from here."

Gian gathered Skye and settled her on his lap with her back to his chest. "There's an easier way, a faster way," he said, his voice a seductive whisper that stroked her core even as his fingers caressed the bite on her thigh.

Skye arched, unable to stop her body from answering his call. Blood rushed to her clit, to the lips of her sex. Gian's fingers moved upward, just barely grazing her now throbbing flesh. Her buttocks clenched in reaction, her legs widened, offering his fingers a place in her wet slit. Gian whispered, "Close your eyes. Picture what you saw as you ran. Allow yourself to be there again."

Her first instinct was to resist, to fight the compulsion in his voice, but Gian didn't allow her time to build her defenses. His fingers grasped and pumped her clit, sending an arching wave of fire through her body. His hand alternated between her breasts, rubbing her tight, hard nipples, making them burn for his mouth. "Let yourself go," he whispered before his lips and tongue covered the bite on her neck. She was only vaguely aware of his fangs sinking into her neck as she dropped into his compulsion.

This time she ran not out of fear, but out of ecstasy. She was *other*, and yet different than she'd ever been before. Everything around her was richer, fuller, her senses wide open, embracing the feel of the air against her sensitive skin.

The smell of lust, of heat, surrounded her. Her labia were swollen, slick, ready. Her body throbbed in time to her footsteps. She felt like a wolf leading its mate on a chase that would end in mating.

Gian was with her, she could sense his presence as she ran, somehow knew that he was communicating what she saw to the others, but she didn't look behind her. He would catch her, and when he did, he would mount her. She leaned forward, pushing herself faster to her destination, aware now that she was panting, that her body was begging for release.

Just as the house she sought came into sight, Gian plunged into her wet channel. In part of her mind she knew that he pumped in and out of her with his fingers, but it didn't lessen the sensation, didn't lessen the pleasure spiraling through her, pushing her to crest and flood his hand with her orgasm.

She came back to herself, panting, her body damp, wet where her juices had soaked into Gian's pants, coating his rigid cock with her essence.

He was rock-hard underneath her, holding himself completely still as though he feared any movement would be unbearable. Need began to build in Skye's body again, but she forced it down, forced her thoughts away from what had just happened, from the presence of the men in the front seat.

Kyle drove until he found a place where the car couldn't be seen from the house where she'd been held. Without a word, he and Nahir slipped out of the car and disappeared into the night.

Gian fought the urge to rip his pants open and mount her. There was too much at stake, too much that had to be done.

He fought the desire, but when her buttocks pressed down on his erection as she reached for the door, intending to follow Kyle and Nahir, his control snapped. He pulled her from the car and pressed her chest to the hood, spreading her legs and freeing his erection in a blur of motion.

The smell of her arousal swamped him, filling his mind with only one thought, to cover her body with his, to fuck her, claim her, to celebrate that he hadn't lost her.

He rammed into her, knowing by her scent, by the blood-connection that deepened each time he bit her, that she wanted this as much as he did.

She moved against him, her hungry moans and writhing body inflaming him further, pushing him to pound in and out of her with fierce hard strokes. He could feel her body opening, coaxing him to move deeper, closer to the hidden recess that allowed an Angelini female to lock her mate's cock into her body. He was only barely able to avoid the temptation of her, only barely able to wrest some measure of control back.

He covered her body completely with his, grasping her hands in his, as he once again sunk his fangs into her neck, this time sharing the orgasm with her.

Kyle and Nahir eased out of the shadows a short while later. "They're gone," Kyle said. "I sense no one in the house."

"I'm going in there," Skye said.

"Of course," Gian said, making no effort to restrain her. The men went with her, pausing and watching as Skye broke a window and started to climb into the house. She hesitated only briefly, aware that none of them was moving forward. A memory of Gian insisting that she invite him into her apartment flashed through her mind. "You can come through here or hold on a minute and I'll unlock the front door and you can come in that way." Gian stepped forward, boosting her through the window and coming after her, the other men followed.

The stench of evil-fouled blood was everywhere. The front rooms a mess.

The men moved toward the back of the house but Skye saw her clothes dumped carelessly next to the sofa and went to them, taking the time to pull on her jeans and boots, to note that her cell phone and wallet were still there, before stuffing her bra in a pocket and tying her shirt around her waist.

Only her panties were missing.

Disgust rolled through her, revulsion at the thought that someone had kept her panties as a trophy or souvenir. She shook it off and went to find the men.

They stood around the altar, staring at the naked body that lay facedown, spread-eagled on the symbol-marked surface. Blood and intestines oozing out from underneath him in a sloppy mess. A smaller measure of blood escaped from the slits on his wrists.

He smelled of semen, of blood and bowels, of death.

Only his ankles were tethered at the corners of the altar, but Skye didn't think they'd been bound in order to restrain him. He'd probably been past caring by then, the chains used merely

Jory Strong

to keep him from sliding off the altar as he'd been butt-fucked during the ceremony in which his blood was drained.

Gian pulled her to him and Skye didn't need to hear his words to know that he was envisioning her lying on the altar instead of the man she'd gutted during her escape. Kyle turned away and moved to the coffins.

Their lids were thrown back. Skye was sure they'd be empty, but Kyle's hiss had the blood freezing in her veins even as her heart sped up. Gian didn't release her as he moved to where Kyle, and now Nahir, stood.

Tension radiated from Kyle and his gaze never left Skye's face. She braced herself against showing any reaction.

The female vampire she'd destroyed lay pale and still in the coffin, in perfect repose other than the gaping hole where her heart had once beat. "Do you know her?" Skye asked, trying not to gather herself in preparation for an attack.

Gian's grip tightened on her and a small hiss escaped. Kyle appeared to back down. "She was a friend of Amy's. I don't know her name."

Skye sensed that the danger had passed. She said, "I want to search the rest of the house."

Gian released her. "Hurry."

Skye looked around the room. "My prints are here. My DNA."

Something that looked like humor flashed in Gian's eyes. He leaned down and pressed a kiss to her lips. "Hurry with your search. We will make the necessary preparations here."

Skye knew instinctively what he meant. The house would have to be destroyed, burned until there was no taint of evil, no clue as to what had happened. The forensic evidence would be lost, any clues that might be unearthed would be destroyed. She paused only momentarily then accepted the cost.

This was not a matter for the police. She'd been lucky to survive the fledgling vampire's attack. She doubted someone not

152

born into this other world, prepared for this task, would be as lucky.

She left the ceremonial room and returned to the front of the house. The witch's room was empty of anything other than clothes. The second bedroom had three mattresses on the floor. Male clothing was jumbled on and around them. A black robe lay folded on the end of one bed, its neat positioning a testament to the fact that it hadn't been used that night.

Skye went to that bed and found fliers advertising discount nights from a couple of strip clubs—Bangers, and the one she hadn't visited yet, Toppers. An empty wallet lay in a corner, stripped of identification and money, but the scent of the man who'd owned it lingered underneath—the man Gian had killed.

She picked up the folded robe. It smelled new, unused.

Her memories moved to the day she'd saved Haley. This smell—his smell—hadn't intermixed with Brittany Armstrong's, hadn't reeked of tainted blood then or on the night he'd almost killed her.

An initiate, not yet a servant, though perhaps all the men hoped to become vampire too. Skye searched her mind for distinctions but found only the knowledge that the Angelini did not use their blood magic to create servants as witches and vampires did.

The second man had cleaned out any thing that might identify him, but mixed in among the dirty clothes were a couple of blackjack chips with a Toppers logo. The final bed probably belonged to the dead man on the altar. She hit the jackpot with a pair of cutoffs. In the back pocket was a wallet with a driver's license. She slipped the license in her pocket and kept searching, moving to other rooms until Gian found her and said, "Ready?"

"Yeah. Ready."

They returned to the SUV together, but Kyle and Nahir didn't join them. Gian got behind the wheel and started driving. As Fangs came into sight, Skye thought about the Harley for the first time since the night's activities had begun. "I need to go to the airport. I need to know if they've got my bike."

Gian took her wrist in one hand and laughed softly. "Not tonight."

Shivers ran along Skye's body, but she wasn't sure whether they were from anticipation or wariness. The smooth flow of his voice promised pleasure but the death of the vampire fledgling might demand retribution. She tested his grip on her wrist and knew that without true violence, she wouldn't be able to break it.

Gian parked the SUV in a reserved parking space behind the nightclub and pulled Skye from the car. A man—a vampire—who she'd never seen before appeared at the back entrance as though silently summoned. His long, deep red hair made her think of a waterfall of blood.

"You will find this of interest, Brann," Gian said as he offered the athame that Skye had taken in her escape.

The vampire nodded. His eyes flicked to Skye and back as he took the knife.

"My companion," Gian said. "Kyle and Nahir are doing what's necessary. They will seek you out when they return."

"Good." The other vampire's gaze met and held Gian's before he turned and disappeared back into the club.

"Not a man of many words," Skye said as she allowed Gian to lead her to the bedroom where she'd awakened after the first attack on her.

"No, but dangerous all the same," Gian said, positioning her against the wall and leaning down to nuzzle her neck as he added, "Just like you are."

Desire pooled low in Skye's body when his lips pressed against the bite mark on her neck, but he didn't do more than flutter a kiss over it before moving up her neck, along her chin, before finally resting his lips on hers as he captured her in his dark gaze.

Instinctively she tried to shift out of his grasp, but he maneuvered her so that he held both of her wrists overhead with one of his hands. There was a deep stillness about him, like a predator about to strike his prey.

His free hand moved to cover Skye's heart before he whispered against her lips, "Did you kill the fledgling?"

She couldn't stop the accelerated beat from pounding against his palm in a quick rush of uncertainty. The flame deep in his eyes grew. She could feel the compulsion to answer, but fought it off.

Gian smiled against her lips before sliding his tongue along the seam and tempting her into a kiss.

Despite the danger—or perhaps because of it—Skye's body tightened with need as her tongue dueled with his. When he pulled away, his mouth went unerringly to the bite on her neck. This time he took it between his teeth and bit down. Skye arched against him in silent pleading, her body fully aroused.

Once again he released her, only to trail teasing licks and kisses upward until his gaze met hers. "Did you kill the fledgling?" There was more compulsion this time.

Skye's heart raced in response. Her survival instincts kicked in. "There was no choice."

The flame in the deep centers of Gian's eyes flared—hot, hungry, possessive—commanding that she immerse herself in it. His free hand moved from her heart and opened first her shirt then his. Pressing his naked chest to hers, he whispered, "Admit that you're my companion, accept the medallion."

Searing heat radiated from the ancient pendant pressed between their two bodies. Fire poured through Skye's veins and she rode the crest of a wave that was equal parts pain and pleasure until she found the strength and escaped from Gian's hypnotic gaze.

She was panting, disoriented, but still able to warn, "You won't control me."

Gian smiled slightly, showing just a hint of his fangs. "You have bound me to you, now I will bind you to me."

His lips covered hers, and as his tongue mated with her tongue, Gian unzipped her pants, toying first with her engorged clit, before covering it with his palm and pressing two fingers deep into her slick, swollen cunt.

She tried to fight the desire, the enthrallment, but her body had already chosen him. As he began pumping his fingers in and out of her, she could do nothing but whimper and arch closer, begging him with her body to form a deeper bond.

Gian pulled her body against his and carried her to the bed. When she felt the cool linens underneath her, Skye's survival instincts rose to the surface for a split second, but he was too strong for her, too fast. He held her down as he stripped them both of their clothing, and then he was on top of her.

"Admit that you're my companion, accept the medallion," he demanded again as his tongue swirled around her nipple before drawing it into his mouth.

Her womb rippled with each hard suck to her nipple. She bucked against him, opening herself and rubbing her wet folds against Gian's penis. But he didn't enter her.

Gian switched to the other nipple, making her whimper and cry out, making her open herself wider and plead silently for him to complete her. The bite he'd left over her heart ached for his touch. The blood roared through her veins like a fire through dry forest.

Skye was shaking with need when he lifted his head and moved up her body, taking her hands and pinning them above her head as he thrust deep into her channel. She cried out, fighting the restraint even as she pumped her body upward to welcome him, to take him deeper. Of their own accord, her lips moved along his neck, traced the pulse until she found the place where it beat hard and fast near the surface of his skin.

At the feel of her lips on his throat, Gian slammed his cock into her, seeking the place reserved only for males lucky enough to take an Angelini mate. She whimpered underneath him, yielding, opening herself so that the tip of his penis could reach her hidden recess.

He held back, driving the hunger and the need to bond higher and higher until all she could think about was his possession. When he felt the sting of her teeth against his flesh, he gave her what she wanted.

Every cell in his body screamed in satisfaction as she locked him inside her, milking his semen with each shuddering orgasm as she took his blood with each deep swallow.

Feelings such as Skye had never known washed over her, through her. She opened herself to them, wanted more of them, knew that she would forever crave them, even as the dark wave of ecstasy consumed her.

She was shuddering, panting, crying when she became aware again. When she would have tried to separate their bodies, Gian prevented it.

With his penis still sheathed in her tight channel, he took her face between his hands, forcing her to meet his gaze. "Admit that you're my companion, accept the medallion."

She closed her eyes, fighting herself, fighting him. But when Gian's fangs sunk into her neck, she was lost. "Please," she begged, wrapping her legs around his waist as she arched into him, pressing her flesh to his and feeling the burn of the pendant between them.

He pounded into her—fast, fierce—striking her clit with each thrust. She writhed against him, begging, shivering, yielding when he sheathed his fangs and brought her face to his chest and commanded her to take his blood. She couldn't resist the compulsion, didn't want to, her mouth closed on his flesh and his blood spilled into her, once again sending her into oblivion on a dark wave of ecstasy.

She was still cradled in Gian's arms when consciousness returned. His dark eyes stared into hers but there was no compulsion, no attempt to pull her soul into his.

"I would never harm you. I want to protect you. Serve you," he whispered, his voice blending with the darkness itself as he tilted her head and brushed his fangs against the sensitive mark on her neck before sinking into her flesh—slowly, like a cock penetrating a vagina—flooding her with warmth and caring, with a joyous sense of belonging.

Do you accept what I offer? he asked, the medallion burning between them.

"Yes," she sighed, yielding for now, but knowing to the depth of her being that she would never settle for less than being his equal.

Satisfaction raged through Gian as he placed the pendant around her neck. The ritual was almost completed. Once again he sheathed his fangs and guided her mouth back to the bite mark over his heart.

"Again," he commanded, knowing triumph when she willingly bound herself to him through blood.

Chapter Fourteen

Skye fought her way through layer after layer of heavy black clouds. They tried to hold her down, keep her from seeing the sun, but the weight of them, the pressure of them, made her stomach roil, her chest compress.

Panic made her fight harder, struggle more desperately. If she didn't break through soon, she wouldn't be able to breathe.

Instinct took over, aided by skills and knowledge painfully gained. Gasping, coming awake to the thundering sound of her heart in her ears, her breath shuddering in and out of her chest, Skye escaped the dark compulsion insisting that she sleep until sunset.

For a split second she was disoriented, confused. But then the events of the previous night came into focus.

Unerringly her hand went to the medallion. It was cool to the touch, quiet where it lay against her flesh.

She tried to remember if her mother wore one. When she couldn't picture it, a hint of panic touched her, but she pushed it away.

Inherent knowledge warned her to block her thoughts and actions, that even though Gian was elsewhere, safely hidden from the sun and any who might hunt him, sharing blood with him had forged an awareness between them that was not blurred by distance.

It took sheer determination to move from the bed to where her clothes lay on the floor, left there when Gian had stripped her. She forced herself to put them on, to walk to the door. Each step felt like a major accomplishment. She hadn't been so weak, so vulnerable since she was a small child.

Leaning her forehead against the wall, she focused on the numbers she'd seen Gian punch on the keypad. Slowly, not wanting to make an error and trip some kind of security lock, Skye repeated them.

A barely heard click signaled that she'd remembered correctly. She opened the door and moved into the hallway, reaching for the cellular phone in her pocket as she tried to decide which direction to go.

There would be guards, to protect the vampires if they slept here, or simply to protect the vampires' property. What little of the life she now remembered with her mother and her mother's mates made her aware of certain facts, but didn't help her navigate this new situation. She'd been so young then, so unaware of how her environment was structured, of the rules that governed her existence. But the weight of the medallion hung heavy around her neck and reminded her of how others might see her. Gian's property.

She chose the way Gian had taken her before, letting her senses flare out as she moved quietly down the hall. Though her body was weak, her awareness of her surroundings seemed stronger. Well before she got to the door leading to the area behind the bar, she could hear Haley's voice say, "Do you think she will rise today?"

A man's voice answered, "Not if Gian really controls her as he said he does."

Haley gave a little gasp. "Rafael, you should watch your words. Just because Brann protects you doesn't mean you can challenge Gian."

The man snorted, "I'm not anyone's pet to speak only when spoken to and behave only as ordered to behave."

Another voice entered the conversation—Kisha, Nahir's companion. "Don't act like you're better than Haley, Rafael, you're the same as we are—you answer to a vampire master."

Haley's soft voice offered peace. "It's okay, Kisha. I wasn't offended." She hesitated then added, "Why is Brann here, Rafael? Did the council send him?"

Rafael said, "And I should tell you *why*?"

"Oh, don't be an ass," Kisha said. "Is he here because of Jen and Amy or because of Gian's Angelini companion?"

Even through the wooden door, Skye could sense the amusement rolling off the man named Rafael. She pictured Brann, the powerful vampire who'd been waiting at the back door when Gian brought her here last night, and wondered what his companion looked like.

Rafael let the tension build until finally answering. "Brann's here to deal with the witch."

Haley's voice was tight with worry. "What about Jen? And Amy?"

"Brann has the skills to remove the witch's taint, though they'll still be vampire." He paused dramatically. "That's if Gian's companion doesn't kill them first. You'd be wise to stay clear of her. I assume you know that she killed a fledgling last night."

Kisha's response was immediate. "You're such a shit-disturber, Rafe. Knock it off. Even Brann believes it was in self-defense. Nahir and Kyle both told us that."

There was movement in the room and Skye tensed, waiting for them to come toward the hidden door.

"You're no fun, Kisha. I'm going to stroll around outside."

"None of us is supposed to leave the building today," Haley said.

"And around we go," Rafael retorted. "I'm not anyone's pet to speak only when spoken to and behave only as ordered to behave."

A door opened and closed. Kisha snorted. "God, what an arrogant ass. I'd like to see him brought down a peg or two. I don't know what Brann sees in him, except maybe a challenge."

There was an unspoken question in Haley's voice when she said, "Brann was here once before, when you and Nahir were away. He didn't have a companion with him, but he…took what he needed from the women who came to Fangs."

Kisha laughed. "I love you, Haley. You are always so polite. FYI, Brann goes both ways, though honestly, I always thought he was more interested in women. I was surprised when he showed up with Rafael as a companion, but Brann's so powerful, he can probably take a female companion also—if he's ever able to find one that can put up with Rafael."

Once again there was movement, along with the clatter of dishes and silverware being gathered. Haley said, "I can do yours, too."

"That's okay, let's do them together then we can watch TV or play some cards." Their footsteps drew near, passing right by the door shielding Skye then grew faint as they passed through another door.

Skye slipped into the bar area and moved quickly to the door leading out of the building and into the parking lot. The lot would be wide open now, free of cars. If Rafael was near, he'd see her as soon as she stepped outside, but there was no choice but to try and make her escape. The switchblade she always kept with her was in the pocket of her jeans but she didn't pull it out. Even if he tried to prevent her from leaving she wouldn't use the weapon on him.

Slowly she opened the door, bracing herself for the sound of an alarm or for Rafael's shout, but neither came. She'd been to Fangs enough times to know which direction would lead her to cover. She hesitated only long enough to make sure that she could sense no presence before committing herself to her path and leaving the building.

Adrenaline kicked in, giving her the strength to run just far enough that she could hide in an alley and consider her next move. She needed to get to the airport and see if the Harley was there.

She reached in her pocket and drew out her wallet, wondering what the cab fare would be, wondering if she dared to go home. The ID that she'd found in the witch's house caught her attention. She needed to know who the man left on the altar was, who the fledgling vampire she'd killed had been. Skye flicked on the cell phone and saw that Rico had called.

Conflicting emotions and instincts crashed through her.

He was her mate. He was safety.

He was a cop. He was dangerous.

This was her world and he was now a part of it.

This was the part of her world that she wanted him safe from.

There was no safety in ignorance.

She dialed his number and couldn't stop the way her heart leaped at the sound of his voice. "Where are you?" he asked.

She told him. "Are you on duty?"

"No."

"Can you come get me?"

There was a surprised hesitation. "Sure."

Skye waited a heartbeat before adding, "When you get here, wait a minute, I'll come to you."

"Shit. You're in trouble. I'm walking out of my house right now. I can stay on the line."

Warmth rushed through Skye. "I'm not in danger. I'll see you in a few minutes."

Rico's voice was cop-firm. "We'll talk about it then."

"I'll see you in a few minutes," Skye repeated before cutting off the connection and silencing the phone.

* * * * *

¡Carajo! He hated this. Hated the worry, hated the fact that he didn't know what she was doing and he was too chickenshit to ask her. Fuck! How could he know and stay a cop?

Rico slammed his fist on the steering wheel. Shit! What was he going to do about this?

Frustration rolled into aggression. They *would* talk. He was starting to get pissed at himself. He'd let himself be led around by his dick long enough. Maybe he wouldn't like her answers, maybe he wouldn't be able to live with them, maybe in the end he'd see if she could make him forget that he'd ever done more than fantasize about her, but at least it would be his choice.

The anger turned to worry when he passed Fangs. He'd been through here numerous times since landing the Brittany Armstrong case. Usually the place was dead, couldn't even get anyone to answer the phone during daylight hours. But now there were a couple of women outside and about a half dozen men. One in particular caught Rico's eye. Despite the long blond hair, the guy oozed power. He was talking and pointing, directing the others. Rico's heart did a nervous tap dance when he recognized the beginnings of a search.

Fuck. He had almost no time to get to Skye.

It was all he could do not to give in to temptation and stomp on the gas. Still, he knew a moment of panic when he got to where she'd told him to meet her and he didn't see her.

Before true fear could set in, she slipped from behind the building and hurried to the car. Rico's jaw tightened when he saw the condition she was in. He'd seen her run all night long tracking and not look as weak and drawn as she did right now. If Gian had done this to her, then he was going to pay for it.

She didn't need to be told to get down so that she wouldn't be seen. Rico didn't need to be told to hurry.

He didn't ask where she wanted to go, but took her to his house. She remained quiet even as he led her into the kitchen and sat her down. "You look like you're getting ready to drop. When's the last time you had something to eat?"

Fire raced through Skye and for a moment she was trapped in the night, in Gian's eyes, remembering the hot, metallic blood that had slid down her throat. Though he could heal her and replenish her with his blood — last night his blood had been neither medicine nor sustenance — it had been magic that bound her to him.

Rico's hand on her face brought her back to the day, to the kitchen where he hovered over her, concern and caring so obvious on his face that Skye felt tears threaten. The surge of emotion shocked her, leaving her momentarily frozen, trapped in his eyes.

"Hey, you're starting to freak me out here," Rico said, the soft way he caressed her face sending a hot flame of love through her.

Skye blinked and turned to press a kiss on his palm. "I'm okay. It was a long night and I haven't eaten since LA."

Rico brushed his mouth over hers. "I make a killer omelet. You like jalapenos?"

"Yes."

"Good. One specialty omelet coming up." Rico turned away from where she sat at the table and began gathering what he needed to cook.

Fuck! How could he resist her when she was like this? Soft, in need of more than just his cock.

He tried to work up some righteous anger, but didn't get any closer than outraged protectiveness. "Did he hurt you?"

Skye's hand went immediately to the medallion. But the gesture made her think of Haley's nervous habit, so she forced her hand back into her lap. "No."

The muscles in Rico's back tensed. "Then why is there a search party looking for you?"

"Gian wanted me to stay until sunset, but there are things I need to take care of."

Rico turned from the refrigerator with a carton of eggs in his hand. "You were being held against your will?" There was anger in his voice, but his expression said that he'd use the law to see that Gian paid.

"No."

Rico's face tightened as though he didn't believe her. Anger radiated off of him as he moved to the counter and began to chop ingredients for her omelet.

An unfamiliar exhaustion settled on Skye. Until the craving to take mates had overwhelmed her, she'd spent most of her time hunting, surrounded by people and yet separate.

Nothing in her life had prepared her for this—for dealing with so many conflicting feelings and realities. She balanced on an emotional razor edge, bound to two dangerous men, uncertain how to integrate them into her life, how to meld what her body needed with what her soul demanded—equality, unity, a cohesive union like her mother shared with her two mates.

Skye rested her head in her hands and let her mind escape to what it was like to run as *other*, to streak across the desert unencumbered by human thought or emotion, to exist, to live, to embrace something greater.

Pain ripped through Rico's heart when he turned and saw Skye. With her shoulders hunched and her face buried in her hands, she looked utterly defeated. The need to comfort and protect her warred with the need to regain control of his life.

Since this thing with her had started, his life had become chaotic, weirdly disjointed. It was starting to affect how he did his job, how he saw himself.

Every cop instinct he possessed urged him to go at her now, when she was vulnerable. But he couldn't bring himself to press her for answers. Instead he put her meal down in front of her and stroked her hair. "Go ahead and eat then take a hot shower. We can talk afterward."

Skye accepted the reprieve and consumed the meal rapidly, barely able to stop long enough to take a breath. Rico laughed and cooked up another omelet, this time adding a couple of pieces of toast. "Either my cooking is unbelievably great or you're starving."

"Both," she said before attacking the second serving. She could feel her strength building with every bite.

"Another?" Rico asked when she'd cleaned her plate.

"No. I'm okay now." She stood and took her plate to the sink then followed as Rico led her through the house, through the bedroom with its masculine scent and huge four-poster bed, and into an equally impressive bathroom. Without a word he began unbuttoning her shirt. She reached over and did the same to his before removing the rest of her clothes.

Rico's face tightened momentarily then darkened as his eyes moved along her naked body. His fingers followed, sending erotic pulses through her as he traced a line from the bite mark on her neck, to the one over her heart, to the one on her inner thigh.

Fuck! It was starting again. He'd wanted a few minutes to hold her, to feel her skin touch his before they started talking. The shower had seemed like a safe enough idea. But now lust slammed through his system.

When her fingers traced a similar line from his neck, to his heart, to his thigh, his cock grew larger, his balls heavier — a male animal on proud display for his female.

Rico ground his teeth against the need pouring through him. He'd never been a biter, never been one to let a woman mark him. But the sight of the marks on her body had him wanting to sink his teeth into her before pressing her mouth to his skin so she could reclaim him.

He fought to stay in control, to keep his body from taking over even as the desire to understand this thing between them was being weakened by the fantasies playing out in his mind.

He forced his words out, trying to keep from touching her. "Did you bite him like this?"

Her whispered "yes" made his cock jerk. Of its own accord, his hand reached down, encircling his penis, pumping once then squeezing when fantasizes of spewing his seed across her flat stomach, across her mound and her breasts seized his mind.

¡Carajo! He'd never been this primitive.

He closed his eyes, tried to close his mind. "Fuck, I don't understand this thing between us."

His tortured expression gentled some of the lust that whipped through Skye's body. She moved closer to the shower, hoping that putting some distance between them would help. She surprised both of them by saying, "I didn't know it would be like this. I didn't understand what it would mean to mark you...to lock you in my body that first night. If I'd known, I would have told you before we joined. I would have tried to give you a choice. I can still try to undo it. I don't know if it will work, but I can try to make the need fade for you."

Rico opened his eyes and saw the sincerity in hers, saw the same glimmer of defeat that he'd seen in the kitchen. Shit, maybe this thing was making a mess of her life, too.

"What about Gian?" When her eyebrows drew together in a silent question, Rico said, "Does he want this...fuck, it's like an addiction...does he want it?"

"Yes." She hesitated, wondering how much to tell him then deciding that in the end he would need to know all of it—maybe not right now, but eventually. There was no safety in ignorance. "Gian knows more about the Angelini than I do. He understands the bond."

Rico's cop instincts snapped into place and with it the feeling of control. He could handle the lust now, hold off until he had some answers. He forced his hand away from his penis and stepped toward her. "Angelini?"

"My race."

His gaze sharpened. "I've never heard of them. Who are they?"

"Hunters, like me. Different, like I'm different."

Shit! He didn't want to believe that there were others like her, that she belonged to a race that was probably the stuff of nightmares—his balls tightened—or fantasies. But his cop instincts said she wasn't lying, the memories of being locked in her body and orgasming over and over again were his proof.

He was close enough to smell her arousal, to feel the heat coming off her body. When her eyes dropped to his penis, it strained and bobbed in greeting. He stilled it with his hand then risked touching her face to draw her attention back to his.

"I thought you had no memory of where you came from. The file says you were found in a ghetto in LA and grew up in foster care. You were mute until you were twelve or thirteen, and even then weren't cooperative when people tried to talk to you."

Her eyes widened and Rico almost laughed at her surprise. "Believe me, the captain has a file that's about five inches thick on you. He's collected every scrap of paper with your name on it. It's almost become required reading for anyone in the department."

She laughed softly and Rico's heart lightened at seeing fewer shadows in her eyes. When she rubbed her cheek against his palm in an affectionate gesture, it was all he could do to stop himself from pulling her into his arms. Only the need for answers held him back.

"There were always vague memories," Skye said, "of my mother and her two mates — husbands. Impressions mainly, nothing to lead me to them or explain how I ended up in Los Angeles. Even now I don't have the answer, but at least I know that I wasn't supposed to be in that city. It's not where I had been before." She shrugged. "The memories only started coming back yesterday when I was in LA."

Rico circled back to what she'd said before. "But Gian knew what you were before you knew?"

"Yes. He knew that I could bind him to me…he knew it before, during and after. He accepts it. He binds me to him in return."

Rico's eyes narrowed when her hand strayed to the medallion around her neck. It was the only piece of jewelry she wore, the only piece he'd ever seen on her.

He reached for it, a knee-jerk reaction that had him wanting to rip it off her neck. But when his hand closed around it, heat seared through his palm and straight to his cock.

"Fuck! What was that?"

Skye shivered. When he'd grabbed the medallion, a rush of power had surged through her—Gian's power. "A safeguard, I think."

"He's Angelini?"

"No. But he's powerful in his own right."

Rico's mind flashed on the blond man he'd seen in the Fangs' parking lot when he went to get Skye. The guy had oozed power. If Gian was the same…

Rico gritted his teeth and reached for the medallion again. This time there was only a small pulse of heat, but it was there, real, and not something he imagined.

He used the medallion to pull her closer. For a split second he thought he saw a flame deep in the centers of her pupils. But as soon as their bodies touched, he threw his head back and closed his eyes as the pleasure of being skin-to-skin roared through him. He could almost believe anything, accept anything in order to experience this.

The damp, aroused heat of her beckoned and his cock responded, swelling further, its tip leaking. There were other answers that he wanted, but right now, he wanted this more.

His hands dropped to her hips and she pressed even closer. But when he would have lifted her, had her wrap her legs around him so he could finally feel the heaven of her tight channel, Skye stilled him with a hand to his chest. "You can't have this and not the bond that goes with it. Every time we join, it deepens, it strengthens."

For a second he fought against the choice she was forcing on him, fought against having to think. All he wanted to do was lose himself in the pleasure of her.

Skye closed her eyes to the need she saw on Rico's face. Her body craved his, but Gian's strength gave her the buffer she needed to resist. She didn't know whether it was the medallion or the blood-magic, but changes she'd only been vaguely aware of since waking came into focus. She understood things that she hadn't understood before — as though some of Gian's knowledge and abilities had become hers.

With a thought she touched Gian's mind and felt his awareness that she was awake and with Rico. He was angry that she'd broken through his compulsion, but there was reluctant admiration too. He couldn't come for her until the sun set, but he could track her to Rico's then. And if she was careless enough to give him Rico's address, then he could send others to retrieve her.

All that she knew with just the brush of her mind to Gian's. She also knew that he waited to see whether Rico would accept the bond. He would be pleased to have her to himself, without Rico to anchor her to a world other than his own. But he would accept the bond with Rico. It was useful, an added layer of protection. And pleasure — he'd shared women in the past.

A spike of savage possessiveness surged through Skye at Gian's remembered pleasure. She would cut his heart out if he ever went to another woman.

Amusement rippled down the psychic line between them. This time she heard the words instead of experiencing them as impressions. *There can be no one outside the bond*, he whispered, his voice fading in a soft caress as his presence became a distant shadow in her mind.

Skye opened her eyes and focused on Rico. His eyes were still closed, his face tight. His thoughts were easier for her to reach.

He struggled to find a way to have her, to reconcile what he feared she was, with what he was—a cop. He couldn't give up his job, his identity, for her.

Skye's mind moved through the past, to the kills she'd made. She didn't regret them, wouldn't undo them if she could, but she could compromise and let others mete out justice in the future. She could give Rico that measure of peace.

She pressed her lips over the bite mark on his neck and whispered, "I'd never force you to give up your job, to be other than what you are. We both want the same thing—justice. I don't need to kill to achieve that goal."

Shock whipped through Rico at her words. His eyes flew open. Fuck, could she read his mind? Or was she just guessing?

She whispered, "I can touch your thoughts."

From Gian's knowledge she added, "When the bond is fully complete, then you'll be able to touch mine as well."

Rico's heart thundered in his chest. He knew he should be scared shitless, but the hot waves of lust that volleyed back and forth between them made fear impossible. He didn't want to give this up. If he could have her and stay a cop, then he was willing to pay any price.

Rico moved forward, pressing her against the wall. This time she didn't resist when he lifted her, urging her to wrap her legs around him.

The smell of her arousal flooded his senses. The feel of her slippery folds against his erection had fire racing along his spine. He'd die if he didn't get inside her.

"Do you agree to the bond?" she asked him.

He thrust into her and groaned against the tight squeeze of her channel.

"Say the words," she whispered.

This time he knew that he wasn't imagining the flames flickering deep in her eyes. If they were the fires of hell, then he was a doomed man.

"I accept the bond."

* * * * *

Trapped in the sluggish daylight sleep of a centuries-old vampire, Gian felt the echoes of Skye's pleasure down their psychic bond. His own penis stirred in anticipation. It was time to meet her other mate, to finish what she'd begun.

Brann's voice cut into his thoughts, sharp with censure. *Even when you were human, you never allowed your cock to rule you. No fuck is worth the risks you take, Gian. She has gained from your blood but you still do not control her.*

And you control Rafael? Do not play the heavy with me...Sire. Gian hissed, letting the other vampire feel the bite of his words.

There was a pause, like the buildup of pressure before a storm breaks. But then Brann laughed across the bond and the tension eased. *You were a disrespectful ass before you became vampire. I don't know why I thought the centuries would improve you. I have called Rafael back from his search for* your *Angelini mate. Maybe when you rise you can put aside the demands of your pike and attend to the business of finding the witch and the fledglings so that I will be free to go about* my *business.*

Gian laughed. *You date yourself, Brann, no one calls it a pike anymore.*

And you remain a disrespectful ass. There was a slight pause, then a more serious warning. *Attend to what needs to be attended to, Gian, before there's more trouble here. Already I hear rumors that another Angelini hunts in Las Vegas.*

Chapter Fifteen

The fuck against the bathroom wall had only whetted Rico's appetite for more. He wanted to bury his cock in her pussy and live there forever. When she raised her arms and bound her braid up before stepping into the shower, his thoughts expanded to latching onto her nipples and swallowing them whole.

He followed her into the shower, glad that when he'd gutted this house and rebuilt it, he'd had the foresight to put in a shower that lent itself to fucking. Just the sight of her smoothing soapy hands over her own body was enough to have him ready again.

Without a word, Rico took the soap from her hands and lathered his own. He'd intended to clean every inch of her body, but the way she watched, the way her gaze traveled over him, lingering on his erection with satisfied, half-closed eyes made him want to show off, to tempt her with his prowess.

He applied the soap to his own skin instead of hers, hesitating over the bite mark on his neck until the hot sparks of hunger shooting from the new erogenous zone had his nipples and cock so tight and hard that he couldn't keep his hand on the mark any longer.

Satisfaction whipped through him when he saw the way Syke's lips were slightly parted, the way her breath moved in and out in short pants as she watched him.

His balls felt huge and heavy. He widened his stance in response and they brushed against the bite on his thigh. His buttocks clenched as a bolt of fire ripped through his testicles.

¡Carajo! She made him feel like a well-hung bull.

His nipples were so sensitive that he couldn't linger over them without fear of coming. When she licked her lips as though she'd like to suckle him, he had to grab his cock to keep from spewing then and there.

Skye moved closer and placed her hand on the mark over his heart. The sound of his heartbeat roared through his head, through his cock, moving at the same rate as hers, thundering in time to the flames dancing in her eyes.

What do you want?

Rico wasn't sure whether she'd spoken out loud or in his mind. He didn't care. Along with the question came the knowledge that he could have her any way he wanted. That she wouldn't turn away from any of his desires.

The breath swooshed out of his body in pants as the fantasies flooded in.

He wanted her tied to his bed. He wanted her sucking his nipples, his cock, taking him all the way down her throat. He wanted her riding his face while he plunged his tongue into her and heard her scream above him. He wanted to mount her. To take her on her hands and knees and have her lock him into her body—a stallion on his mare, a wolf on his mate.

He tightened the grip on his penis when her eyes darkened, when she wetted her lips and leaned closer, licking at his mouth, tempting him, coaxing him to cover her body with his.

All thought left him then. He took her down to the shower floor, reveling in the way she went to her hands and knees, in the way she held her body to expose the slick, wet folds of her vulva.

The steam trapped the scent of her arousal and held it against his body. The hot water pounding against his back sharpened the need.

His. She was his mate.

He mounted her then, thrusting deep, demanding with his body that she acknowledge what he was to her. She yielded, squeezing him, teasing him to plunge deeper, harder. In a frenzy he moved in and out of her, not sparing her from the weight and power of his body.

She writhed underneath him in ecstasy, driving them both to the brink of oblivion until finally that last little bit of her opened to admit him, to lock him to her. Then there was nothing but the white-hot pleasure of orgasm after orgasm as his body jerked and shuddered above hers.

Even when he knew that they were no longer locked together, Rico couldn't bring himself to pull away. He nuzzled her, licking and kissing along her neck until he got to her ear. She shifted and he almost whimpered when his penis slipped out of her hot channel.

Skye's laugh was soft, affectionate, covering him like a warm blanket. "You must have a huge hot water heater. We'd be lying in cold water if we were at my apartment."

Rico grinned and got to his feet then helped her stand. His cock stirred when their wet flesh touched, skin sliding against skin, but for the first time since he'd been with her, the need to have her again didn't threaten to consume him.

They had a lifetime to fuck, to play, to mate, to make love, to give in to their fantasies. That knowledge settled over him, left him in control of himself again.

He let her leave the shower first. After they'd dried off, he said, "My sister leaves some of her clothes over here. You're about the same size. They're in the bedroom at the end of the hall."

Skye stilled, alarmed but curious at the same time. Except for Rico's friendship with Captain Rivera, she'd never given any thought to how his life might be connected to other people—how her life might now be tied to others.

"I didn't know you had a sister."

Rico snorted. "One sister, five brothers. All of them in law enforcement." His expression grew somber as he pulled Skye to him. She could read the question without touching his mind. She repeated the words she'd said earlier.

"I'll never force you to give up being a cop. We both want the same thing—justice. I don't need to kill to achieve that goal."

He nodded once then pushed her gently toward the doorway. "Get dressed before I decide that I can't resist your body any longer."

Skye laughed and moved toward the open doorway, feeling lighthearted, complete. With a thought she touched Gian's mind and found him in the heavy daytime sleep of a vampire, though a part of him was aware of her.

His anger at her escape had passed, though his resolve to find her had not. *Do you think I'll run and hide?* she chided.

You will let me find you when you're with him? he countered.

Skye's body quickened with reawakened need. *Yes.*

The link faded but remained like a tiny nightlight in a vast, darkened hallway. Skye got dressed, stopping only long enough to retrieve her wallet and the ID she'd taken, before returning to the living room.

Rico was talking on his phone. "Look, I'll go with you, Cia… Yeah. I know it's my day off, but I want to get this thing closed up and you're on to a good lead… Jackson would stand out like he's wearing a neon sign. He's got rookie stamped all over him and besides that, he hasn't been on this case since it started. He'd spend most of the night staring at the strippers and the freaky-looking kids… Yeah, okay… I'll meet you at the office to discuss strategy. Bye."

"The Armstrong case?" Skye asked and watched as his face closed off, as he braced himself against thinking about the case. "I can help you. You can help me. The cases I'm working on are connected to your case."

Rico didn't know what to do with her offer. He wanted to bring whoever killed Brittany Armstrong to justice, but he knew that Rivera wouldn't want him to share any information with Skye. His chest went tight thinking about the captain. He needed to tell Rivera about this thing with Skye. It wouldn't stay hidden for very long.

"I can't tell you anything without talking to the captain first," he finally said.

Skye was warmed by his answer, by the underlying willingness to try and find a way to compromise. "Do you have a copier here?"

He blinked at the change of subject. "Yeah. In my office."

She pulled the ID of the man she'd gutted out of her jeans and handed it to Rico. The faint stink of foul, evil-cursed blood floated along her senses, more memory than reality. "His scent was in the woods along with Brittany's."

Rico's face tightened. "How did you get this?"

"We struggled and I took it."

"When?"

"Yesterday. When I got back from LA. He was waiting for me, along with another man."

"Why didn't you call me!"

"Gian found me first."

Rico's body tensed. The cop in him warred with the man.

It was like navigating through a minefield. There was more going on here than she wanted to tell him. Maybe more here than he could handle right now.

He chose to stay on safer ground. "You're sure he was in the woods with Brittany Armstrong?"

Skye's mind ranged back to the scent of two men—the witch's servants—and to the vampire fledgling that she'd killed. They smelled the same, as though the magic that controlled them also stamped out their individuality. There'd been five people with Brittany, probably the three fledglings and the two servants. The man Gian had killed hadn't smelled of tainted blood. "His scent was there," she told Rico. "Tell the captain that if you find out who this man hung out with, you might find the killers."

Rico looked down at the driver's license. The name was probably fake, but he could scan the picture in and see if he got a hit. Fuck. It was a lead. Something to bargain with. He started to put the ID in his pocket then figured he should treat it as evidence. Maybe they could even take a few prints off of it. When he headed for the kitchen to get a baggie, she said, "I want a copy of it to show around."

"No." The word was an automatic response, but as soon as he said it, he knew he meant it. If this guy had already attacked her once, there was no way he was going to make it easy for her to go against him again. Maybe this was why Gian hadn't wanted her to leave Fangs. His mind shied away from thinking about what he shared with the other man. Instead, Rico braced himself for her fury. When it didn't come he stopped and turned back to her.

She stood with a bemused expression on her face, as though she was torn between being mad and laughing. Amusement won out. She shook her head and strolled over to him, winding against his body like an affectionate cat. "Having mates is going to take some getting used to." She pulled his head down and rubbed her nose against his before biting his lip in a small warning. "I'm going to let you get away with this—for now."

The tension eased from his body. Fuck, he loved this, the feel of her body against his, the challenge of her. She made him feel alive, complete.

"I've got to get to the station. You can stay here if you want." He frowned at the thought of her going back to her apartment. Fuck. It galled him, but maybe he should take her back to Fangs. On the heels of that came a question he should have asked before this. Cop intuition tightened Rico's gut. "Where's the Harley?"

"I'm not sure." Her eyes flickered to the ID Rico was still holding. "After the scuffle, I ran. There wasn't any time to try and get to the Harley."

"You think he took it?"

"Maybe." She half-smiled. "Too early to report it stolen if that's where you're going."

Rico didn't want to agree with her, but in the end he did. He could circle back to this later, maybe take her down to the station and make sure she stayed long enough so an artist could do up a composite of whoever had been with the guy who'd attacked her.

Shit. What he really wanted was for her to stay here, safe, but he knew that wasn't going to happen.

"You can borrow my truck." His gut did a little summersault. The truck was his baby. "You can drive something other than a bike, right?"

Her eyebrows rose and he wanted to kiss the challenge right off her face. "Okay, right. Let me bag this, then I'll show you the truck."

The truck was a monster. Gleaming black metal and enough power to pull a house, but it was the bed that caught Skye's attention. Long, covered, with plenty of room to carry a couple of coffins.

* * * * *

Rico's gut tightened when he walked into the bullpen and saw the captain sitting next to Caldwell's desk. Fuck, he couldn't sit on the information Skye had given him, but he wasn't ready to talk to Rivera about her. Shit. He didn't even know what he was going to say. The captain was half older-brother, half-uncle to him. Not really family, but close enough.

Rivera and his father had grown up in the same neighborhood, gone into police work a few years apart, and still got together and played poker together once in a while. Telling the captain that he was involved with Skye was like a dress rehearsal for introducing her to his family.

Dread settled like ice in Rico's gut. He'd rather look down the barrel of a gun than face that. Even if Skye wasn't who she was, curiosity would get the better of at least one of his siblings and they'd do a background check on her. Not that they needed to go any further than the file Rivera had.

Rico took a deep breath and did what he had to do. He pulled the bagged driver's license out and dropped it on Caldwell's desk. "This is one of the people who was in the woods with Brittany Armstrong. Name's probably fake, but the picture's accurate. If we're lucky, we may pull a print."

Rivera was too good a cop not to jump immediately to the point Rico wanted to avoid. "How'd you get this?"

"Skye Delano."

Cia's mouth went tight with disapproval. The captain's hand twitched and Rico knew that Rivera was fighting the urge to cross himself. He used to do it every time Skye's name was mentioned, but after a couple of the guys started mimicking the behavior, Rivera stopped doing it.

"We'll talk later," the captain said, his voice making it clear that the discussion wasn't going to be pleasant.

Rico felt his gut twist a little tighter, but he didn't look away. It was time he faced up to this. He'd made his choice.

The captain stood and picked up the bagged ID. "I'll get the techs working on this. If something breaks, I'll have them call you. In the meanwhile, follow up on Caldwell's lead but don't get in too deep." He looked at Caldwell then. "This is your angle, but if it looks like the civilian may get hurt, do what you can to intervene. The last thing we need is another killing like Armstrong's. We got off lucky that none of the newspapers got a hold of it."

Caldwell nodded. "Yes, sir."

"Keep me posted," the captain said before striding out of the bullpen.

Caldwell's chilly disapproval washed over Rico even as she pushed a fax toward him and brought him up to date. "This is Marina, the girl I told you about. There may be others, but she's the only one I've been able to get close to online. She's from LA. Pacific Palisades to be exact. Her father is a wealthy lawyer, her mother a dedicated socialite. Probably started the Goth thing as a way to get attention." Cia grimaced.

"She's supposed to go to Fangs first, so she can see for herself that vampires exist. After that she's supposed to go to Bangers where she'll be 'tested', whatever that means. If she passes, then she'll start the initiation process. That's the same drill Brittany went through—or close enough. I talked to one of the detectives in Virginia yesterday. They were able to recover some files she'd deleted. She was supposed to go to Fangs first, then Bangers. There wasn't anything about being tested before she was initiated, but it's still close to the same MO. And the threads leading her from public chat rooms to very private chat rooms are almost exactly the same—like the same people who trolled for Brittany are trolling for someone new."

Rico didn't want to admire Caldwell. He'd rather stay pissed. The captain had saddled him with her and right from the start she'd done her best to keep him away from Skye. But fuck, this was good work, most of it probably done on her own time.

"This is a great lead," he said.

Caldwell's face lightened. "Thanks. You ready to go?"

"Yeah." Rico's chest tightened and the mark over his heart burned. Gian would be waiting at Fangs. Rico didn't know how he knew that, but his gut told him that he was going to meet Skye's other mate tonight.

* * * * *

Old vampires didn't need to sleep in coffins, but for fledglings who'd not mastered the magic necessary for survival, coffins were essential.

The knowledge came from Skye's past. From a barely remembered conversation with her mother's mate, Sabin. It made her heart ache that she was still gathering bits of information, trying to piece together her life before… Even now she didn't remember how she'd been separated from her mother and fathers.

Details that should have been engraved in her soul, a part of who was, remained illusive. But at least it was coming back.

When the time was right, she would start searching for her family.

Skye parked Rico's truck and got out, her quick strides carrying her across the asphalt parking lot and to the funeral home's main entrance. She didn't need to look at the sky to know that sunset was approaching. She could feel it on her skin, in the way Gian's power was building.

As she entered the funeral home, a dark-suited man stepped forward. "May I help you?"

Skye didn't hesitate. She trapped him in her eyes. "Have any coffins left here in the last twenty-four hours?"

A struggle took place across the man's features and victory shot through Skye at the hint of compulsion that she could feel in his mind. The fledgling's touch was no match for her own.

Skye let him fall deeper into her own eyes and repeated the question. His features cleared. A movie played out in his mind and she saw Amy's glowing eyes as she'd held the man enthralled.

"Yes. Two of them." His words were matched with more images. This time of him loading the coffins into a hearse and driving them to a storage unit. Jen was waiting there. Skye paused the memory in order to examine Haley's younger sister. She was flush with a blood feeling, but nervousness poured off of her. The man slipped the coffins into the storage unit and turned to leave. Out of the corner of his eye, he saw the witch, but it was just a fleeting impression.

Skye probed harder, making sure she was seeing the truth. She could sense the warmth that preceded the sun's rising along his skin, his sudden urgency to get back to the funeral home, the compulsion to forget about the coffins. She let him drop from her eyes, leaving only a vague memory that she'd been here but hadn't found what she was looking for.

* * * * *

"There she is," Caldwell said.

Rico studied the girl who'd just joined the line of black-clothed, body-pierced kids waiting to get into Fangs. How could Skye stand to hang out here?

"You know what really gets me about this?" Cia asked, but didn't wait for Rico's response. "Most of these kids have it made just by being born into families with money. All they have to do is keep their noses clean and do okay in school and their lives are set. Most of them probably were given cars at sixteen and already have a college fund set up for them. But instead they do this to themselves."

"Money's not everything. A lot of these kids wouldn't be here if they had what they needed at home," Rico said, and surprised himself by feeling a spark of compassion for the misfit kids in line. He'd gone to school with a lot of kids who had money but no family life. Not that he'd ever known hunger, but his mother had never worked outside being a homemaker, and with seven kids on a cop's salary, they'd never had a lot left over. But they'd had family, and lots of it, and he'd known growing up that he was rich in a way that most of the kids he knew envied.

Caldwell shot him a hard stare. "What's going on with you? Now you're identifying with them? Oh, right. This is one of your girlfriend's hangouts when she's not doing business with scum like Big Daddy." There was a wealth of disapproval in her voice.

Rico shifted in his seat. He'd never wanted a partner, but if Rivera was going to pair him with Caldwell, then he needed to get this out in the open. "Look, Cia, if you've got a problem with me having a private life that includes Skye, then talk to the captain and see if he'll reassign you. Otherwise, keep it to yourself."

Caldwell looked like she'd bitten into shit. "Fine. But you're a damn good cop, Rico, and I hate to see you throw it away over her."

"I'm not throwing it away."

Cia snorted and opened the car door. "That's bullshit. I'm going to go stand in line behind Marina. It's probably better to split up anyway." She started to close the door, then added. "Have it your way. I'm not going to say anything to the captain, unless *you* have a problem with me being your partner." She shut the door firmly and stalked over to the line.

Rico shut his eyes briefly. He'd be glad when this case was wrapped up. He had a shitload of stuff to work through and he didn't need this on top of it.

A small wave of excitement rippled through the kids waiting in line. Rico's attention turned and locked onto the man who'd just stepped out of Fangs. His gut clenched when he saw the long dark hair and aquiline features. He didn't need Skye here to tell him who he was looking at. Gian.

Goddamn. He wasn't ready for this. But when the line started moving, Rico got out of the car.

* * * * *

They hadn't chosen the storage locker for security, probably because they'd only intended to "stay" long enough to find a new place. Skye's lips tilted up in a half-smile as she used the bolt cutters she'd gotten at the hardware store to snap the lock.

The sight that greeted her when she rolled the door back turned the half-smile into a full smile. The Harley was here, waiting to be reclaimed. And wrapped in the smell of foul blood and dark magic were both coffins.

Skye set the bolt cutters aside and pulled out the knives, both purchased from a man who wouldn't remember selling them. The sun would drop in a few minutes, but she didn't intend to wait. She closed the door and plunged the locker into darkness.

Her night vision had been sharpened by Gian's blood. It took only a second for her eyes to adjust so that the inside of the storage unit was as visible as a room in daylight.

The thin wall that separated Gian's mind from hers still shimmered in place, but she could feel his power building on the other side, aware that she was hiding from him.

Skye moved to the first coffin. Preparing herself to strike fast.

The hand holding the knife began its descent even before the casket lid had completely opened.

There was only time for a startled hiss and a flash of red, glaring eyes before the knife was driven home and Amy Weldon's fate was suspended. Jen's life force was weaker and just as easily subdued.

* * * * *

Gian sent another strong summons to Skye before turning his attention to Detective Rico Santana. He didn't need the Angelini marks to know who the man in the parking lot was. He recognized him from the first night that Skye had come to Fangs—the night when he'd seen her dancing and felt the undeniable call of her blood to his.

Echoes of the pleasure Skye felt when she mated with Rico whispered in Gian's mind. His cock grew hard, his blood heated.

Unlike Brann, Gian had never been attracted to men, but tonight he would enjoy sharing blood with this man. He would enjoy the feel of another cock against his as they both mated their bodies to hers, amplifying the pleasure and closing the bond so that no other could enter it.

* * * * *

Rico didn't bother joining the line. He leaned against the car and watched as the first bunch was allowed in. When the line stopped moving, the bouncer he'd seen before began walking along the line, handpicking more people. Their excited squeals sent anger rushing down Rico's raw nerves.

What a fucking power trip. How could Skye stand this?

The bouncer got to where Marina and Caldwell stood next to each other and Rico held his breath. He wasn't worried about getting into Fangs, the badge would take care of that, but it would be less suspicious if Caldwell got in on her own.

She'd at least dressed in black. It gave her a tourist-checking-out-the-freak-show look but he wasn't sure she could pull off Goth even to follow through on her lead. When the bouncer nodded, Caldwell at least managed a credible smile. She said something to him and tilted her head toward Marina. The bouncer gave the go-ahead and it was done.

Rico straightened away from the car and headed toward the doorway — toward Gian — just as Gian began moving toward him. With each step forward, the primal instinct to fight for sole possession of a mate warred against erotic fantasies. It was too easy to picture Gian fucking Skye, too easy to imagine them both doing it.

They stopped a few inches apart and studied each other. Rico's gut tightened at the sight of the flames in Gian's eyes. But he held out his hand anyway and felt a jolt of heat through the bite marks, through his cock, when Gian's hand clasped his and skin touched skin.

Chapter Sixteen

The buzzing in Skye's head was getting stronger, more painful, as Gian's summons became more insistent. The barrier between them was weakening under his assault.

She'd been lucky so far—lucky that she hadn't lost much time finding a place to hide the Harley, lucky that Rico's truck had a winch so it was easy to pull the coffins into the truck bed, lucky that she knew an area where she could bury them without too much risk of being seen. But luck didn't hold indefinitely.

She pushed herself to throw the last shovels full of sand over the hole and escape before Gian began tracking her.

* * * * *

"You are *way* lucky," Marina said. "Your first night here and one of the vamps is interested in you." She leaned closer to Cia, as though someone could actually eavesdrop in a place as loud as Fangs. "There's a girl I sometimes hung out with in LA, she's from Pacific Palisades, same as I am. She tried for months to get one of the vamps interested in her, not to be a companion—that's not much better than being a sex slave—but to make her a vampire. She finally gave up and found another way. But it cost her a lot of money. If I were you, I'd go over and ask him to dance or something. Don't worry about those vamp-sluts hanging off him—he hasn't given them a second look."

Detective Cia Caldwell shivered despite the heat being generated by all the bodies packed into this place. She'd busted her ass to get this lead, spent every spare moment in cyberspace or on the phone to the cops who were going over Brittany Armstrong's computer, but right now, every instinct she had was screaming for her to get out of there, before it was too late and her life was changed forever.

This whole scene was creeping her out. There wasn't enough money in Vegas to make her read a Stephen King book, much less step into one, yet here she was in the middle of a horror show.

God, she wasn't cut out for undercover work, that was for sure. She'd been so sure she had Marina figured out... Now it only pissed her off more to see these kids being sucked into this stuff. Her eyes landed on Rico, then Skye. She had to clench her hand to keep from making the sign of the cross. She had to let it go—along with the last of the crush she'd had on him.

Mind over matter. That's what her mother had always preached.

What was more important to her career—a one-sided, nonexistent love affair with Rico, or having him as a partner?

Having him as a partner. That won hands down.

And she didn't have a chance against Skye Delano. Never had, never would, especially if Rico was willing to get in the captain's face with it.

Cia's gaze wandered around the bar, finally settling at the doorway where the bouncer who'd let them in had now taken a position leaning against the wall. Her eyes met his and a tendril of icy-heat washed through her. For no reason at all, he scared her.

She shivered again and prayed that this night would hurry up and end.

* * * * *

Rico knew the minute Skye walked into Fangs. Every cell in his body tightened with awareness.

He shot a look to the private table where Gian was sitting with three other guys. From where Rico was standing, he could feel the tension building there, like an argument getting ready to erupt into a fight. As he watched, Gian stood and Rico knew that the other man was aware of Skye's presence, too.

Rico swiveled to watch Skye, felt his heartbeat kick into overdrive as she walked toward him. She stopped only inches away from his body, close enough that her scent and heat surrounded him. "You're working?"

"Yeah."

A small smile played across her lips and he wanted to cover it with his mouth. "So I guess you can't dance," she said.

His cock hardened at the thought of rubbing against her. But he didn't get a chance to answer before Gian was there, his hand wrapped around Skye's arm, menace radiating off him.

Something primitive flashed through Rico. Arousal shifted to aggressiveness, protectiveness.

Skye pressed a hand over his heart, distracting him, making him look at her face before he could follow through on the impulse to put himself between her and Gian.

"It's okay," she whispered, leaning into Rico and pressing a soft kiss against his lips.

It took a minute for the adrenaline to fade. There wasn't any fear in her—at least not that he could see. But Rico couldn't keep himself from saying, "I'm here if you need me."

Skye rubbed her lips over his. "Later, I want us to spend some time together."

Rico's cock got harder wondering if she meant the two of them—or the three of them.

* * * * *

Skye allowed Gian to lead her to the private table where Brann and Kyle and Nahir waited. She wanted to touch Gian's mind, to see how much of his menace was directed at her and how much of it was purely for show. But she didn't dare lower the wall she'd placed between them...not yet anyway.

His grip tightened momentarily as he placed her in a chair, then moved behind her, his hands on her shoulders so that she was trapped in front of Brann.

Once again the other vampire's hair made her think of a waterfall of blood. Skye opened her senses as she studied him. Ancient memories stirred but remained hidden. A small shiver of uneasiness wormed its way into her consciousness as the knowledge that they shared a blood link flowed into her. *Gian's sire.*

Brann's nostrils flared then narrowed. "She has found the fledglings. I smell the dark magic on her." He looked to Gian. "Can you see what she has done with them?"

Skye didn't wait for Gian to try and force the answer out of her. She said, "They wait for judgment, nothing more."

Kyle's voice was low and angry as he asked, "And who will judge them?"

Skye flashed on the face of the hunter she'd seen at Big Daddy's house. "The Angelini."

"This is not their business," Kyle said.

From Gian's knowledge, Syke said, "It is always their business when humans are killed."

Kyle snorted. "The servant they destroyed was already tainted by the evil he played in. You can't mean to seek justice for a man who would have raped you as you bled to death on the altar."

"No. I want to see justice for Brittany Armstrong."

When Kyle would have said something else, Brann made a small motion with his hand and silenced him. "Justice will be served by the death of the witch and her remaining servant. Where are the fledglings?"

"They're safe." Skye allowed Gian to see the coffins as they'd rested one on top of the other before she'd covered them with dirt.

Brann's hand snaked across the table and cupped her face, forcing her eyes to meet his. For an instant she felt the full force of his power and knew soul-deep fear, then Gian's hands loosened and she wrenched away.

"No," Gian said when Brann moved to take Skye's face again. "She is my companion. She answers to me."

Brann's eyes flashed. "And you answer to me."

The air thickened and swirled with violence. Gian's hands tightened on Skye's shoulders—a warning, a promise of protection. He gave a small nod. "The fledglings are safe. Give me some time alone with my companion…Sire."

Like a gust of wind across a desolate plain, the tension cleared. Brann's eyebrows rose and a small smiled hovered. "Ah, finally the respect I deserve."

* * * * *

Rico's cop instincts were on full alert. He didn't like the feel of what was going down at the private table with Skye and he didn't like the way Caldwell seemed to be getting too tight with the girl they were tailing.

Fuck! They were cops, not social workers.

But even from this distance Caldwell's body language radiated concern and her expression earnestness. Goddamn, he could just picture her sitting there trying to convince the girl to pull the body piercings and wear white instead of black.

The situation was making him edgy as hell, and his cock wasn't helping matters. What had Skye meant when she said she wanted them to spend some time together?

He tensed when the girl reached in her pocket, then relaxed when she pulled out a cell phone. Shit, what was he thinking? That she was going for a gun?

Marina got up and moved toward a less crowded spot. Rico eased away from the bar and tried to get close, but by the time he was in hearing range, she'd already pocketed the phone.

He waited, seeing which way she'd go. She headed toward the bathroom but at the last minute bolted outside.

Fuck!

Caldwell was out of her seat and after Marina in a heartbeat. A new song kicked in and a group of kids surged out of their chairs, slowing Rico down. By the time he got through the door, he saw Marina climbing into a dark Yukon, Caldwell close by but not close enough, yelling something, then moving in front of the car like something you'd see in a bad cop movie. A horror movie. The Yukon lurched forward with a squeal of rubber against asphalt, pulling Cia underneath it then backing over her, before roaring forward and screaming down the road.

Fast-forward and slow motion blended. Suddenly Skye and the others were there, hovering over Cia's broken form. Rico's heart thundered in his ears as he checked for a pulse. Despite the blood leaking from her nose and mouth, she was still breathing, still alive. He reached for his cell phone only to have his wrist grabbed by one of the men who'd been at the table with Skye. Fear took the form of rage. But before it could erupt into violence, Skye touched Rico's arm and said, "There's no time for that." Every cell in Rico's body screamed in denial.

The man with the long red hair actually smiled and Rico's body reacted, struggling to strike out, to free himself so he could call for help, but the other man never took his eyes off of Skye. "True. Even if she lives, her spine is crushed in several places. She may never do more than breathe on her own. A trade, Skye? Her life thrown into the mix of justice?"

"Healed—not enslaved, Brann," Skye said.

Brann laughed. "Gian has met his match in you. Done. She'll be healed, not enslaved."

Gian leaned down and Rico tensed, wanting to scream that Cia not be moved, not be touched. Skye's hand tightened on his arm. Somehow Rico knew that whatever Gian was going to do, it was intimate, personal, and Skye didn't want to share Gian in that way, but she said, "Trust him, Rico. I was in worse shape, closer to death than she is."

The bouncer stopped Gian's movement by saying, "I'll do it…Sire."

The men around Skye froze, identical expressions of surprise surfacing briefly on their faces. Gian moved back. "As you wish, Terach."

Only the gentle way in which Terach lifted Caldwell kept Rico from struggling and fighting against the hands holding him in place. Skye said, "She'll be okay, Rico. Trust me in this. She'll be okay…better than if you send her to the hospital."

The nightmare reality played though Rico's mind in a never-ending loop and he exploded. "What the fuck was she thinking about!"

Skye stood and he shot to his feet, all raw energy with nowhere to go. The others also rose, moving and intermingling with the kids that had gathered behind them, watching the drama unfold.

Gian stepped close enough so that he touched both Rico and Skye. The jolt that whipped through Rico's body broke the cycle of his thoughts. His eyes met Gian's and he couldn't look away. Like dark seduction, Gian said, "Let your mind be at ease. Your partner will be all right."

Instinctively Rico fought the voice. Skye's arm slipped around his waist. Her voice soothed as it moved through his mind. *Trust this. Trust us. She will be okay.*

He couldn't fight both of them. He couldn't fight against the sureness he sensed in them. He had a sudden picture of Skye's broken body and knew that he was seeing the truth. Somehow Gian had healed her so that only faint bruises had remained. Slowly he nodded, accepting the peace of mind they offered.

Gian moved back then and some of the intensity faded. His head tilted slightly, toward the kids that still gathered. "I will come to you after this is dealt with."

For a second Rico's heartbeat rabbited in his chest. Then realization dawned. None of the kids would have a memory of what had happened to Cia.

He couldn't fight the shudder of horror, though his mind argued that it had to be this way. It was better for everyone.

"They're Angelini, too?" Rico asked as the men who'd been at the table with Gian and Skye began winding their way through the thinning crowd of onlookers.

Gian's teeth flashed white. "Only in their nightmares."

Chapter Seventeen

Rico could understand why wounded animals holed up in their dens. Now that he was home, showered and in fresh clothes, he could face what had happened, could even believe that Caldwell was going to come out of it okay. What was she thinking—that she was supercop? It had happened so quickly that he hadn't even gotten a license plate number. Fuck, and the kid, Marina…if he ever caught up with her…

Rico moved over to the refrigerator and pulled out a beer, pressing it against his forehead for several seconds before opening it and taking a swig. He was still tense, still wound up.

The doorbell sounded and his body tightened another couple of notches, but lower down this time, in his cock and balls. He waited a heartbeat, hoping that Skye would yell that she'd get it, but she didn't. She was still in the room his sister used, showering, getting dressed, ratcheting up his need to fuck by making him wait.

Rico set his beer down and went to the door, opening it, knowing that it would be Gian. He stepped back but Gian didn't come inside.

Edginess about the situation made Rico terse. "You waiting for a formal invitation?"

Amusement lurked in the other man's eyes. "An informal one will do."

Rico's heart rate spiked up for a second as scenes from vampire movies he'd seen as a kid rushed through his imagination. He shook them off and said, "Come in. Anything on Cia yet?"

Gian moved through the door and closed it. "She heals."

How? But Rico didn't ask the question as he led Gian further into the house, to the den, with its thick carpet, its oversized couch and chairs, though neither took seats.

His mind skittered back to the crazy thoughts he'd had at the doorway. *¡Carajo!* He didn't believe in vampires.

And what about Skye? What about the things she can do? He was saved from his thoughts when she slipped into the room and what little blood was left in Rico's head went straight to his cock.

She was wearing one of his sister's dresses, something some well-meaning relative had given Nicki with the advice that if she looked more feminine, she'd be able to catch a husband. Goddamn! He didn't know what his sister looked like in that thin little scrap of material, but on Skye... Fuck, he wanted to kneel at her feet and crawl right up underneath the dress and get his mouth on her.

Just the image of burying his face in her cunt while the soft cloth trapped the smell of her was enough to make Rico feel short of breath. The sensation only got worse as his eyes roamed upward to the tight hard points of her nipples.

His cock got harder, tighter and he had to close his eyes against the temptation of her, had to remember that Gian was here and he couldn't fall on Skye and fuck her right now. But the thought of Gian's presence only made it worse.

Between one heartbeat and the next Rico accepted what was going to happen, wanted it to happen—needed it to happen.

* * * * *

Skye's body tightened, her womb clenched. She was already swollen, her inner thighs wet with her own juices. The call of Rico's lust was as compelling as the call of Gian's blood.

She'd thought it would be awkward this first time together, but now there was no room for apprehension. There was only the urgent need to be with them. To finish what had begun. To complete the bond.

The medallion burned against her skin though she didn't need it to amplify what Gian was feeling. His craving, his desire, burned through her veins.

Skye moved forward, the dress caressing her skin like a lover's hands. Gian and Rico were standing next to each other, making it easy to touch them both, to give herself over to them.

Like floodgates being opened, as soon as Skye touched him, Rico gave up any thought of holding back. His knees buckled and he went to the floor in front of her.

Skye whimpered as Rico's fantasies flooded her mind. When his hands stroked along her legs, she closed her eyes and leaned back against Gian's chest.

Gian gave a soft laugh against her throat before his lips touched her skin, his hands moving to slide the straps of the dress down her arms. *We will linger another night*, he whispered in her mind, *but not this time*.

She hadn't worn a bra or panties so there was nothing to hinder their access. Rico's tongue scraped against her inner thighs, his mouth sucked away her juices, but more gushed toward his lips.

Gian's hands cupped her breasts, his fingers tight on her nipples, squeezing, causing her to arch and press her lower body tighter to Rico.

She reached back and circled her arms around Gian's neck, stretching her body between the two men, leaving herself open and vulnerable, like a female wolf offering a show of submission. Gian's fangs grazed against her neck and a sob escaped her.

Rico moved away long enough to pull the dress down her body. The sight of Gian's dark hands on Skye's breasts, of his mouth against her neck as she offered herself to both of them made his cock jerk with anticipation.

He unzipped his jeans, intending only to ease the pressure, but the desire on Skye's face had him pulling his cock out. She made a soft, hungry sound and Rico's eyes went to her mound.

He didn't need to open her with his fingers. Her cunt lips were already parted, the wet pink flesh glistening and begging for his kiss, his tongue. What man could resist that sight? Rico dug his hands into her ass and held her in place as he buried his face into her pussy, inhaling the heady scent of her, licking and biting like a starving man then plunging his tongue in and out of her channel, taking her first orgasm into his mouth.

Explosive pleasure rushed through Skye's body, but the orgasm only fed her need for a more thorough joining. She untwined her arms from around Gian's neck and moved her hands to Rico hair as she sunk to her knees, the weight of her body urging him backward onto the floor.

In a frenzy she stripped him of his shirt so she could feel his flesh against hers, but she didn't have the patience to do more than shove his jeans further down his legs.

His cock was wet, swollen, hungry and she wanted to eat it whole but Rico forced her upward with a whispered curse. "I won't last if you put your mouth on me."

Possessive pleasure ripped through her at the sight of him underneath her, at the way he smelled of her and bore her marks. She covered his lips with hers and met the thrust of his tongue as he speared her with his cock, ramming all of him into her with one forceful stroke.

Gian's body straddled hers and she whimpered when she felt the swing of his testicles against her buttocks. Underneath her Rico stilled, and then his hands moved around to spread her ass cheeks.

Skye was soaked in her own juices, but Gian still took a moment to prepare her further, to work his fingers in and out of her anus, coating her with extra lubricant as Rico teased her with short strokes until she began writhing and pleading with Gian to join his body to theirs.

Gian covered her then, working his penis into her slowly. Rico groaned and arched upward as the space he was occupying tightened and grew smaller. Skye clamped down on Gian's cock, fighting against the painful pleasure of his possession even as she welcomed it. She could feel the tension in his body, the burning need to shove himself into her and fuck—he was only barely able to control himself, to hold back for fear of hurting her.

But Skye didn't want control, she didn't fear being hurt. She dropped the barriers separating one from the other and Rico's lust poured into her, joining with her own need before swamping Gian and washing away any control.

He drove his penis all the way in, stroking Rico's cock through the thin barrier that separated them. Rico groaned and bucked, moving in and out of Skye's tight channel, feeding the pleasure that all of them experienced.

Gian held himself still for several heartbeats, then hissed and began thrusting, sometimes in counterpoint, sometime in concert with Rico's strokes.

Skye writhed and screamed between them, her cries driving their lust higher.

Rico's thrusts became more aggressive as he fought to lock within her. Gian's fangs emerged in anticipation.

Then in the moment Skye trapped Rico in her body and his semen began jetting into her womb, Gian struck, sinking his fangs into her neck as he too filled her with his come.

The pleasure of their shared orgasm left them panting, holding each other as their bodies solidified and became separate entities rather than one.

Gian eased his face away from Skye's neck, making no effort to hide the fangs from Rico as they retracted into their sheaths. Rico's heartbeat accelerated, and he knew by the expression on Gian's face that the sound of the blood rushing through his veins was a heady temptation.

Rico wanted it to be a trick of his imagination, but he knew it wasn't. Some part of him had known—fuck, he'd had a premonition of this when he'd had to invite Gian into his home, but he hadn't believed. How could anyone be expected to believe that vampires really existed?

Skye brushed a kiss against the bite mark on Rico's neck and Rico's cock stirred inside her pussy. He never wanted to leave her silky, wet channel.

She tightened on him and he could feel the need, the bond between them. Then she laughed softly, moving so that his cock slipped out of her and Rico wanted to howl at the loss of her warmth.

After she'd wriggled out from between them and stood, she said, "I vote for a shower and a soft bed."

They followed her through the bedroom and into the shower. As the hot water washed over Rico, he grew hard just remembering what had taken place the last time he was in the shower with Skye. Despite what had already happened, he wanted to take her down and mount her.

As if reading her thoughts, she moved closer and ran her hands along his body, stopping when one hand cupped his testicles and the other encircled his shaft.

Rico couldn't stop himself from stroking into her hand.

She laughed softly and loosened her grip, teasing him with the promise of pleasure, making him frantic to feel her fingers wrapped firmly around his penis.

Skye whispered a kiss across his lips and down his neck, stopping over the bite mark and sucking gently.

Rico arched into her, silently begging her to tighten her grip on his cock. When she did, he closed his eyes and groaned as her hand pumped him, sending waves of ice-hot need up his spine.

Gian moved up behind him and fear started to rise in Rico, but Skye's soft laughter brushed it away before it could take hold. "Gian doesn't want your body. That belongs to me. He wants your blood—at least this one time—to complete the bond." Her mouth licked and sucked from the mark on Rico's neck to the one over his heart, then along his ribs and over his abdomen before brushing a kiss over the mark on his inner thigh.

When she looked up at him, her eyes were dark with the promise of pleasure and Rico's cock throbbed in anticipation. "Do you freely offer your blood to Gian?"

"Yes."

Rico almost went to his knees when she took him into her mouth and began sucking. The hungry sounds she made threatened to turn him into a rutting animal.

He groaned and buried his hands in her hair, fighting against the need to thrust violently. Her hand tightened on his cock and balls, staving off orgasm after orgasm until he was shaking, desperate to spew his seed.

" *¡Carajo!* Please!"

She took him all the way back in her throat and in the instant that his semen jetted through his cock, Rico felt Gian's fangs sink into his neck. The pleasure was extreme, like nothing Rico ever known, and even when there was nothing left in his sac he continued to pump and orgasm.

* * * * *

Rico woke with the feel of the sun on his skin. His heart let out an instant shout of joy. He wasn't a vampire.

Skye's soft laugh drew his gaze down to where she curled against him. *You have nothing to fear. He can't turn you into a vampire, can't make you serve him, though he'll probably have to be reminded. The Angelini bond protects you as it protects me.*

Even after everything that had occurred, Rico's heartbeat accelerated at the sound of her voice in his head. Shit! He wasn't sure he liked this, her knowing his thoughts, her being able to talk to him this way.

You have the same ability now. I'll teach you how to put up shields. You'll have your privacy, as I'll have mine.

Real privacy, or an illusion?

I won't betray your trust, Rico.

He trusted her, but he couldn't let the conversation drop. *But the truth is that you can know what I'm thinking any time you want to.*

She turned then and traced her fingers along his jaw. *Yes, as least when we're close together. The sun weakens Gian's ability to move through my barriers, as does distance.* She shrugged. *I don't know if it will always be this way. I can't touch any of the details of what my mother's relationship with her two mates was like. They were bonded, they were happy. I am a part of all three of them, but the hows and whys and possibilities are blank spaces.*

Rico rolled over on his back and pulled her on top of him. *We can work on building shields later,* he growled. *But right now, no barriers seems like a good thing to me.* She smiled and opened her legs, welcoming his morning erection, welcoming him.

* * * * *

"Are you going to work today?" Skye asked as they sat at the table and ate another one of Rico's creations.

Rico's face hardened. "Only long enough to grab Cia's file and see if I can figure out where the girl might have gone and who she was meeting. I don't want to run into the captain and have to answer questions about last night. He's more than just my boss."

"The dark-haired girl that your partner was sitting with?"

He hesitated and Skye was careful not to touch her mind to his. Finally he said, "Yeah. Cia's been putting a lot of time in on this case. The kid we were tailing has been in some of the same Internet chat rooms as Brittany Armstrong, wants the same thing that the Armstrong kid wanted — to be a vampire."

A sick expression settled on Rico's features. "Guess that's not as crazy an idea as I thought it was."

Skye couldn't stop the small laugh from escaping. "No, though it's not as easy as the movies and old stories make it out to be. It requires strong magic, more than most people can survive."

Rico looked at her sharply. "You knew when you found Brittany's body that they were trying to turn her into a vampire."

"No." She laughed again and teased, "If you'd told me that you thought vampires existed and that's what had happened in the woods, I would have wondered why my body craved such a loco mate."

Rico's heart took a hit of pure happiness. His mother and father teased each other like this. And until this moment, he hadn't realized how much he needed all of it—the fantasies, the intense sex—but the tenderness and teasing, too.

He dared to touch her mind, to feel what she was feeling, and found that even though she was different in so many ways, in this she was the same. She wanted a home, the love of her mates.

There were flashes of memory, of her mother and her mother's two mates, and Rico realized something else. He'd always seen Skye as powerful, desirable, a mystery and a fantasy that were impossible to resist. But she'd been alone since she was a small child—not lonely, but alone, without family, without anyone who cared whether she lived or died.

Rico ached for the child she'd been. He reached across the table and covered her hand with his. He showed her images of his own family, flipped through them like the pages of a photo album. "They're a lot to take in all at once, but for better or worse, you're stuck with them now."

Skye's laugh was soft. "For better or worse." She sent him the picture of her mother and her mother's two mates. *For you as well. When this is done, I will hunt for them.*

Rico gave her hand another squeeze then released it, standing to gather dishes and take them to the sink. "I'd better get in and get those files."

Though his back was turned to her, Skye could feel his thoughts turn to his partner, could feel his need for reassurance. "Your partner will be fine. When she's healed, Terach will return her."

"Will she remember all of it?"

"I don't know what she'll remember. Terach will get word to us about what he's told her so that our stories agree."

Rico nodded, not liking that he'd be forced to lie to the captain, but accepting it, even with humor. If Rivera wanted to cross himself at the thought of Skye, what would he do if he stumbled into Fangs and found that vampires existed?

Skye rose and came over to stand behind him. When she circled her arms around his waist and pressed against him, hugging him, offering comfort, Rico wondered how he'd ever lived without her.

Some primitive part of his psyche leaped to take advantage of the thought. "Are you going to move in?" he asked.

She stilled against his back. "Do you want me to?"

"Yeah. I want that."

He could feel her smile against his back. "What about your captain?"

"He'll have to deal with it. The other guys in the department will have to deal with it." Rico turned then and met her eyes. "I won't give you up. I wouldn't change what we have together even if I could."

Skye's eyebrows went up and she teased, "Including Gian?"

Heat rushed across Rico's face. He didn't want to think about that too closely. Not only had the sex been intense, but the bite… Fuck…

Skye laughed. *He can tone it down if he wishes. He didn't want you to fear it in the future.*

When every nerve in Rico's body went tight, she added, *Gian has never been interested in men, not in that way.* Her hand teased along Rico's cock. *This is mine. There may be times when the blood exchange between you and Gian is necessary, but that's between you and him.*

Rico buried his face in Skye's hair. "I don't have to invite him to live here, do I?"

"No." She laughed again. "And you don't have to start hanging out at Fangs."

At the mention of the club, Rico's thoughts circled back to Caldwell. What the fuck was she thinking about jumping in front of that car?

Skye said, "There's still time to save the girl—Marina."

For a split second Rico was tempted to say that Marina deserved what she got, but he bit the words off. Maybe Caldwell saw something in the girl, maybe that's why she'd tried to stop her, or maybe Cia was just being a good cop and didn't want to see someone she was sworn to protect end up like Brittany Armstrong.

Rico felt the barrier go up between his mind and Skye's and wondered about it until she asked, "Can you tell me about Marina?"

For a second Rico's training warred with his new reality. Fuck. This wasn't simple police work anymore. The rules he'd always accepted didn't apply easily to this. He sighed, refusing to fight a battle that no longer made any sense. "I don't know that much about her. Rich family." He paused as his mind leaped to form a connection that he'd missed earlier. "From LA. Pacific Palisades." He moved so he could watch Skye's face. "You said the cases you were working on were connected to the Armstrong case. You went to LA."

The half-smile that drove Rico crazy formed on Skye's lips. She said, "I went to Pacific Palisades."

Cop instinct made him ask, "Did you find the girls you were looking for?"

"I found them."

He braced himself, he knew there was more. "Were they dead?"

She studied him for a long moment before he felt the barrier lift between their minds. In the span of several heartbeats he saw her stake two girls as they rested in their coffins, saw them flare to life then cease, awaiting judgment for the death of Brittany Armstrong. With the brush of Skye's mind to his, he understood the trade she'd made for Caldwell's life.

It shocked the shit out of him that he could accept it. That he could let the vampires mete out justice if he didn't find the witch and her servant first.

Skye kept the barriers down, but spoke out loud, "I'm going to hunt at a place called Toppers."

Rico cringed at her choice of words and at the thought of Toppers. It was a rough, dangerous place even for cops—even for Skye. His heartbeat quickened—especially for Skye now that she'd bound herself to him. She'd been lawless before—no, not lawless—but not governed by human law. Now the promise she'd made to him put constraints on her. A shot of fear rushed through Rico.

He pulled her body against his. "If you ever think your life is in danger, do what you have to do. Don't worry about me being a cop." He hugged her tightly then released her. "I'll go to Toppers with you. Just let me call in and check my messages first."

Skye nodded and moved away. He picked up the phone, praying that the captain hadn't left orders for him to call and report on how it went at Fangs.

There was only one message of interest. The lab had gotten fingerprints and a positive ID on the driver's license Skye had given him. David Olney. No aliases, but he did have a sealed juvenile record and a long string of arrests for assault and battery along with a notation in his file that he was attracted to cult and alternative religions. Rico grunted at the last and hung the phone up.

Skye was watching him and he realized that the barriers between them weren't closed. Rico braced himself for her answer. *Should I bother looking for this guy, or is he dead?*

She answered with a picture that had Rico's stomach threatening to heave its contents and his soul shivering with dread. He could feel the evil that surrounded the altar and the body raped and drained of blood there.

* * * * *

The moment Skye stepped out of Rico's truck, she smelled the tainted blood. It was faint, the scent scattered by time and by the people that had entered and exited Toppers. "He's been here recently," she said as Rico joined her.

Rico looked around with cop eyes. The sun had set on their way over and only a handful of lights illuminated the parking lot, not nearly enough for the kind of crowd that hung out here. It was a crime scene waiting to happen. "How long ago?"

Skye shrugged. "I don't know."

They moved past the bouncer and paused in the entrance of the loud, smoky nightclub. It was easier to use the mental link than to talk above the noise. *I don't see him,* Rico said. *Let's aim for the bar, there's a good view of the place from there.*

The scent is scattered. I need to walk around before it dissipates completely.

Rico's hand gripped her upper arm. *I'll stay with you.*

She laughed softly. It warmed her that he was protective, that both of her mates were protective. Even now she could sense Gian getting closer, coming to her.

Her body reacted and she momentarily forgot that she was hunting as memories of the three of them together flooded her mind.

Rico's hand tightened on her arm. *Don't think about that!*

She could feel his swift arousal, the blood pounding in his cock as it strained against his jeans. Along the bond with Gian, she felt the same need, the same desire.

Reluctantly, she forced her mind away from her memories, but there was no instant relief from the demands of their bodies.

Later, we can seek our pleasure, Gian whispered in her mind. *Brann comes with me now, as does your mate's partner.*

Rico's relief and hope flooded the bond. *Cia's okay?*

She is well, Gian said.

Rico hesitated then dropped his hand from Skye's arm. *I'll wait here.*

Skye nodded and moved deeper into the club. It was a rough place, worse than many she'd hunted in, but not as bad as some.

Lust and anger and desperation filled the air as thickly as the cigarette smoke did. Violence hovered, ready to explode into existence at the slightest provocation.

Skye weaved her way through people and tables, moving cautiously even when she knew that Gian and the others had arrived. She could smell the guns that some of the patrons wore and knew that others carried knives. This was a place to tread lightly.

Several times she hit pockets of the scent she was tracking, as though her quarry was close, but she didn't see him. In the periphery of her mind she monitored the conversation between Rico and his partner and was satisfied that Caldwell seemed…normal.

Gian's amusement found her. *Jealous?* he teased.

I do not worry that my mates will be unfaithful.

Gian laughed. *She is no longer unclaimed anyway.*

Skye had maneuvered to the hallway that housed the bathrooms and led to the emergency exit but Gian's comment had her stopping and turning to look across the club to where Cia and Rico had their heads together in conversation. Unerringly her eyes went to the pendant that Caldwell now wore around her neck.

Fury rippled through Skye, but before she could say anything, Gian said, *We do not view our companions as our slaves. You bargained only that she not be enslaved. I did not know that Terach intended this. When I found out what he'd done, I ordered that he stay away from her until justice has been meted out. After that he must…court her…and gain her willing acceptance of the companion bond.*

And he'll obey you?

He is my creation. A hint of amusement crept down the bond. *In this he has chosen to obey rather than to risk the wrath of my Angelini mate.*

Skye shifted her gaze to Gian, and next to him, Brann. If she was to live in this world, then she needed to learn its intricacies.

Caldwell moved then. Her gaze clashed with Skye's and her lips disappeared in a familiar frown of disapproval and suspicion.

Skye's earlier anger melted into amusement. Let Terach deal with the consequences of his actions.

Instinct snapped Skye's mind back to the hunt as the smell of tainted blood grew stronger. She turned, her eyes drawn immediately to the slowly opening exit door. She felt Gian and Rico moving quickly toward her. But before they could reach her, the stench of evil-fouled blood rolled over her as the bathroom door opened and the man she'd been hunting stepped out. She saw his instant recognition, his knowledge that she wouldn't be here alone.

Chapter Eighteen

Years of fighting and surviving had made Skye smart and fast. She had her knife out within a second of seeing him.

He attacked immediately, swinging his thick, meaty arm at her head as he reached for a weapon. She slashed out, cutting through his shirt and deep into his arm. Blood gushed from the wound.

In a heartbeat she smelled the metal of a gun. It glinted in the dim hallway and she ducked instinctively, slashing out at his stomach as he fired.

The sound exploded in the small space. The strip club filled with screams and shouts and the wild scramble of people trying to get out of the way.

As blood soaked the front of his shirt, he struggled to take aim again and Skye saw it in his eyes that he knew he was a dead man and that he intended to take her with him. She slashed again, this time feeling the searing hot pain of a bullet along her side.

The roar of his gun deafened Skye to the report of another gun. But just as she would have lunged forward and struck again, her attacker's head rippled, blood and brain matter spraying across the walls and Skye, painting them with the foul taint of evil.

Skye looked to where Caldwell stood, eyes dazed, face pale and pinched as she slowly lowered her police-issue revolver. Rico moved to Caldwell and began talking to her.

Brann stepped forward then, a pleased look on his face. *It would seem we made a good trade*, he purred in Skye's mind. His smile widened as his gaze shifted between Skye and Rico. *Interesting. You stand there wounded and yet your mate comforts another. Perhaps the magic of the Angelini bond has been greatly exaggerated.*

Skye felt Gian tense as she lifted her lip in a silent snarl and said, *Go to hell, Brann.*

The older vampire threw back his head and laughed. *Why is it that those who have my blood running through their veins are so disrespectful?*

Rico came to Skye then, his face tight, his thoughts conflicted, torn between his duty and his desire to protect her. Gian's voice was cool with censure, *Do not trouble yourself. I will see to her needs.*

¡Carajo! Cia's a cop, my partner, and until tonight she's never even drawn her gun on anyone, much less killed someone! He turned his back on Gian and leaned in to get a closer look at where the bullet had grazed Skye's side. Resentment flashed through him along with relief. *He'll heal you?*

He can. But we need to get out of here. I'm sure someone has already called the police.

Fuck! I can't just let you walk away. This is a crime scene — there'll be an investigation.

There are plenty of others who saw the attack and can witness that your partner did what needed to be done. You'll be here for hours and I am injured. Does the law require that I stay here and bleed — her eyes shifted to include Gian and Brann — *when someone could take me for treatment? You know where to find us.*

Rico's nostrils flared and she could feel him searching the connection between them to ensure that his will was his own. A different type of pain shimmered through her at his distrust and she started to turn away from him.

His hand shot out and grabbed her wrist, forcing her to turn and face him again. *Fuck. I'm sorry. I couldn't get a clear shot.* His hand trembled slightly and she could feel him trying to get control of his emotions. *Go — I'll take care of things here.*

Skye allowed Brann and Gian to take her arms as though she needed their help to leave. Sirens filled the night, but when they would have hurried her, she said, "If we can find the servant's car, we may find where the witch has gone."

Brann nodded and disappeared into the night. Gian swung her into his arms and moved through the parking lot quickly, his mind touching hers as she followed the scent of tainted blood down the darkened street.

They found the servant's car a block away just as several squad cars screamed past with their lights flashing. *We'll return later*, Gian said as a blood-red Viper stopped beside them, its passenger door opening to reveal Brann behind the wheel. Amusement flickered through Skye and she wondered why she'd thought Brann would want to avoid attention.

Gian eased into the cramped confines of the car, the movement sending pain through Skye's side. While she'd been tracking her assailant, she'd been able to keep her mind off the gunshot wound, but now the pain rushed in like a fiery explosion. She couldn't stop the sharp intake of breath, nor the way her body bowed and tensed when Gian shifted to close the car door.

Another patrol car screamed by before Brann pulled away from the curb. In the darkness Skye could see Gian unbuttoning his shirt and despite the pain radiating through her side, her body tightened with anticipation.

His eyes met hers and she was caught in the flame deep in their centers. *We can wait until we are alone, or we can do this now*, he offered.

Skye hesitated and Gian stroked her hair. *You are my companion. Among our kind, the sharing of blood with a chosen one is often done in front of close friends.*

She wavered for a second then leaned forward and gave a small lick across his tiny male nipple. Gian hissed and the flames in his eyes leaped and danced. One fingernail elongated, sharpening and curling into the beginnings of a claw. He scraped above the nipple and blood instantly welled, beading and rolling across the tight brown areola.

Skye hesitated again and he said, *I can blur the reality of this if you wish.* She shook her head and covered his nipple with her mouth, her mind focused solely on him, on the way his body tightened as intense pleasure whipped through him each time she sucked, each time she drew his blood.

The bond between them intensified along with the need to join physically. The throbbing pain in Skye's side changed form and became a pulsing, raging hunger in her cunt. Her body grew damp, her pussy soaked and the smell of her desire filled the car.

Along the blood-link, she heard Brann growl, *Finish it, Gian!* in the second before Gian slid his hand into her pants, pushing her legs apart and exploring the wet slickness of her, then plunging his fingers in and out of her tight channel, striking her clit forcefully until she arched and sobbed in release.

The orgasm left her almost as weak as the gunshot wound would have. She lazily lapped at Gian's nipple then buried her face in his chest.

He was rock-hard against her buttocks and she rubbed back and forth, her thoughts focused on his erection. He was close to coming.

Don't, Gian warned. *There is no time. In a minute Rafael will join us. He may have located the witch.*

The sexual lassitude dissipated slowly at his words. Skye shifted and Gian hissed as her buttocks rolled across his cock. She looked out the window and saw that they had neared Toppers. The parking lot was crowded with police cars. The patrons who hadn't fled were corralled with yellow crime scene tape.

They drove past without slowing and Skye's mind cleared enough to ask, "Did Rafael break into the car?"

Brann chuckled. "Yes. My companion has his share of useful talents."

Skye studied him then, taking in his long blood-red hair and aquiline features. He reminded her of a powerful jungle cat — as lethal and deadly as he was sensuously masculine. It was hard to picture him with another man.

Brann turned toward her, trapping her with the full force of his gaze. *Be careful where your thoughts take you*, he warned in the silky voice of a predator.

Gian hissed and shifted Skye, freeing her from the trap of Brann's eyes. Along their bond he warned, *Never forget that Brann is a force to be reckoned with*.

Skye acknowledged his warning with a shrug, her eyes already drawn to the man that waited next to Gian's car. *That's Rafael?* she asked, taking in the long blond hair, the muscle shirt that showed off his upper body, the faded jeans that emphasized his huge cock. He was gorgeous — a fantasy man who looked like he belonged on a poster, or in a centerfold.

That's Rafael, Gian growled, censure in his voice at her thoughts.

Skye laughed and pressed her mouth against his, teasing along the seam of his lips with her tongue. *I took mates, I didn't go blind.*

Gian's fangs extended and he captured her lip, biting down just hard enough so that several small droplets of blood welled to the surface in an erotic warning. Skye's nipples tightened at the threat.

Brann eased the car over to where Rafael waited and Gian slipped out with Skye still in his arms. "So this is the missing Angelini mate?" Rafael said, his voice holding a hint of some private amusement.

Gian flashed his fangs, but didn't answer. From the car, Brann said, "What have you got?"

Rafael pulled a folded newspaper from somewhere behind him and the smell of tainted blood washed across Skye's senses. "Three addresses circled," Rafael said. "Kyle and Nahir have checked two of them already. They're on their way to the third now." He grinned. "It's only a short distance from the last house they burned."

"Get in," Brann ordered.

Rafael's eyebrows went up. He turned and looked to where Gian still held Skye in his arms. He sniffed the air and his eyes went dark, his mouth soft in a parody of arousal. "Ah, restraint always wears on Brann's nerves."

This time the command was stronger, silent, though Skye could feel the whip of power in the air. Rafael shrugged and got in the Viper.

* * * * *

Except for the color and rundown condition, the house was the twin of the one Skye had escaped from. "Is she here?" Skye asked as Gian parked his car behind the Viper.

"She's here."

Kyle and Nahir emerged from the darkness as Skye got out of the car. Something had changed since the last time they'd hunted together. Before there had been caution, but now they gathered in front of the witch's house like people going to a party.

Rafael slid out of the Viper. When Skye's gaze flew to the fresh bite mark on his neck, his lips curled with insolence and he gave her a sketchy salute.

Her mind flashed to the conversation that she'd overheard between Haley and Kisha, and Skye agreed with Kisha's snorted comment. *God, what an arrogant ass. I'd like to see him brought down a peg or two. I don't know what Brann sees in him, except maybe a challenge.*

Gian touched Skye's arm and brought her attention back to him. "You and Rafael will have to go in first. The witch will have felt the death of her servant, she'll be waiting. Do not let her lure you into the circle with her."

When Skye would have asked why, he showed her horrifying pictures of demon-guarded witches then said, "If she is powerful enough to create vampires using her dark magic, then she is powerful enough to summon greater forces to protect her. She is not invincible against our shared power. When I call you to me, you must come immediately, you must yield to me instantly." Skye nodded though her heart pounded hard and fast. Gian leaned down and brushed his lips against hers. *Go now. When you're in the room with her, move around the circle, distract her.*

Skye and Rafael walked in silence to the front door, the vampires only several steps behind them. This way of hunting was foreign to Skye, almost unnerving. "Shouldn't one of us take the back?" she asked.

Rafael smiled and proceeded to kick the door in. "You watch too much TV."

For a second Skye was stunned by his arrogance, but once she'd taken in the fact that there was no immediate danger, her sense of humor surfaced. She bent forward and turned the doorknob, illustrating that it hadn't been locked and gaining a genuine smile from her aggravating companion.

Behind them one of the vampires hissed, not amused by the byplay. Rafael turned and made a sweeping gesture. "Please come in."

Black candles lined the walls, their flames flickering over symbols that held no meaning for Skye but caused her survival instincts to rise to the surface and her soul to shudder.

"Same old, same old," Rafael said. "You'd think they'd be more original." He grabbed Skye's arm. "Don't worry, we've got this covered. The symbols are there to lure the weak, especially new vampires with a greed for more power."

The scent of tainted blood and dark magic was heavy in the air. Skye could feel the witch's waiting presence in the room at the end of the hallway.

"Kind of like being cannon fodder," Rafael quipped after the two of them had traveled the hallway and stepped though the doorway.

As Gian had suspected, the witch waited at the center of an ash-lined circle. As soon as she saw Skye, her eyes narrowed with hate. "There's a special place in hell waiting for you, Angelini."

Skye laughed and her heart settled into a controlled rhythm. This she understood. Her hunts had ended this way many times, with a game of cat and mouse played around insults.

"And for you," Skye said as she moved to the left. "Where's Marina?"

Rafael went to the right, Gian and the other vampires fanned out in equal distances around the circle, chanting low and in a language that Skye couldn't understand.

The witch's laugh was an unpleasant sound against Skye's skin. "Go look for her, Angelini. See if you can save the poor pathetic human."

Skye shrugged. "There'll be plenty of time for that. I doubt this will take long. If you were so powerful, you wouldn't be here like this, your fledglings lost and your servants dead."

The witch screamed in fury and the vampires chanted louder.

Inside the circle, the air shimmered, like heat off the desert, and Skye sensed something powerful fighting to break free and take shape. She edged closer to the circle and the witch lunged at Skye.

But Skye was quicker, jumping away and asking, "Ready for justice yet?"

The chanting grew louder then stopped abruptly. Into the silence Brann said, "A fair question, and because I'm a fair man, I'll give you a choice—a quick death or an ugly one…Iselda." At the use of her name, the witch shrieked.

Before Skye could react, Iselda leapt halfway out of the circle and grabbed Skye's lower legs. The shimmering power that Skye had seen before surged forward and true terror kicked in. From the depths of her soul came the word *demon*.

Skye fought the witch's hold, struggling to keep from being dragged into the circle as the vampires started chanting again, their voices layering one on top of the other.

Brann's voice rose above the rest and as they reached a crescendo, Skye heard him say the witch's name in the instant before he plunged the witch's own athame into her heart.

Blood gushed from her every opening, rancid and evil. It should have been a killing blow, but Skye could sense that Iselda wasn't dead.

Gian's voice commanded, *Come to me*, just as Skye fought her way free of the witch's hands.

Without thought, without question, Skye went. He pulled her against his body and she let her soul and mind flow into his, joining all that she was to him.

Oaths and blood-magic united the vampires. As one, their power pushed the witch's body back into the circle, trapping it with the demon she'd summoned.

With the knife driven through her heart, she could do nothing but shriek and scream as the demon devoured her, leaving behind only blood-soaked clothes and the black athame that Skye had used to save herself from being a sacrifice.

The vampire voices lowered to a whisper and once again Brann spoke, invoking a different name…and the vibrating shimmering energy disappeared.

Chapter Nineteen

They found Marina in one of the bedrooms, drugged and bound, but unharmed otherwise. "She is a friend of Amy and Jen's," Kyle said. "I will do what needs to be done."

Skye tensed, but before she could question or argue, Gian pulled her against his body. *The girl will not be harmed. Kyle means only to explore her thoughts and alter her memory if necessary then send her on her way.*

Amy and Jen are mere fledglings. They will be placed under a master's care until they are strong enough to stand on their own and cause the rest of us no harm. Until that time, they will have no contact with anyone from their past.

Brann will be their master?

Gian's soft laugh whispered along her spine. *No, while Brann can remove the witch's taint and remake them, he has no patience for training fledglings. There are others among us who relish that role.*

Skye nodded, her mind lingering for a moment on the images that his words created. Though she wasn't drawn to the BDSM scene, she had hunted among its participants in the past.

Amy's half-brother will not give up looking for her now that I've told him that I think she's alive, Skye said.

Then he must be convinced that she is dead.

Skye nodded. *His personal aide is in town, waiting for my call.*

Gian licked along her neck then scraped his fangs over her pulse. *I have met very few humans who couldn't be hypnotized by us, by the Angelini. Call him to you. Let him carry the news of Amy's true death back to her brother.*

It would be better if we could also send proof.

Gian looked to Brann and Skye knew that they talked, though she had only the impression of words and not their sound. When Gian shifted his attention back to her, he said, *Amy possesses a ring that she stole from her brother. Brann has commanded that she surrender it. Haley will give it to you when we return to the club.*

As soon as they were in Gian's car, Skye used her cellular to call Martin. "Have you located her?" he asked without preamble.

"Yes."

"I want to meet with you. Immediately."

His manic, nervous energy flowed down the telephone line. "At your hotel?"

"No. I've got a rental car. Name a place where no one will notice us and I'll pick you up."

"I'm on my way to a bar named Fangs. I can wait for you there. Do you need directions?"

"No. I'll get them. How long?"

"Thirty minutes."

"I trust you've been discreet and no one else knows that you've located Amy."

Skye's instinct warned that the question was more important than it seemed. "I've got a silent partner. He knows."

There was a tense silence. "None of the research indicated that you had a partner."

On a hunch she said, "He doesn't want the police department to monitor him as they do me."

"Ah."

"I'll see you in thirty minutes," Skye said, snapping the cellular closed and returning it to her pocket.

"He's nervous," Gian said. "Untrustworthy."

"Yes."

"I'll go with you."

Skye laughed even though warmth flooded her heart at his unspoken concern. She moved closer, her body touching his, and the warmth became heated need.

Later. His voice was a husky caress in her mind. *Let us deal with this and get it behind us, then there will be time to love and play at our leisure.*

Skye reached to find Rico. He was still at Toppers, but close to being finished. She could feel his body respond as her thoughts and needs brushed against his.

* * * * *

Haley was waiting for them as Skye and Gian moved through the back entrance of Fangs. Her hand fluttered nervously to her pendant as her gaze moved back and forth between Gian and Skye then finally settled on Skye.

"Kyle said that you'd been injured and that your clothes were bloody. I left something for you to wear, in the room you were in before."

"Thanks," Skye said.

Gian pressed a kiss to Skye's temple. *I will meet you in a few minutes.*

As he walked away, Haley handed a heavy, masculine ring to Skye. "I'm supposed to give this to you. Amy said that her brother stole it from his grandfather. It was supposed to be buried with his grandfather, but her brother paid someone to remove it before they buried the coffin."

Skye studied the ring and knew instantly why Amy had stolen it from her brother. It had the look of something old and mystical, though she could feel no magic attached to it. "Somehow that's fitting."

Haley twisted the pendant she was wearing. "Thanks for finding Jen. And for not killing her...them." In a rush, she added, "They didn't mean for Brittany Armstrong to die. They wanted to make her a vampire—their vampire and not the witch's. But they weren't strong enough." She took a deep breath, her eyes both pleading and hopeful. "I hope we can be friends. This life is...it's hard sometimes...not being able to talk about...things."

The request surprised Skye. She'd had people ask her for many things, but no one had ever asked for friendship. Feeling oddly disoriented, she nodded and said, "I'd like that."

Haley's smile was brilliant. "Thanks." She moved back. "You probably want to take a shower and change."

* * * * *

Skye found it amusing that the senator's aide drove past Fangs several times before finally parking in a remote, pitch-black area of the lot. If he only knew what lurked in the dark, he'd park directly under a light.

She watched as Gian glided toward the car, toward the unsuspecting man. She followed, sure to stay in the light, to keep Martin's attention away from the unexpected menace that was Gian.

When she was close, she heard the click of electric door locks being released. *Front seat or back?* she asked.

The night grows short. I will take the front and with it the blame for whatever happens. Your other mate comes to us now. Let's be done with this.

Even if Skye had wanted to argue, there was no choice. Just as Martin frowned his annoyance that she was getting in the backseat, Gian joined him in the front.

Martin whirled and stood no chance at all. The instant his eyes met Gian's, he was trapped, his thoughts and intentions spilling out like the insides of a gutted fish.

He makes it easy for us, Gian said, satisfaction in his voice at the aide's plan to kill Amy and bury her in the desert.

Skye laughed silently and pulled the ring from her pocket. Gian took it and offered it to Martin, along with the suggestion that he go to the place where Skye had buried the now-retrieved coffins and sleep until the sun rose. The disturbed dirt and the shovel in the trunk of his car, along with the ring were all the proof his mind would require that his plans had been successful.

Martin took the ring and slipped it over his finger. Skye could sense the glee in him, the expectation of having the senator in his debt for taking care of this matter. Through the aide's memories, she could see that it was a debt the senator willingly took on, though he'd been careful never to give the order directly.

Kyle appeared with a shovel. At Gian's command, Martin unlocked the trunk. As soon as the shovel was in place, Kyle said, *Your mate has arrived*, then blended back into the night.

Gian said, *I will finish providing him with the details of his crime and meet you in the club.*

Skye slipped from the car and went into Fangs.

Rico was leaning against the bar. At the sight of him, Skye's pulse quickened and when he looked up and smiled, joy rushed through her.

She skirted the dance floor and got to him, wrapping her arms around him and pressing a kiss against his lips in greeting. *Everything's okay?* she asked.

He closed his eyes and leaned his forehead against hers. *Yeah. There were plenty of witnesses, so I only got a little bit of my ass chewed off for letting you guys leave the scene.* He gently ran a hand along her side. *He healed you?*

Yes.

Good.

I didn't think you'd come here.

Rico laughed at that. *Well, what happened last night kind of put a new slant on things.* He opened his eyes and stared into hers. *They towed the guy's car in and supposedly found a link to his blog. Brittany Armstrong's murder is detailed in it, along with the deaths of three girls and David Olney. All of them were supposedly in the woods that night. According to what he wrote, they all died attempting to turn into vampires and he burned the bodies so they wouldn't be recovered. The captain is ready to close the case.* Rico hesitated several heartbeats before adding, *I've never had a case tie together so conveniently before. But I wouldn't mind seeing this one shut.*

Skye could almost hear Brann's laughter in her mind as she remembered his earlier boast. *My companion has his share of useful talents.*

There would be other hunts, but this one was over. She pressed a kiss to Rico's lips. *Justice has been served.*

Rico nodded and relaxed against her, content with her answer. Content with being here with her. He would never get enough of her, of what they had together.

Skye could sense the moment Gian entered the club. Her blood heated and her body moistened. She turned in Rico's arms and watched as Gian glided toward them. She could feel their anticipation, their desire, their need for her. Love was a pale word for the bond that held them together and yet that was there too.

Gian came to a stop in front of her, his penis as heavy and engorged as Rico's. *The night disappears quickly and I would feel your mouth on my cock. I would see you mounted and mount you myself. Shall we go play?*

Skye laughed, her heart light, her soul complete. She looked at Rico and knew that the flames danced as wildly in her eyes as they did in Gian's. *Shall we?*

Lust roared through every pore in Rico's body. He pressed her back against his erection. *Yeah. Let's go play.*

Enjoy this excerpt from
Binding Krista
© Copyright Jory Strong 2005

Adan d'Amato grimaced as he studied the scene in front of him. Gambler's Paradise they called this place, but it was more likely Gambler's Hell.

Humans were packed in like miners on an old Ewellian transport. Between the noise that their mechanical machines made, and the sound of their voices, it was enough to send a less-seasoned warrior running for cover.

At Adan's side, Lyan d'Vesti wore a fierce scowl. His mood was echoed in his mind-thought. *The Council wastes our time. We'll find no bond-mate here.*

Adan laughed softly at Lyan's impatience. *Our mate will arrive. Whoever watches over her would not send us to this location if she were not going to be here.*

Lyan snorted. *You have too much respect for the infallibility of the Council and its genetic scientists. Their predictions and equations do not always hold true in the real world. Have I not told them so each time I was hauled before them to explain my actions? It would amuse them to send us on a wild chase, or mate us to a human with nothing of the Fallon in her. But if this human mate is unsuitable, then I will have one of my own choosing. The Vesti take what belongs to them when the time is right to take it. We do not beg at the table of the Council.*

Adan didn't bother hiding the amusement in his thoughts. *No doubt you have managed to offend someone on the Council, if not all of the members. But I have been a model citizen. When the marker in your genes was matched to the human's, the scientists had to know that you would choose me to complete the mate-bond. No doubt they would have welcomed the extinction of your traits, but because of the respect they hold for mine, they told you of the woman's existence.*

Lyan shifted impatiently. *We will see if you remain amused as this plays out.*

In front of the warriors, a red light suddenly began flashing. A siren screamed and an elderly human female with blue-tinted hair squealed in a tone pitched high enough to shatter Sarien glass. Only reflexes honed by hours of training and years of experience kept Adan and Lyan from using the Ylan crystals on their wrists to transmute the offending machine into particles so small that it could never be recovered.

Coins began tumbling out of the machine the elderly human had been hovering over. Lyan shook his head in amazement. *Coins! It has been thousands of years since our ancestors were here and yet these humans continue to evolve at the creeping pace of a Tresor slug. No wonder our appearance gave rise to their legends of angels and demons!*

Adan shrugged. *Be glad that some of the Fallon were drawn to these humans and bred with them. If not for the genes of our shared ancestors, there would be no hope for either the Vesti or the Amato and both of our races would be doomed to extinction.*

Lyan fought down the fury that always threatened to consume him at the mention of the fate awaiting those on Belizair. His heart raged at the pain his elder brother and his brother's mate endured. Unless the genetic scientists found a solution to the bio-gene virus the Hotalings had let loose on Belizair, his brother's pairing would produce no children. Nor would there be children for any of the Amato or Vesti females.

So far the scientists had found only one way to defeat the Hotaling virus. Now the Council's agents searched among the humans in order to identify those females who had the genetic marker of one of the Fallon—the shared ancestor race of the Amato and Vesti.

All hope to avoid extinction rested on the unmated males, yet each male carried both the fear that there would be no match and the knowledge that it required a Vesti or Amato co-mate in order to produce offspring.

Lyan forced the tightness out of his chest. He was the first of his family to be matched. The continuance of their line rested with him—and Adan. He had never been drawn to females outside of his race but... Even as the thought took form, a woman entered the casino and need shot through him.

Suddenly he had to fight for air, fight even to keep his balance. The purple-colored Ylan crystals woven into the wristbands bearing the symbol of Lyan's clan-house burned against his skin, echoing the searing heat swirling through his very bloodstream.

Adan took a sharp intake of breath, his eyes zeroing in on the woman. The deep gold Ylan crystals on his wrists swirled as his emotions surged in recognition of their mate's presence. "By the Council, she is exquisite," Adan murmured as he placed a hand on Lyan's shoulder.

Lyan's nostrils flared as every predatory instinct within him focused on their mate. She was small, even among her own people, and dressed in black—the color of a warrior's clothing. And yet her body was made for pleasure, not fighting.

Against the black material, her hair was a golden torch. Lyan could imagine the silky heat of it burning its way across his skin and inflaming him further as it flowed over their writhing bodies. The mating fever of the Vesti race shimmered just below the surface of his control. He was rock hard, ready. Instinct urged him to pounce now, to take her, join with her, make her completely his. A low growl vibrated along his throat.

Like a cool wind, Adan's voice whispered, warned, *And to take her that way is to guarantee there will be no offspring, for either of us. It is not one or the other, it is both or there is no conception at all.*

The growl in Lyan's throat deepened. He snarled, *Curse the Hotalings and their get. Let our people hunt them down one-by-one and rid the universe of them for their use of the bio-gene weapons.*

And we will. But for now let us be glad that our scientists have found a way for us to avoid extinction. Our mate awaits. Do we stand here and argue what cannot be changed, or do we go and secure her so that through her womb our lines may both survive?

Adan didn't wait for an answer, but stepped forward. As he did so, the woman sensed his movement and looked at him. He was too skilled a hunter not to see her tense, ready herself to escape. Her reaction flooded his being with the desire to protect her even as blood pounded through him in anticipation of a chase. Let her run. The victory and mating would only be that much more intense. On his wristbands, the gold crystals swirled in tune to his anticipation of a mate, an heir, the survival of his race.

Lyan's voice growled in his mind, *Now whose lust threatens to leave us without a mate? She must accept us willingly or there is no bond.*

Adan laughed softly. *Do you really doubt our ability to secure our bond-mate? Before this night is over, she will belong to us in all ways.*

About the author:

Jory has been writing since childhood and has never outgrown being a daydreamer. When she's not hunched over her computer, lost in the muse and conjuring up new heroes and heroines, she can usually be found reading, riding her horses, or hiking with her dogs.

Jory welcomes mail from readers. You can write to her c/o Ellora's Cave Publishing at 1056 Home Avenue, Akron OH 44310-3502.

Why an electronic book?

We live in the Information Age — an exciting time in the history of human civilization in which technology rules supreme and continues to progress in leaps and bounds every minute of every hour of every day. For a multitude of reasons, more and more avid literary fans are opting to purchase e-books instead of paperbacks. The question to those not yet initiated to the world of electronic reading is simply: *why?*

1. *Price.* An electronic title at Ellora's Cave Publishing and Cerridwen Press runs anywhere from 40-75% less than the cover price of the <u>exact same title</u> in paperback format. Why? Cold mathematics. It is less expensive to publish an e-book than it is to publish a paperback, so the savings are passed along to the consumer.

2. *Space.* Running out of room to house your paperback books? That is one worry you will never have with electronic novels. For a low one-time cost, you can purchase a handheld computer designed specifically for e-reading purposes. Many e-readers are larger than the average handheld, giving you plenty of screen room. Better yet, hundreds of titles can be stored within your new library — a single microchip. (Please note that Ellora's Cave and Cerridwen Press does not endorse any specific brands. You can check our website at www.ellorascave.com or

www.cerridwenpress.com for customer recommendations we make available to new consumers.)

3. *Mobility.* Because your new library now consists of only a microchip, your entire cache of books can be taken with you wherever you go.

4. *Personal preferences are accounted for.* Are the words you are currently reading too small? Too large? Too...**ANNOYING**? Paperback books cannot be modified according to personal preferences, but e-books can.

5. *Instant gratification.* Is it the middle of the night and all the bookstores are closed? Are you tired of waiting days—sometimes weeks—for online and offline bookstores to ship the novels you bought? Ellora's Cave Publishing sells instantaneous downloads 24 hours a day, 7 days a week, 365 days a year. Our e-book delivery system is 100% automated, meaning your order is filled as soon as you pay for it.

Those are a few of the top reasons why electronic novels are displacing paperbacks for many an avid reader. As always, Ellora's Cave and Cerridwen Press welcomes your questions and comments. We invite you to email us at service@ellorascave.com, service@cerridwenpress.com or write to us directly at: 1056 Home Ave. Akron OH 44310-3502.

NEED A MORE EXCITING
WAY TO PLAN YOUR DAY?

ELLORA'S
CAVEMEN

2006 CALENDAR

COMING THIS FALL

THE
ELLORA'S CAVE
LIBRARY

Stay up to date with Ellora's Cave Titles
in Print with our Quarterly Catalog.

TO RECIEVE A CATALOG,
SEND AN EMAIL WITH YOUR NAME
AND MAILING ADDRESS TO:

CATALOG@ELLORASCAVE.COM
OR SEND A LETTER OR POSTCARD
WITH YOUR MAILING ADDRESS TO:
CATALOG REQUEST
C/O ELLORA'S CAVE PUBLISHING, INC.
1337 COMMERCE DRIVE #13
STOW, OH 44224

The premier magazine for today's sensual woman

Lady Jaided magazine is devoted to exploring the sexuality and sensuality of women. While there are many similarities between the sexual experiences of men and women, there are just as many if not more differences. Our focus is on the female experience and on giving voice and credence to it. Lady Jaided will include everything from trends, politics, science and history to gossip, humor and celebrity interviews, but our focus will remain on female sexuality and sensuality.

A Sneak Peek at Upcoming Stories

Clan of the Cave Woman
Women's sexuality throughout history.

The Sarandon Syndrome
What's behind the attraction between older women and younger men.

The Last Taboo
Why some women – even feminists – have bondage fantasies

Girls' Eyes for Queer Guys
An in-depth look at the attraction between straight women and gay men

Available Spring 2005

www.LadyJaided.com

Lady *Jaided* Regular Features

Jaid's Tirade

Jaid Black's erotic romance novels sell throughout the world, and her publishing company Ellora's Cave is one of the largest and most successful e-book publishers in the world. What is less well known about Jaid Black, a.k.a. Tina Engler is her long record as a political activist. Whether she's discussing sex or politics (or both), expect to see her get up on her soapbox and do what she does best: offend the greedy, the holier-than-thous, and the apathetic! Don't miss out on her monthly column.

Devilish Dot's G-Spot

Married to the same man for 20 years, Dorothy Araiza still basks in a sex life to be envied. What Dot loves just as much as achieving the Big O is helping other women realize their full sexual potential. Dot gives talks and advice on everything from which sex toys to buy (or not to buy) to which positions give you the best climax.

On the Road with Lady K

Publisher, author, world traveler and Lady of Barrow, Kathryn Falk shares insider information on the most romantic places in the world.

Kandidly Kay

This Lois Lane cum Dave Barry is a domestic goddess by day and a hard-hitting sexual deviancy reporter by night. Adored for her stunning wit and knack for delivering one-liners, this Rodney Dangerfield of reporting will leave no stone unturned in her search for the bizarre truth.

A Model World

CJ Hollenbach returns to his roots. The blond heartthrob from Ohio has twice been seen in Playgirl magazine and countless other publications. He has appeared on several national TV shows including The Jerry Springer Show (God help him!) and has been interviewed for Entertainment Tonight, CNN and The Today Show. He has been involved in the romance industry for the past 12 years, appearing on dozens of romance novel covers and calendars. CJ's specialty is personal interviews, in which people have a tendency to tell him everything.

Hot Mama Cooks

Sex is her food, and food is her sex. Hot Mama gives aphrodisiac a whole new meaning. Join her every month for her latest sensual adventure -- with bonus recipe!

Empress on the Mount

Brash, outrageous, and undeniably irreverent, this advice columnist from down under will either leave you in stitches or recovering from hang-jaw as you gawk at her answers to reader questions on relationships and life.

Erotic Fiction from Ellora's Cave

The debut issue will feature part one of "Ferocious," a three-part erotic serial written especially for Lady Jaided by the popular Sherri L. King.

COMING TO A BOOKSTORE NEAR YOU!

ELLORA'S CAVE
2005
BEST SELLING AUTHORS TOUR

Discover for yourself why readers can't get enough of the multiple award-winning publisher Ellora's Cave. Whether you prefer e-books or paperbacks, be sure to visit EC on the web at www.ellorascave.com for an erotic reading experience that will leave you breathless.

www.ellorascave.com